A MARKED WOMAN

JOAN FOOR

ISBN 978-1-63452-106-2 (paperback)
978-1-63452-107-9 (ebook)

Published by Foor Publishing
Palmdale, California

Author: Joan Foor
Editor: Kathryn Jordan
Cover Illustration: John MacFarlane
Cover/interior design and layout:
Mark E. Anderson, www.aquazebra.com

Printed in the United States of America

ACKNOWLEDGMENTS

I would be amiss if I didn't start with my brother Les Foor, poet, author and publisher who encouraged me in all my endeavors.

Much thanks to my best friend Pamela Ahlgrim, RD who read and re-read chapters over the years and challenged me to push onward with this project.

My editor Kathryn Jordan provided me with positive suggestions and her comments for tweaking were extremely helpful.

The members of my critique group over the last few years provided me with constructive ideas and support advising me never to give up: Marilyn Dalrymple, author; Felix Mayerhofer, author; Edward Mooney, Jr., author; and Cynda Thomas, author.

Dancers of the Boogie Woogie Mamas listened to my story line in between performances and events inspiring me to finish writing this story. They were in attendance at book signings sharing the excitement of my three prior book debuts: Patty Dagata, dancer; Kay Strait, dancer; and Kim Wright, dancer.

My first cousins spent several evenings during a much needed vacation in Sarasota, Florida several years ago reading out loud chapter after chapter from a rough manuscript. They stayed up until almost dawn giving me feedback. There was much laughter, high energy and support for me to continue writing until completion. Many thanks cousins: Debbie Darnell; Karyn Espenlaub; and Linda Raneri. And my other first cousin, Donna Carson who has spurred me over the telephone lines to get this story published while her eye sight is in good enough condition to read it.

DEDICATION

For my mother, a brave, courageous, free spirited woman who faced unsurmountable odds in life sustained by her strong faith as a Christian.

At the Threshold
Emerging from the chasms of time
Behold the threshold gate.
There are no warning bells to chime
The future will not wait.

Time it seems, has naught to tell
Of future days in stock
Life has so many wares to sell
So many doors to knock.

Future urges us along
The past is close behind
Praising that eternal song,
"So seek and you shall find."

Every road lies straight ahead
No end is in our view;
We've made our past, made our bed,
No other rest will do.

Step lively down the rutty road,
Tread not the beaten track;
Aim for your objective mode
There is no turning back.

By Leslie R. Foor

A MARKED WOMAN

Based on a True Story

By

Joan Foor, MN RN

CHAPTER 1

Muted sun-light through the window joins the sterile whiteness of the walls creating a golden glow. This welcomed light projects into the dreary cubicle where my bed is lined up with all the rest. The clatter of stainless steel basins, along with a symphony of moaning and gibberish, swells the anger within my chest as women around me begin to wake and fuss from their beds.

"Good Morning, Naomi. It's time to get you up now," utters nurse, Claney. My hunch is she's a practical nurse; there's no R.N. on her name tag. She places a towel and washcloth on my army green metal bedside stand and leaves. Mrs. Claney is one of the more innocuous attendants. Her uniform is disgusting, more gray than white, with yellow perspiration stains at her armpits. Her hair hangs like a horse's mane past her shoulders with gray roots visible through her dyed reddish brown hair.

What bothers me most are her shifty eyes—she always looks away when ours meet. I don't trust her, nor do I believe everything she tells me. She's soft spoken with a thinly masked contempt she covers up with a minimum of pleasantries. I'm angry at her and the rest of the staff for holding me captive. No one will tell me why I'm here. Was it my husband alone who committed me to this horrendous existence? If so, he will pay. There must have been others involved. Was it Dr. Hill? When I find out I'll get even. What did I do to deserve such punishment? My son will be home soon. He'll find a way to rescue me. These nurses and attendants refuse to let me use a phone.

Nurse Claney continues to blabber about her daughter who is away at college while she guides me to the sink. I half listen, while my mind fights the humiliation of her ordering me around, laying out the clothes I'm to wear.

"We need to get you all cleaned up, Naomi. Your daughter, Jan, will probably be coming to visit today." She keeps up with aimless talk, "I'm so proud of Denise. Her grades are good even with her working on the weekends." Claney hands me a wash cloth. One relief this isn't Thursday—the day of the week we are forced to take a tub bath. And not a day we generally receive another horror, referred to as a "treatment." She gives me a plastic stick with a pink foam sponge smeared with tooth paste. How can I get a good teeth cleaning without a regular tooth brush? I can barely hold onto the short handle, let alone brush my teeth. I struggle to move the sponge up and down over my upper teeth. Mrs. Claney grabs it!

"Here, give me that. You're making a mess!" She smears toothpaste on the easiest to reach enameled targets. She holds a cup of water to my mouth and pours. She knows the rinse water sometimes chokes me. She takes a little too much pleasure banging me across my back. This day is turning out to be no different from most.

She motions for me to sit on a straight-back wooden chair. I wait for her to lay out my clothes. These clothes are unfamiliar, a white muslin slip with wide straps, nothing like I ever wore at home. A common, cotton house dress which reminds me of the ones mother made for the poor from flour or feed sacks during the depression. Today the dress is checkered brown and white with short white capped sleeves, and no belt. *I wonder who wore these.* I'm forced to wear white ankle socks, never the sheer stockings I love. The socks rarely match and have black numbers on them. Each step of Mrs. Claneys' daily ritual seems designed to tear at what little dignity I've left. I reach for the ties of my hospital gown. She shoves my hand away.

"Naomi, stand while I pull your undies up," she orders.

"Where's my own underwear? These are too big. The crotch of these cotton pants is sagging along the inside of my legs. And, where's my brassiere?"

Mrs. Claney raises her eyebrows, "Naomi we've been over this before. You don't need a bra for now. Don't go getting yourself all worked up." I snapped back, "I want my own clothes? Is it too much to ask?"

"Now, now, Naomi, calm down. I've told you before. This is what your family brings you to wear."

"You're a damn liar! My kids wouldn't bring me these rags. Someone has stolen my things." I sense her changing tactics.

"Shhh, mind what I say. Causing a fuss will only get you into trouble." She keeps glancing over the cubicle block wall to see if anyone is close enough to hear. The sound of metal trays gets louder as the food carts approach.

Mrs. Claney takes my arm, leads me to the nearest wooden bench on the opposite side of the block wall which partitions our beds from the other half of a large room. She knows I get upset when other women try to take food from my tray. I never get enough to eat—I'm always hungry. Breakfast is nothing to brag about, the oatmeal reminds me of the paste we used for glue in grade school. A watery liquid runs from the scrambled eggs, onto my toast. My eggs are gray, not yellow. Mrs. Claney tries to cut my bacon and it breaks into small pieces like charcoal.

"Mrs. Claney, there's the woman who keeps grabbing food from my tray."

"Give me a tray, honey. Give me a tray, honey." The woman repeats over and over as she shuffles her feet in my direction.

"Get her out of here! Can't I have some peace for a change?"

"Gracie, go on now. Leave Naomi alone. You've had your breakfast," Mrs. Claney, turns this tall thin women around, sending her away from me. I hear Gracie repeating the same thing as she shuffles in the other direction, "Give me a tray honey. Give me a tray honey..."

She never stops at meal time. She's got to be crazy. *Do they think I'm crazy too?* Oh, God, am I dreaming? Let this be a nightmare about to end.

I watch the staff as I try to pick up bits of bacon. The nurses are busy feeding women or delivering trays. Mrs. Claney hurries to the other side of the room to help with the rest of the trays. Everyone is bustling about except for the women with sheets wrapped around their waists securing them to the back of straight chairs waiting to be fed. Other women sit on benches around the room or wander about. No one is looking in my direction. This is my chance to get out of here. Trying not to draw attention, I raise up, slowly edging my way around the block cubicle wall past my bed to the back of the room. Staying close to the wall, keeping my eyes on the staff, I make it to the glass encased Nurses Station which is now empty. Usually, a nurse or two are sitting there. I pick up speed and head for the propped open swinging doors.

Finding myself in a long corridor, I glance over my shoulder, and hurry toward the door ahead. The door knob won't turn. I push my weight against this gray obstacle standing between me and my freedom. It won't budge. I look back. I'm still in the clear. Two open windows are side by side in the corridor. I press the palm of my hand against the window screen, but it's fastened tight from the outside. I glance again to see if Mrs. Claney or any nurses are in sight. I rush toward the next set of doors. With all my strength I thrust my body against it. I back up and slam myself into the door again and again with all my might. I pound the door with my fists, feeling no pain. The realization that I can't escape breaks a dam of frustration and anger.

"Let me out! Let me out of here," I scream. "Do you hear me in there? I don't belong here. This is a terrible mistake!" Suddenly, I'm grabbed under both armpits from behind and lowered to the floor. I struggle to get free, but two attendants pin me down. I can't see their faces. I kick and squirm to get free.

"Stop it, you're hurting my arms, let me go!" Someone tries to slip a stiff unfamiliar garment over my head. I keep kicking and swinging my arms wildly. I look up and spot the big, buxom nurse with the heavily starched cap standing over me. The wings at the sides of her cap look like devil horns. Her attendants apply more pressure against my arms, while she slips this heavy canvas over my head. A short male staff member unravels the long straps of this garment and wraps them around my waist. Someone pulls the straps tight at my back, pinning my arms across the front of my chest. My arms begin to throb with each beat of my heart. The big bosomed one leans over and gives an extra pull to the straps at my back.

"Let me go! Get me out of this contraption. I'm going to tell my son!" I scream. Perspiration runs down my forehead stinging my eyes. But I keep right on kicking. The sweat makes it difficult to make out all the faces hovering about me.

"Calm down, Naomi. You're only making matters worse. Stop kicking!" It's Mrs. Claney's voice from behind.

"Mrs. Claney, help! You know I don't belong here." I look for an ally to rescue me from this rigid cocoon. She does nothing to assist me. My voice begins to fade from screaming at the top of my lungs. I've little energy left to fight. The attendants grab hold of the straps at my back, and my feet slip as they pull me backwards my bare legs dragging against the cold tile floor like a rag-doll down the hallway.

"You're hurting me. Let me out of this thing." My lips begin to quiver from yelling. It's hard to catch my breath. Why doesn't Mrs. Claney say something, try to help me? The devil-horned nurse bends over and shakes her finger in my face making me blink. "See how you like spending time in a strait jacket. You'll learn the hard way!"

My tears make it hard to see everyone, but it's certain the staff follow her orders. That's it, Claney is afraid to take a stand against this one—she must be her supervisor. I hear the rattling of keys and the sound of a metal door banging farther down the hallway. They continue yanking me by the straps.

"Please let me go." My hip hits the bump of a door jamb and before I know it, I'm in a dim room with thick blue mats running across the floor and up the walls. The nurses swing me around, with the door at my back. The devil-horned nurse steps in front of me, her arms crossed under her huge bosom. "This is what you get for carrying on. We'll teach you to behave, one way or another."

"Don't leave me in this contraption. I can't get my breath. How can you be so cruel? You will have to answer to my son. He will be here soon to rescue me, you'll see." I turn my head away so she can't see my tears. My voice is fading to a whimper. I'm bound too tight across my chest. I try to shift my arms, but can't. Looking up, I see no glimmer of softness in the eyes of my captors.

The devil-horned nurse turns sharply away heading for the door. "Leave her! She'll learn we don't tolerate this type of behavior here." The attendants follow behind. The loud bang of the door shutting, the sound of the key turning in the lock, and their footsteps fading away, these are the answer to my pleas.

I push with my feet to rotate my body around facing the door. The small slit of a window has what resembles chicken wire between two panes of heavy glass. My arms continue to throb and the more I struggle to re-position them the worse they ache. Perspiration is running down my back and between my breasts. I lay down on my left side exhausted. My legs are cold against the mat. I draw them closer to my body.

"Dear God in heaven, help me." Tears flow down my cheeks forming a puddle on the mat. As I lick my lips for moisture, I can taste the salt from my tears. My mouth is dry and fluid from my nose runs over my lips and drips from my chin. I can do nothing but let it drip. Exhausted, I've reached the lowest low of my existence. I don't know how long I lay bawling and sobbing uncontrollably. All I'm certain about is that I'm at their mercy. My forehead throbs pulsing into my ears. I can sense my heart pumping at my wrists. I cry out, "Please, someone help me. Please, I'm sorry. Let me out!" I repeat it over and over until my voice is a mere whisper.

In a fetal position trying to keep my legs warm, my mind begins to spin. There were twists and turns in my forty-three years of life. God knows I made mistakes, but surely this isn't to be my punishment. I've tried to follow the strict religious beliefs of our church and the New Testament, be a devoted wife, and care for my children the best I could. How did it go so terribly wrong?

CHAPTER 2

Raised on a farm in central Pennsylvania, Russ, my husband, was old-fashioned and a tight-wad. I believed nothing was too good for our kids. My son Leslie was born first. Jan came two years later. Russ didn't want to spend money for their dancing and piano lessons. He took his manly responsibilities seriously and was a good provider. In the early forties, Pennsylvania Railroad men were bumped from one job to another. Russ had to bid on jobs with lower hourly wages. He got upset when I ran out of money before his payday.

I loved taking the kids to a restaurant for lunch or supper and to the movies. Russ was pessimistic and had no interest in movies or the arts. I worked as a seasonal sales clerk at Woolworth's in order to buy Les and Jan more toys and clothes. Working was my only chance to find out what life could have been as a woman of independent means. I enjoyed the holidays, bright lights, decorations, and got a kick out of frenzied shoppers, especially at Christmas. Russ only went to church when Les or Jan were singing or reciting. He was a scrooge, but tried not to spoil the fun on Christmas Day. I wanted our children to have the advantages I enjoyed growing up, but we lived on a blue collar income. I put clothes on lay-a-way. He would see the bills come in.

"Woman this has got to stop. How many times have I discussed your buying clothes on lay-a-away or credit? We will never get ahead this way."

"Those clothes were on sale, Russ. I can't wait till payday if the kids need clothes for school, or I need an outfit right away."

"Lay money aside after payday for unexpected expenses. If you don't have the cash during the sale, it's simple, nothing should be bought! Do you understand, woman? I'm struggling to keep us out of debt, dammit!" He pounded his fist on the table.

"You don't get it, Russ. There are times when the kids have events or recitals. Do you want your kids and I to be embarrassed?" I raised my voice. "Am I to deliver the message to Jan and Les that they can't participate because their father said so? Or, forget what you're asking for, it isn't payday week?"

"You heard me, woman! I'm telling you you're spending too much money for these lessons, costumes, and clothes. And what about all those books?"

"So that's what this boils down to. For your information, I borrow most of the books from the library and trade with my sisters. I don't buy them."

"This argument is over. I'm warning you to stop spending money we don't have!" He turned and stormed out the back door letting the screen door slam behind him. He resented the money spent for Les and Jan's lessons. But when Les and Jan performed their rendition of the Star Spangled Banner in Uncle Sam costumes at the Elk's, Moose club, or wherever, he was all smiles. He turned and faced his drinking buddies saying, "Those are my kids."

Russ had become grumpy and irritable. Not at all like when we first met. I remember driving Dad's Model A Ford on a dirt road when suddenly the car became difficult to steer. I pulled to the side of the road and stepped down carefully from the running board. I didn't want to get dirt in my new pair of open-toe shoes. The left front tire was flat. I wouldn't change a tire even if I knew how. It was too far to walk in either direction to reach a farmhouse. Pop surely would come looking for me once darkness set in. It was a clear, warm and sunny day. Not the typical hot and humid weather in Pennsylvania. I sat on the edge of the running board, waiting for someone to come along. A shiny cherry red open roadster passed me heading in the opposite direction. I wanted to wave my arms to indicate I was in trouble, but knew it wasn't proper. To my surprise, the car turned around and drove up beside me.

"Looks like you could use some help." That's the first time I met Russ. From the driver's side he jumped over his door like an acrobat. I nodded yes, but knew I shouldn't talk to strangers. I stood and pulled at my dress to smooth any wrinkles from sitting. He walked over to the spare tire mounted on the left front fender and pounded it with his fist.

"Your spare looks okay. I'll change your tire and get you on your way in no time." Our eyes met as he spoke.

I quickly glanced away. I wasn't accustomed to looking straight into the eyes of strangers, especially men. "Thank you, well, I mean, I would be most grateful."

"I'm Russ, Russ Bryar," as he started unbuttoning his shirt. I tried not to stare, but at nineteen, I had never seen an entire man's bare chest. He wore no undershirt. I had caught glimpses of Pop in his undershirt every now and then when he was shaving.

"Here, hold my shirt. I don't want to get grease on it."

Our eyes met again. I could feel the blood rushing to my cheeks—it must have been obvious. My eyes followed him as he got tools from his roadster.

"You can sit here while I jack up your car", he opened the door on the passenger side of his roadster and motioned for me to get in. I sat down carefully trying not to wrinkle my chiffon dress. I folded his shirt, and laid it across my lap.

He removed the spare tire from the fender well and leaned it against the front bumper. He didn't notice me staring at the large muscles across his back while he worked. He threw the flat tire into his car's rumble seat and walked toward me. I stepped down, grabbed his shirt, as it fell from my lap almost hitting the ground.

"I can patch this tire at the garage where I work and get it back to you. Where do you live?" I tried not to stare at his chest and looked away when he came closer.

"Fairview," I replied, handing over his shirt. He slipped his arms through, and left it hang open.

"Whereabouts in Fairview?"

My heart began pounding faster. I knew I shouldn't be giving my house number to a stranger, but I had no choice.

"What's the matter, don't you remember your own house number?" He wiped his hands on a rag, closed the door behind me, and with a puzzled gaze our eyes met once again.

"Well, yes, that is, we've not lived there long. It's 1804 6th Street, on the left side heading up the hill toward the cemetery." My voice quivered as I spoke. He turned and walked to the driver's side of his roadster. He jumped over the door and slid down behind the steering wheel.

"I'll drop your tire off tomorrow evening." I could tell his car was his pride and joy. He turned the roadster around and headed in the opposite direction. Looking over his shoulder, he smiled, and waved as he drove away. I started my engine, and began thinking how I would break the news to Mom and Pop. I'd just given our address to a stranger, when I've been told never to speak to strangers. I would have to be careful how I described what took place. Mom will be upset, but hopefully calm down when I explain what happened. Rather than continuing my journey to Aunt Minnie's I turned the car around and headed home.

Mom looked up the moment I walked through the front door. Her hands were white from dusting pie dough with flour. I knew what was coming the moment she halted that rolling pin.

"Naomi, where have you been? You should've taken Genevieve or Viola with you. It isn't proper to be driving around alone. You know better!" Whips of gray hair had managed to slip out from under her baking cap. Several pie tins were lined with dough and empty pans were ready for dough. She was in a baking frenzy with little patience left for me.

"Why do I always have to drag one of my sisters with me? I'm old enough to take care of myself." I didn't want to show too much excitement about meeting Russ. "Within minutes after getting a flat tire along came this kind young man." Actually it was about an hour before Russ came by. This was one of those little white lies to avoid confrontation.

Mom showed concern, "Well, you've proved today things can happen beyond your control, and it would've been good to have Genevieve with you. She was upset when you left without her."

Mom was right, but I wasn't going to let on I purposely left without a sister.

Pop glanced over his National Geographic Magazine, "What did you say about a flat tire and a young man? What's his name?"

"He goes by Russ, Pop. He promised to fix the tire and return it tomorrow evening."

"Andy, we don't know the first thing about this fellow and our daughter has invited him to the house. Naomi, you'll stay in your room when he comes. Your father will handle this."

Pop, once again to my rescue, "Jen, don't be too harsh. After all, we owe him our thanks for helping Naomi."

Pop was such a kind and dear father and always stood up for me. How he remained so cheerful was beyond me. What he must have been going through, losing his job repairing and engraving watches and fine jewelry. People didn't have money to spend for either of Pop's services. He no longer could bring in enough money for the family. It wasn't easy for him with my three younger sisters, Genevieve, Viola, and Shirley and their demands. My fourth sister, Bern, two years younger, was engaged to be married. Bern worked at the shoe factory and paid a few dollars board to help Mom with expenses.

Pop's plan to send me to Indiana State Teachers College after high school was out of the question. Not only a disappointment for Pop, my heart ached when I realized my college dreams were shattered. Pop and Mom would barely be able to afford Bern's wedding.

Mom was short tempered, more resentful toward Pop, and unhappy with all of us lately. At least we were able to enjoy our new house on the outskirts of Altoona for two years before Pop told us his life savings was gone. For an entire year he kept the loss of his money in the 1929 stock crash a secret. Pop, along with hundreds of other men, traveled by train to The New York Stock Exchange. What a shock it must have been to find his stock certificates were worthless. Pop hoped to find another job and avoided telling us about his financial trouble. He was unable to find other work.

Pop continued to go downtown and wait for customers needing watch or jewelry repair. To spare expense he took public transportation to his office. He had to walk five blocks to catch the streetcar, and about the same distance from where he got off to reach his office.

I remember the day I was in my cousin's barber shop getting a haircut. I saw Pop limp past the window. The barber closest to the window remarked, "There's that old drunk going up the avenue. I can time my watch by him." I felt the blood flushing my face and my ears were hot. I was so angry I wanted to slap him. I yelled across the room, "You don't know what you're talking about. He's not a drunk and has never had an intoxicating drink in his life!"

"How would you know, young lady?" He snapped back, sarcastically. Everyone stopped what they were doing and stared.

"Because he's my father!"

The barber's face and neck turned red. There was absolute silence-like a movie with no sound. My voice quivered, "Pop lost his leg as a child. A freight car broke loose and rolled down a siding area where he was playing. Scared, he tried to get up, but his shoe caught in the track. A nearby switchman witnessed the accident. He jumped from a side car and used his belt as a tourniquet to save Pop's life. His foot and lower leg were crushed ending with an above knee amputation. Pop has a wooden leg and it's hard for him to get around."

Pop wouldn't have wanted me making explanations for him, but it was time they stopped their foolish gossip. The shop talk softened and everyone glared at the barber who had made the accusations. I wish I could've kept quiet. My eyes began to tear, I looked away, so the men couldn't see how upset I was. How my heart ached for Pop.

Pop was a proud man. He would never hear anything from me about this incident. As long as I can remember, each evening Mom would take a basin of warm water and a washcloth to the parlor for Pop. I looked away when he lifted his stump from the socket of his old wooden leg. Too many times I had seen the bright red blood oozing from what looked like the raw end of a pork loin. It sent chills up and down my spine. I knew there must have been pain with every step he took. Pop never complained about his handicap.

We were forced to move into a one hundred year old creaky, creepy, run down four-story house next to the cemetery. It was all we could afford. The landlord said the house was condemned and scheduled for tear down. He felt sorry for our family and rented it to us. Mom became the sole breadwinner. She started doing neighbor's washings, ironing, baking, and cleaning. Money was slow to come at two or three dollars for a large wicker basket of clothes—washed and ironed. Heavily starched white shirts were always hanging from a curtain rod between the parlor and kitchen, for pickup. It took Mom about thirty minutes to iron a man's heavily starched cotton shirt.

Mom looked older than her years and had no time for herself. Her hair was already gray at the temples, pulled back into a bun, covered by a hairnet or white baking hat. Her cotton housedresses were the norm, always with a full apron, unless it was Sunday. She never wore makeup, except to church. I watched on Sunday mornings when she sparingly applied a nearly white powder on her nose and used some lipstick to dab her high cheekbones and lips. The mole above her upper lip was perfectly positioned for a natural beauty mark. She slipped on a jersey silk dress, dark stockings and black leather oxford shoes with a Cuban styled heel. Unless very sick she never missed a service.

The Fourth Street Church of God was where all of us were baptized. After church, we girls were expected to act like young ladies. We would sit around the parlor in our Sunday best. Sometimes we played games with my youngest sister Shirley and I drummed my favorite hymns on the piano. We enjoyed singing until Pop sold the piano-it went with everything he considered no longer essential.

It was common for family and friends to drop by unexpectedly especially on Sundays. They were always welcome, whether at mealtime, or just for a piece of Mom's pie, cake, or a cup of coffee. Whatever food on hand was stretched and shared with whoever came. I remember adding more green beans and potatoes each time more arrived until the whole batch was like soup. Pop served it as if it were perfect. When no one was looking he winked and we both had difficulty keeping from busting out laughing. After supper it was back to church. My sisters and I attended a Christian Endeavor Class, followed by an evening service.

I loved singing in the choir and sometimes sang both at morning and evening services. I never did like sitting about the parlor in my Sunday best waiting until time to go back to church. During the week Mom repeated a predictable routine of dusting, cleaning, and washing. Even in freezing weather, Mom would complete her chores. Windows were washed every Thursday. She held me by the belt at my waist, as I balanced my backside on the windowsills of the second and third floors. I reached the top window panes with a rag on the end of a yardstick.

In the winter, I hated to get out of bed. I stretched my arms outside the covers to see how cold it was. I would look over at my sister, Bern, as she yawned her breath was like hot steam forced from the tea pot. Bern and I slept together and many times one of my other sisters jumped in bed with us to keep warm. We had heavy quilts and feather beds. The heat never reached upstairs. The house walls had no insulation as if inviting the cold breeze. In winter snow collected on the windowsills. When Bern refused to get up from a warm bed I threw a snowball at her. I could hear Mom throwing wood into the kitchen stove in preparation for breakfast. Once my feet hit the cold linoleum floor, I'd dance back and forth to stop the frigid stinging of my feet, except for an occasional slip when the slop-jar wasn't tucked far enough under the bed.

One spill was a sure way to start an un-welcome day.

When I started the job at J.C. Penney's Genevieve and Viola took over my chores. They walked together downtown to clean the public restrooms twice a day. Our family resented this requirement to qualify for The Emergency Relief Fund. The toilets were located beneath the sidewalk by The City Hall Building. Men in dirty ragged clothes hung around this corner using curse words, smoking cigars, chewing tobacco and spitting on the street.

My sisters were given skim milk in jars-it used to be thrown away. The WPA handed out clothing, two pair of shoes a year for my sisters and food. Genevieve and Viola with Grandpap's help borrowed a wagon and picked up surplus food. It took the three of them to pull the load of surplus items home. The bakeries handed out stale donuts; we heated them in the oven to soften before eating. Mom was given ration/coupon books and tokens to buy meat and butter each month. Some months there was none available. Genevieve eventually got a job at the grocery store at $11.00 a week working long hours. The Mother's Assistance Program held back $1.00 for every dollar Mom earned. Mom was spending about $8.00 a month for groceries.

Each morning, I would put on house slippers and start making my way toward the cellar, my younger sisters following behind. We mumbled a weak good morning to Mom standing at the stove preparing breakfast. The wooden steps creaked as we made our way down to the unfinished dirt cellar. A dim light bulb hung from a wire cord at the bottom of the stairs. Daylight peering through the small cellar window helped us navigate across some heavy planks spanning a pool of icy water leading to the toilet. Pop had laid 2 by 10 boards across to reach solid ground. He and Mom escorted us the first few times. Pop told us, "Stay on the boards, the water is deep and dangerous." The neighbor said, "It's a natural spring under the old house, and the ground is like quick sand."

I usually was first across the boards to the toilet. The throne had a cracked wooden seat and was perched on a mound of dirt against a faded out whitewashed cellar wall. It did flush most of the time. Before long we made fun out of our trips across the water. I would act like I was going to force one of my sisters from the planks, but jogged around them. It took a balancing act to pass one another. When it was little Shirley's turn, we didn't tease her. She remained scared at the age of seven. One of us held her hand when she crossed.

Then we marched back up to our room, dressed quickly and hurried down to a warm kitchen. Mom had our breakfast ready, eggs, scrapple, toast, or hot oatmeal with milk, and hot chocolate. We were not allowed to drink coffee. "It stunts your growth," Mom insisted. We knew the neighborhood kids drank coffee for breakfast, but Mom didn't like being challenged about her decisions and besides we preferred hot chocolate. Pop already had a cup of coffee or two, and was reading the daily newspaper when we joined him at the kitchen table.

CHAPTER 3

I resumed the topic I hadn't finished the night before. I was totally obsessed with anticipation of Russ's visit and my mother's edict banning me to my room. "Mom, I didn't get a chance to thank him. Can't I at least do that much," I pleaded. She looked up with those almost black eyes and gave me a dark stare, her eyebrows arched—a sign when she disapproved of my actions or comments.

Pop glanced over at Mom, as if asking for her permission, "Its only proper Naomi thank him personally. I'll handle this, but Naomi should be present."

"That girl has gone too far this time, Andy. I will have no part of this, mind you." Mom was moving her iron faster across the board. If Mom had her way I wouldn't see Russ. After church, I hurried through dinner and ran upstairs to look for the right dress to wear. I thought of excuses to run downstairs when Russ arrived, in the event that Pop didn't call me. The air was still and the heat of the day was settling in my room like a heavy wet blanket. My mind was made up. I would go downstairs even if Pop didn't call me. I don't know how long I was lost in thought fixing my hair and looking in the mirror, when I heard a car pull up out front. I quickly changed into my pink chiffon dress, as if I were late for a wedding. I ran to Mom and Pop's room on the same floor and looked out the window. I could see the back of Russ's car, but not Russ-the porch roof was in the way. I rushed to the stairwell pausing to pull at both sides of my dress to smooth out any wrinkles from being jammed into the wardrobe. I waited at the top of the stairs. I was certain Pop would answer the door. I knew Mom would be uncomfortable and stewing, but Pop would keep his promise and call me.

"Naomi, honey, come on down. That young fellow Russ is here."

Pop winked from the bottom of the stairs. Genevieve and Viola were fussing with each other over the dishes in the kitchen. They looked at me and started giggling when I appeared in one of my best Sunday dresses. Mom was cutting strips of dough for homemade noodles at the kitchen cabinet. Mon's mouth dropped open, but she held her tongue. Her eyes said it all. She was upset seeing me in one of my Sunday's best. I rushed past Mom into the parlor. I didn't need her to embarrass me with any remarks about my outfit.

I heard Pop asking the usual questions, "Where do you live, Russ?"

"In the East End, near Kettle Road."

Before Pop could continue, I entered the room. I could feel Russ's eyes going up and down my body and then our eyes met straight on. I looked away. Trying hard not to blush and show too much excitement, I walked closer to Pop and rested my hand on his forearm. "Russ, how nice it is to see you again." He wore a tight tan T-shirt. His hair was combed straight back with brown eyes that sparkled. "I really owe you an apology. I didn't thank you yesterday for changing the tire. I told Pop how nervous I was about having a flat. I simply forgot my upbringing."

"No problem, it's okay. You must have been scared all alone on a deserted road. I'm glad I was able to be of help."

He smiled as he spoke. I returned a half smile. I felt the warmth of blood rush up my neck to my face and ears. I avoided turning toward Mom. She would've noticed it immediately.

"Stay and have a piece of Jen's pie," Pop said.

Russ grinned happily, "Wish I could, but mother's expecting me any moment. However, I'll take a rain check for sometime soon." He turned and walked toward the screen door.

"You're welcome anytime. Come by and see us," Pop continued. We followed Russ out to the porch and watched as he got the tire from his roadster and laid it on the porch.

"What do I owe you, son?"

"Not a thing. It was a small nail, an easy patch."

"Well, we certainly appreciate your help. Are you sure we can't talk you into some of Jen's pie?"

"Wish I could but I really have to go."

"Thanks again, drop by when you're over this way," Pop insisted.

I watched Russ drive up the street, turn down the hill by the cemetery and disappear. I had a feeling I would see Russ again.

It wasn't long afterward, Pop sold our car to help with the bills. About the same time Russ began visiting. Mom was pleased when he complimented her on her pies or cakes. She would blush slightly, and tuck wisps of gray hair sticking out from her baking hat away from her face. She gave a slight smile of approval, but didn't want to show how much she was beginning to like him. Russ and I always sat in the parlor, or on the porch swing within view.

One day Pop was sitting on the other side of the porch reading the newspaper when Russ asked, "Do you want to go for a short ride in my roadster?" I glanced over at Pop; he looked up over the newspaper and nodded his approval. Without hesitation I jumped up, "I'll get my sweater." I opened the screen door grabbed for my sweater and almost knocked the clothes-tree over. I didn't look toward Mom ironing for fear she would protest. I hurried down the porch steps with Russ. He opened the door on the driver's side. I slid under the steering wheel and moved close to the passenger door. I kept watching nervously toward the porch expecting Mom to rush out with an objection. Russ started the car and I sighed with relief when he pulled away from the curb.

"Don't sit so far away," he said with a smile. I grinned happily and moved closer to the center.

"Where would you like to go?" Russ asked.

I hesitated at first, "What about driving through Sinking Valley? I love looking at the farms and countryside."

He stepped on the accelerator, looked into my eyes, and said, "Sinking Valley, here we come."

It felt good driving in the open air. I worried about my hair getting tangled and kept running my fingers through to smooth it back.

Russ patted the seat beside him, motioning for me to move even closer, "Let your hair blow. Don't worry, you look fine." I moved a little bit his way, and he chuckled. It was a wonderful Saturday afternoon. We stopped at a road-stand in the middle of Sinking Valley.

"What would you like to drink?"

"I'd like a root beer if they have it." Thanks for asking. I followed his every move as he walked to the fruit stand. His stride was purposeful and masculine.

This was our first time alone without family peering at us. I loved watching his mannerisms and facial expressions. Russ was two years older than me, always well shaven with fair skin. His chestnut brown hair receded from a high forehead. He stood about six foot tall, had broad shoulders and well developed biceps. Russ looked straight into my eyes as he spoke. I was accustomed to looking away from men. It took time for me to let our eyes meet. I hoped Russ was not psychic, for I was wishing he would kiss me. I was sorry when the afternoon ended. He walked me to the porch, the family looking on as we said our goodbye.

A few days later, he picked me up after work. On the way home, he veered the car to the curb. With the engine still running he pulled me close. I tingled when he took hold of my chin with his left hand, slid his right hand around my waist pulling me gently to him and kissed me. My warm feelings for Russ were different from those I experienced with other fellows.

How I looked forward to his kisses! At times he lifted me up and sat me on the edge of his roadster door. He balanced me with my legs dangling down. Russ was strong and when he pulled me close, I could barely get my breath. I loved to hear his ideas, about the different race cars he was working on, and his plans for winning.

"Why did you quit high school a year and a half from graduating?"

"I was bored. The only thing I liked was Mechanical Drawing and The Auto Body Shop Course."

I thought it would've been best had he graduated, but passed it out of my mind. He was fun to be with, and I was discouraging other fellows who came by the house or saw me at church and wanted a date. Guys I dated before Russ were younger and immature.

Mom said, "I'm glad you are sticking with Russ. I don't have to make excuses when young men come by asking for you."

When I was still in high school and different boys walked me home, I never was sure if they were hanging around for Mom's cake, pie, or trying to get enough courage to ask me for a date.

The young men in their twenties who lived on our street stopped by frequently. Most couldn't find work and visited with Mom—she always had something freshly baked sitting on top of the stove for them. It was a kind of refuge to come and get advice. She loved the attention, but didn't let on. It didn't take long for Russ to know how to get around Mom. "This custard pie is the best I ever had."

She answered, "You don't say," with one of those silly grins on her face.

He joked with her and continued to rave about her cooking. Of course, who didn't, she was a great cook and baked pies and cakes every day. The church women and the neighbors all complimented Mom. She took meals to sick people and sent food for every church supper.

Russ and I always hurried back by dusk, unless he picked me up after work. Mom and Pop sat on the front porch swing and waited for us. One night we drove Kettle road to the dam and parked. "Do you see how wide the breast of Kettle Dam is?"

"Yes, why do you ask?"

"My buddies bet me I couldn't swim across the crest. It's off limits and there's a strong undercurrent. One night we had a few beers and they dared me to jump in. They watched as I crawled under the fence, dove in, and swam to the other side. I had to rest awhile before I had strength enough to swim back." Russ told me how his friends would bet one, or two beers to challenge him at hand wrestling. "They always lost," he bragged. His eyes lit up telling me how the first day of hunting season he shot more rabbits than his three brothers put together. Time slipped away between kisses and stories we shared under a clear moonlit sky filled with millions of stars.

One kiss led to another and another, until we were swept away with desire and passion. Words ceased. It was my first experience at making love and Russ was gentle. He helped me climb to the back seat while kissing me intermittently. Gently, he removed my shoes, silk stockings, one by one, from my garter belt and quickly pulled his T-shirt over his head. He placed our clothes over the front seat. I could see his muscular shoulders and hairy chest in the moonlight. Running his hands up under my skirt along my thighs, I shivered from a tingling sensation throughout my body like never before. He unfastened the garter belt hooks at my waist and removed it from beneath my slip. His large fingers fumbled trying to open the small silk buttons of my blouse. With some hesitation, I helped unbutton the last few. I slipped my arms from the sleeves. He laid it with our other clothes.

Russ pressed my shoulders gently against the back seat. Kissing my shoulders one by one, he slid his tongue down inside my brassiere between my breasts while sliding the straps of my slip down my arms and removing it along with my skirt. His rough hands snagged the front of my satin brassiere as he caressed my breasts reaching my nipple with his tongue. With his left hand he unfastened my bra. My breasts fell out to the sides, wanting to be free.

He threw my bra aside, "You are beautiful!" he whispered. Russ gently pressed his bare chest against mine. The kisses kept coming, to my breasts, his tongue swirling around my nipples. I could feel the warmth of his breath as he nibbled around my ears, up and down my neck and finally my mouth—I opened my lips for his tongue to enter. I was hot all over. It felt like a sunburn followed by chills. My upper thighs throbbed as he slid his tongue back across each breast, suckled each nipple, and slid his wet tongue down toward my navel. My mind was overcome by desire.

Russ pulled my panties down until they were around my ankles. I kicked them loose. The air was hot and humid and our bodies lathered. Like a magnet we were drawn into one. My arms reached around his waist, but the thrust of his lower body caused immediate discomfort followed with an ecstasy I had never known. My arms fell down to my sides—I could not hold on, "Oh, Russ, I have never."

"Shh, honey," he said, in a whisper.

I lost all my strength. Russ took control over my entire body. I was swept away like the pedal of a rose caught in a sea of water swirling away from shore in the vastness of a moonlit night. I lay speechless with my legs in a cramped position in the back seat of his roadster. He smoothed my hair back, kept kissing me, and at the same time reached with his left hand for his T-shirt draped over the front seat.

Breaking away from my lips, Russ slipped his shirt over his head and began handing me my clothes piece by piece, to get dressed. I couldn't get my brassiere re-fastened. He reached around and helped hook the fasteners while kissing my shoulders. He spun me around and pressed his lips gently against mine. I didn't want it to end. The silence was broken, "I've got to get you home, honey." He pulled up his trousers, stuffed in his T-shirt and pulled up the zipper. It took a lot of effort on both our parts to find each piece of clothing and put me back together. I could see Russ's face in the moonlight. A deep crease appeared on his forehead as he combed back his hair.

"C'mon, let's hurry. I've got to get you home. It's late." I knew he was worried about Pop and Mom. My heart was still pounding with excitement, but at the same time a cool realization began to set in. What had we done? I let all my defenses down in a matter of minutes. My strong religious teaching was overcome by an uncontrolled desire to let myself be loved. Did I let this happen because I knew there would be no college, or were these feelings the same between every man and woman alone like this under a moonlit sky? What I had been saving for marriage was now gone. A romantic encounter such as this was to be saved for a honeymoon. My mind lost control over my body. Russ didn't say he loved me. Did he really love me, or was this something else? I just didn't try to stop his advances, nor did I want to. It was as though I was caught up in a romantic fantasy in the middle of a novel. But, this was real and happening to me. I wanted to experience being loved, what it was like to be in love and now I knew. Or did I? Being kissed over my body caused such strong sensations. Russ holding me in his arms, and expressing his love and desire for me. He even said, "You're beautiful."

Pop was the only one who ever told me I was pretty. He treated me like a princess. Was I about to let my religious background play on my conscience and ruin it for me? I just didn't want to try to reason out what I had experienced. My thoughts were interrupted when Russ looked over with concern.

"It's later than I thought. I hope your father didn't stay up and start to worry." He didn't want to destroy Pop's or Mom's confidence in him, nor did I. There was silence between us as he started the engine and headed for Fairview. He took hold of my arm and pulled me across the seat, I could feel his warm body close to mine. Not a word was spoken until we reached the first stop sign, "Are you okay?" He asked.

"Yes, I'm all right." I answered quietly looking down toward the floor board, then back up at him. He smiled and picked up speed as we drove up 4th Street. When he entered 6th Street he turned the headlights off, drove slowly, cut off the engine and coasted with the arc lights and the full moon guiding us to the curb. Russ took hold of both my hands pulled me under the steering wheel, and out his side of the car. With my bare feet on the running board he placed one arm around my waist and reached up with his other hand, taking hold of my chin with his fingers, and kissed me with warm slightly open lips. I leaned over and gathered my garter belt, stockings, and shoes under my arm. Russ raised the sleeve of my blouse and kissed my bare left shoulder as we walked to my porch. Lastly, he slid his lips slightly open down my arm, turned my hand, and kissed my palm gently. I turned sideways and took one stair at a time with my shoes, stockings, and garter belt under my arm. I tiptoed barefoot into the house. The table lamp was lit in the parlor. I turned it out and watched Russ drive away without his head lights on.

Everyone had gone to bed. My hope was they were asleep. I tiptoed to my bedroom, removed the rest of my clothes in the dark, and slipped into my nightgown. Being extra careful not to arouse Bern, I crawled in bed on top of the bedspread. I lay still and wide awake recalling moment by moment with Russ. I wished Russ were there in bed beside me instead of Bern. The night lingered, as I struggled with my thoughts.

The next morning, I felt some muscle soreness at my inner thighs as I walked about. There was a slight redness and some chafing about my breasts and nipples. My face was sensitive to a hot wash cloth. I'm sure it was from his short whiskers. Yet my entire body was less tense and more relaxed. The muscle soreness was more pleasurable than bothersome. I wanted to jump into the air like a ballerina and shout to the world, *I'm in love, I'm in love!* But how could I? This had to be my secret. I wanted to share it with Bern. After all, she was in love. She'd understand, or would she? I wasn't sure how she would accept my letting go like I did. I expected the worst from Mom at breakfast, "You came in late last night. Where did you and Russ go?"

"After the movies we went for a drive in the country to spot deer, near Kettle road. We lost track of the time." I looked up to see her expression. She looked satisfied, I couldn't believe it—no stern stare of suspicion for a change. Russ had won her over like the boys in the neighborhood with all their fussing over her pies and cakes.

From then on the entire family saw my excitement each time Russ came to call. Mom was not happy with my going out several nights a week, especially when I had to be at work early the next morning. Had she forgotten what it was like to be in love? Russ and I had favorite romantic parking spots around town. We were in each other's arms necking from one date to another, hours seemed like minutes.

I was determined not to let myself get out of control. It was a constant struggle for both of us to put the brakes on our desires. In between our necking we paused, drew hearts and played tic-tack-toe on the steamed up windshield.

The weeks of being swept into a dreamland, consisting of love and kisses came to an abrupt halt when my menstrual period didn't come. I waited anxiously for days. Maybe it was late this time due to all the excitement—a week later I began to really get worried. Making matters worse I couldn't tell anyone. There was nothing to do but wait it out for another month. It probably was my imagination and I was worrying over nothing. Falling in love with Russ and getting emotionally involved was out of the ordinary-that must have interfered with my cycle. The next month's due date came and went with no signs of menses. I began to feel sick to my stomach each morning. I thought, *Is this God's punishment for deviating from my religious upbringing?* I had to walk through the kitchen each morning to get to the front door. Passing Mom preparing individual breakfasts made matters worse. Each day my feelings were more intense. There was always a repeat of the same thing.

"Naomi, do you want eggs or oatmeal this morning?" I was running out of excuses why I didn't want to eat. It got to the point I couldn't remember what excuse I used the day before.

"I'm eating while I do my inventories," I said.

She looked up from the stove with those deep penetrating eyes, "You need a good breakfast before rushing off to Penney's. What's got into you?"

"Nothing, Mom, I'm just not hungry this early in the morning any more. I've got to go." I hurried to the door before she could coax me into taking a piece of toast. Just smelling food made me sick to my stomach.

Every day I was sick till noon. Sometimes it lasted the entire day. I got immediate relief after eating a few dry soda crackers, but within a half hour I was nauseated again. I had the same symptoms I heard people with ulcers talk about. This gnawing feeling of emptiness in my stomach didn't help what was going on in my mind. After ten weeks I knew in my heart I was pregnant. I couldn't keep it to myself any longer. I wanted to wait until the moment was right to tell Russ. I kept hoping by some miracle my period would show.

One night we drove to kite hill, one of our favorite romantic spots when I broke the silence. "Russ, I missed my menstrual cycle. It's now over two months since I've had a period." My voice quivered as I spoke. "And I'm so sick in the morning I rarely eat for fear of throwing up."

"What are you saying?" He lifted my chin up to kiss me again, but paused looking straight into my eyes. He had a worried look, his eyebrows raised and the creases across his forehead deepened.

"I'm pregnant, Russ, and I don't know what to do." My eyes began to tear. I could tell he wasn't prepared for the news.

"Are you sure, honey? Couldn't it be due to all the excitement? The getting to bed late and you've been working a lot of overtime lately?"

"Yes, I'm sure. Russ there's no room for doubt any longer. You know I can't go to our family doctor. It would be too embarrassing." He pulled me close and held me tight in his arms a long while before he spoke. It was all I could do not to bawl my eyes out. How I wanted to hear him say, "I love you."

Complete silence, then he loosened his grip and placed his hands on both my shoulders, "Well, I guess, we'll just have to get married."

"Get married without telling anyone? I can't disappoint Mom and Pop. They would expect a church wedding. I'm scared about what people will say."

Russ took his thumb and brushed away a tear rolling down my cheek.

"Stop worrying that pretty little head of yours. We will have to elope when the time is right and surprise everyone."

"I'm not sure eloping is the right thing to do, Russ. I worry about what the Bible has taught me about starting a marriage this way. It's a bad omen!"

"Don't be ridiculous." Russ insisted it was a bunch of nonsense. "Don't get into superstitious stuff like Mom. Remember when the bird flew into your house and what havoc it was to chase it outside. Your Mom wouldn't enter the house until the bird was gone. She fretted about it for days. Even your Pop thought it was a sign someone was about to die. As far as I know, not a soul died. We love each other and with a baby on the way—it just happened sooner than we planned."

Uncontrollable tears streamed from my eyes. I turned my head so Russ wouldn't see me out of control.

Russ reached over, took hold of my chin, and turned my face toward him, "Stop crying, it'll be okay. You do love me, don't yah?"

"Yes, but I worry about us sneaking around and starting our marriage this way."

He ran his fingers along the edge of my hairline smoothing my hair back behind my ear as he spoke, "You do too much worrying. You're superstitious. And it's what you read in all those books that upsets you." He gave me a little kiss. "Just concentrate on being together, and married to boot," he offered, reassuringly.

I tried my best to smile. This wasn't how I pictured myself getting married. Russ had proposed, and I was grateful. I did love him, the touch of his hands and warmth of his smile. Was this part of God's plan for my life, had I met my soul' mate? How could I be sure? Would Russ feel trapped into this marriage later on? Too many thoughts ran rampant through my mind. In high school, I had planned for college. Marriage was to come later surrounded by family and a large church wedding. Under these circumstances it wasn't going to happen.

CHAPTER 4

Two weeks later, Russ and I drove to Cumberland, Maryland. We were married by a Justice of the Peace. It was exciting sitting close to Russ driving across the state line. But this wedding wasn't at all like I'd dreamed or read about. Not that I expected to be carried over a threshold, but I would have liked to have been married in our church, along with the usual serenade by the kids on the street. There would be no banging of pots and pans and yelling in front of our house for Russ and I. And we would have no lollipops and candy to throw out to get the kids to go away. It wasn't that long ago when I was one of those kids out there banging for candy from newlyweds on our street.

Our plan was to get back to my house at a decent hour to avoid suspicion. Russ gave me a nice 14 karat white gold wedding band trimmed around in yellow gold. On our way back to Pennsylvania I sat close to him and we kissed at almost every stop light. Sometimes we got the sound of a car horn from behind. Russ didn't jump on the accelerator the instant the traffic light changed. Normally, he would raise his eyebrows and those creases in his forehead would deepen with the blow of a horn, but not on this trip.

"Our honeymoon will have to wait," he said, jokingly, with a big smile, as he pulled up the emergency brake in front of my house. He helped me slide across the seat and out his side of the car, took hold of my chin, and gave me a long wet kiss. My heart began to beat wildly and ached at the same time, because we had to part on what should have been our honeymoon night.

"Good night, my husband," I whispered as our lips parted. I placed my two fingers on his lips and smiled. I was disappointed with the ceremony, but the day turned out as planned. Now I was Mrs. Bryar and I had a husband. This would have to be enough for now. I removed my wedding band, slid it into my purse, and blew him a kiss as I walked up the porch steps. The parlor light was still lit as I entered the house. I turned out the lamp, and watched through the bay window as Russ, my love, drove away. I was happy and sad at the same time. Russ made it easy for me, but I still had to deal with the guilt of having to get married. Keeping this secret from my family would be difficult.

I wanted to turn on the lights and bang on a few pots and pans myself. If only I could wake everyone up, spill the entire story, but I knew I couldn't. We continued to live as before, Russ with his parents and me with Mom and Pop. Russ and I both worked all the overtime we could to save our money to start housekeeping. As I watched my sister Bern and her sweetheart Ray get married at church, I was happy for them. But I removed myself from their wedding because I regretted the fact that this beautiful, well arranged wedding, was the one I had pictured for myself. I was envious that she could share these moments openly. Was I happy for Bern? Sure, but she would be leaving and I would no longer be able to share my thoughts with her. Lately, it was all superficial anyway. I wanted desperately to tell Bern I was married, but had to keep my secret for a future date. When Bern came home from a short honeymoon I wanted to blurt out about Russ and me, but I couldn't take away from her excitement. She moved out of our house and for the first time in my life, I had a room to myself.

Russ and I began looking for a place we could afford to rent. We found a small house not too far from Mom and Pop's. Russ was friendly and not the least concerned about talking with strangers. He and the landlord talked like they had known each other for years. The landlord promised once the house was vacant he would rent it to us. Once we knew the little house was available I asked Russ to come over for dinner. Finally, we could quit hiding our secret. It was a burden I had carried way too long. I had sleepless nights thinking over and over how to prepare Mom and Pop for what was coming. Mom had homemade pot pie with ham and potatoes topped off with egg custard pie. After clearing the table we all went into the parlor. Mom and Pop had barely sat down when I stood there full of excitement, "Mom and Pop, Russ and I have something to tell you." I took hold of Russ's hands and pulled him up from the chair. Russ had a great big smile on his face.

"Russ and I are renting that small house on Howard Avenue. It's the two story close to the sidewalk, near Third Street."

"You and Russ are going to do what?" Mom stood and faced me.

"Russ talked with the landlord, and its all set now that the house is vacant."

"Andy, did you hear what your daughter just said. You're not moving anywhere! Where did you come up with such an idea? You'll not get our permission if that is what you're asking. There is no way!" Mom scolded. Her dark eyes were penetrating just like when I did something horrible. When she plaited my hair and I moved because she was weaving too tight, she would slap me over the head with the comb. I could feel the same tension and knew I couldn't prolong teasing her. I walked over with my hand stretched out in front of me so they could see my wedding band.

"Mom, Pop, we were married weeks ago." I stepped closer, and pointed to my ring finger. Russ just stood there pale and speechless, like he had seen a ghost and was scared almost to death.

"So that's it! Why would you sneak around and do this without telling us?" Mom asked. I could tell she was angry and hurt at the same time.

"Jen, quit getting all worked up and let them explain," Pop interrupted.

Finally Russ got the nerve to speak, "Well, you see, sir, I wanted to marry your daughter, but I didn't want all that fancy wedding and church stuff. Naomi was hesitant, but I convinced her and, well, we were married by a Justice of the Peace in Cumberland. See, here's the marriage certificate, it's all legal. We're husband and wife." He unfolded the certificate and walked over to show Pop.

"It's okay, son. I believe you, and I don't question your intentions. Of course, this comes so unexpected, you understand."

"We didn't want to tell you until I had the means to support her, and we could set up housekeeping. Heck, I thought you wouldn't be opposed to our running away to get married if I had a good job and could take care of her."

Thank heavens Russ spoke up. I could see Mom steaming up minute by minute.

"This is a fine way to start a marriage. Look at how proper a wedding your sister, Bern had. I thought I brought you up better than this, Naomi." Mom's face was red and her eyes teary. I knew she was hurt by our eloping, but more disappointed because there was no including her in our plans.

"But, Mom, you like Russ, and we didn't mean to upset either one of you. We just wanted to be together. It will be okay, you'll see."

"Jen, come now. There's no harm done." Pop struggled with his leg, got up from his overstuffed chair, walked over and shook Russ's hand. He followed with a big hug and patted him across the back.

"Welcome son", Pop said. He grabbed me around the waist, squeezed me tight to his chest and kissed me on the cheek. I looked over at Mom. She was wiping her tears with the edge of her apron. She got up slowly, walked over to Russ, gave him half of a hand shake and looked up at him with that half smile of hers. Glancing away from Russ, she took a long look straight into my eyes. I knew that look, and it would be sometime before she would accept what I had done, if ever. The silence was broken when her voice quivered, "Excuse me, but I've dishes waiting to be done." With that, she headed for the kitchen.

The next day, I was sitting in the back seat of Russ's father's car when Russ broke the news. I could tell his father was terribly upset. He wasn't an ordained minister, but close to it. Russ told me he started the first Rescue Mission in town. He was quite aware I was in the back seat when he scolded, "I hope you know what you are doing, son." I pretended not to hear. Russ turned and winked. I was so relieved to get everything out in the open, even though there was more to tell.

We began moving our personal belongings into the rental house. It was fun trying to arrange the bits and pieces of odd furniture we'd picked up here and there. The rental house had a gas refrigerator and small stove. Russ would flop down on each piece of furniture as we positioned it and pull me by the arms till I was sitting on his lap. That was all we needed to get carried away with kisses and love making. I scrubbed the wood work, cabinets, and lined the shelves with new shelf paper. I bought some curtains on sale and hemmed them to fit the windows. Our little square house began to take shape. It was sad leaving my old house on Sixth Street, but I was happy to have a place we could call our own. Finally Russ and I could be together as a married couple.

I wore loose clothing to conceal my weight gain as long as I could—but Mom and others I'm sure figured it out. No words were exchanged about it, I was grateful. Our family was so active in the church I knew there would be questions about why we eloped.

Church women do gossip. I could imagine them whispering behind Mom's and my back. I had rehearsed what to say if they questioned me. "Russ didn't want to wait long enough for a big wedding—we were too much in love." My encore," Russ wanted to get married right away so we could start a family. The truth of the matter was I would have to deal internally with the fact these were all lies. To make it easier, I convinced myself it was telling white lies of sorts. To face the facts, I just couldn't control my emotions, nor could Russ, that magical night. We were carried away by desire and lost in our embraces. I was disappointed not being able to go away to college and Russ gave me the attention I needed. I had left my guard down and somehow cast aside my religious teaching and what I understood from the Bible in the heat of that night.

Responsibility for my actions came rather quickly—just seven months later I gave birth to my son, Leslie, named after Russ's father. My labor lasted for over 24 hours. I delivered at home with a mid-wife from our neighborhood. I never had experienced such pain! I continued to deal with my religion by blocking out the fact we had to get married. It was as though I took a part in a movie as the devoted wife and mother. I read Dr. Spock's books and every baby book I could get my hands on. Mom was very helpful, and those years I had helped with my baby sister, Shirley, made handling my son easier. The most difficult part and what I hated most was changing his diapers. Russ helped a lot with dirty diapers and emptying the bucket I used for soaking and bleaching. Being a mother and wife took up my day. There was no way I could go back to work. Hanging diapers outside with the weather permitting, or in the attic, was daily, along with all the cooking and house work.

We planned our second child carefully and hoped for a girl when Leslie was two. This time my labor was easier, and we named our baby girl, Jan. She had thick coal black hair and black hair all over her little body. I was scared by a rat in the cellar before she was born and I showed everyone the hair on Jan's back. It looked like an ink and pen sketch of a large rat. She was a more demanding baby than Leslie, who we nicknamed, Les. At ten months she was walking. Jan took off crawling so fast, it was hard to catch her before whatever she was after was already in her mouth. Her favorites were shaving cream, tooth paste, and bugs on the move. And, when she could get her hands into her diaper she smeared it around like finger paint. I didn't see a future artist in the pattern of the mess all over herself, her crib and the wall.

Those early years of marriage and motherhood were a challenge. The kids had the usual diseases, chicken pox, whooping cough, three day and German measles. I hated the quarantine signs we had to post on the front door when the kids were sick. The doctor came to the house and there couldn't be visitors until the kids were taken off quarantine. My sisters, Genevieve and Viola, became my primary baby sitters. Besides, they came down to use the bathtub for their weekly baths, since the old house had no bathtub. Russ and I were able to go out on Saturday evenings due to my sisters being at the house.

I decided to become more active in the church again. It was important I introduce religion to our kids. I joined the women's Faithful Follower's Class and began to sing in the choir as I had done before I was married.

CHAPTER 5

It was Russ's idea to purchase almost an acre of ground in the Pennsylvania woods along the Juniata River. The river carved a long bend through tall evergreens, reflecting their mirror image in the water. The green brilliance of the trees on the mountain side against the blue sky and sparkling water below were picture perfect. Russ picked a lot which had the steepest embankment from the river's edge. Russ remarked, "Storms up river have caused floods washing out cottages miles upstream. The twenty foot bank will protect our cabin from high water. I'll build farther back in the event water would ever approach a height close to the 1936 Johnstown Flood."

The woods were thick along the opposite river bank. Saplings growing close to tall evergreens created a thicket you could barely crawl through. Fir trees 50 feet or taller on the mountain ridge block the sun in late afternoon casting dark silhouettes onto the river. A single lane dirt road of rich red clay followed the same path as former horse and buggy's. Russ's father said, "I used to hitch ole Nell to the buggy and travel for hours to reach my favorite fishing hole a couple miles downriver. We caught eel and salmon before they built the dam." I heard his fish stories many times over.

Les was two and Jan was still a baby when we started pitching a tent facing the river. At night, when I gazed at the heavens, I saw the blackest and scariest sky I'd ever seen. Bright stars flickered on and off like tiny flash bulbs. The dippers looked dimmer in the city. Country living was new and exciting for me.

The kids pointed and giggled as squirrels, birds and wildlife appeared. We did have a floor in our tent preventing some insects from crawling in. Russ did a sketch to show me his plan for a two-story cottage with dormer windows. Mom had a fit about me taking the kids into the wilderness. She was worried about snakes and mosquitoes. Russ taught me not to be afraid of wild animals. Deer came to the river for water and muskrats were busy building dams with sticks along water soaked logs. Gray and red squirrels, groundhogs, porcupine, possum, turtles, rabbits, owls and raccoons were abundant. The kids and I loved to watch the animals scurry along the riverbank.

"I'll build the cottage right here," Russ drew a line in the dirt to show us where the porch would be facing the river. He dug a four foot square hole at the rear edge of our property and poured a cement foundation. The outhouse became our formal place to pee. I hated digging cat holes using the woods as my bathroom. Lucky the kids were still in diapers. An occasional spider hanging from the rafters in the outhouse did bother me. When I heard something rustling in the trees I would point my lantern in that direction. Eyes peered back at me. Scared, I yelled for Russ, "Hurry a wild animal is out here. I'm afraid to move!"

He came running with a bright flash light, "C'mon", he said. It was always a possum, porcupine, owl, or raccoon and nothing to be afraid of. Before long, I was able to tell them apart. At night owls hooted, whip-poor-wills called and the bullfrogs bellowed. These strange sounds were topped off with a million crickets. It took getting used to this crescendo before I could fall asleep. It was scary knowing all there was between us and these wild animals was thin canvas. But Russ had a rifle, and I knew he would protect us. Jan, Les, and I learned to identify these wild sounds.

A small creek ran along the edge of our lot. The water came from a natural spring located several acres uphill near an old abandoned farmhouse. The remains of and old Spring House made of tongue and groove logs surrounded the crystal clear water. The water was cold as ice water even in the heat of summer. There was an old gray speckled porcelain dipper we drank from. We let the kids drink and play around while we filled empty glass water jugs to carry for drinking and cooking. I was able to rustle up hot dogs, beans, and picnic food on a portable Coleman two-burner kerosene stove. I transported meat from the city in an ice chest and cooked the perishables first. We dammed up the water from the Spring House that trickled down hill onto our property. This became our fish pond and a place to store milk and butter.

One night, on my way back from the outhouse, I saw bright eyes peering back at me from the pond. "Russ, come quick! There's a big animal out here." I froze on the spot, and held the lantern still. Russ came running with his rifle and flashed his spot light toward the pond. Two huge coal black eyes were staring at us. It was a raccoon washing one of the fish we caught earlier and were saving for a future fry.

"It's an older one helping himself to our fish." Russ laughed and walked toward the coon. The raccoon ran away with our fish in its mouth. I was relieved it wasn't a mountain lion or something more dangerous. During our tenting I only saw one black bear slowly wade across the river one morning at daybreak. With each experience, I was less afraid, but anxious to get our cottage built. When the tent got soaked after several days of pouring rain I was ready to go back to the city. Dampness was not good for any of us.

Les was four and Jan two years old when we poured the deep post holes for the foundation. Russ placed large long bolts down into the cement. "I'm anchoring our frames in case flood waters ever reach our cabin. It will never wash away." With a hand saw he cut each board one by one and hammered it into place. I helped hold boards and pound nails, but not without bruising myself. Once the bottom floor was nailed down we pitched our tent on what would be the first floor.

I was plenty busy keeping two kids out of ivy and oak poison, away from bugs, snakes and unknown creatures crawling about. Jan would eat anything she could pick up with her two little fingers including bits of dirt. Les was beginning to listen and understand what "No" meant.

Once Russ was ready to raise the side frames he invited his friend, Louie, my brother-in-laws Ray, Edgar and my Uncle Herman who had a cottage up the river. When the side frames were nailed into place our cottage took shape. Russ built a large picnic table and bench by the riverbank. My sisters, Aunt Ted, who was Mom's sister, and Louie's wife and I prepared food for a picnic. Russ built a bon fire and hung a kettle on a tripod to boil corn and hot dogs. It was fun to sit at the table and watch the river go by. Our cottage became the place for relatives and friends to visit. We went swimming and fishing as weather cooperated, while Russ continued to build from dawn to dark. It took a little over two years of weekends, holidays and summer vacations until we had a two-story cottage and could say good bye to tenting. Russ rarely took time out to fish or swim with the kids and me.

When I got pregnant with my third child on the way we rented a larger house down the street from where Mom and Pop lived. This was great as Les and Jan were getting older and we needed more bedrooms. Besides we had my sisters Genevieve and Viola close as baby sitters. Carol Lee was a more difficult birth than Les or Jan. I had a rough three weeks due to the jagged tears from child birth and my hay fever returned the same month. Mom, Genevieve and Viola were a big help. After the first frost in early October I was fine. Carol Lee was such a happy baby. She rarely cried and slept through most nights. Jan saw her as a doll baby and wanted to hold her like a play thing.

Russ hung a clothes line in our attic for drying diapers on rainy days. Mom agreed to take Les and Jan up the street to her house while I washed several loads of clothes. It had been raining for days. I placed Carol Lee in her basinet in the attic and ran back and forth to the washer in the cellar. I had finished the diapers and carried a bushel basket of Russ's work clothes to the attic. When I reached the attic, I glanced over- Carol Lee was gone! I looked down and there she was lying on the floor. I dropped the clothes basket and ran to her. I picked her up and ran my hands over her head and felt over her little body. She didn't cry and looked at me with a big smile. I was frantic with worry. I wrapped a receiving blanket around her and ran downstairs and next door to the neighbor's. I pounded on their screen door. Mrs. Steiger, opened the door, "I need to use your telephone, my nine month old baby fell. Help me! It's an emergency I need to reach Dr. Mattis, right away."

"Sure, Naomi. I'll find the number." She got the book and thumbed through the pages quickly. "I've got it, I'll dial it." Mrs. Steiger handed me the phone. "Nurse, please get Dr. Mattis. My baby fell and I'm afraid she's hurt bad"

"This is Dr. Mattis, who am I speaking to?"

"It's me, Naomi Bryar. Carol Lee fell from her basinet onto the hardwood floor, doctor."

"Take her to the hospital emergency right away, Naomi, I'll meet you there."

Mr. Steiger drove me to the hospital. I ran into the Emergency Entrance holding my dear Carol Lee in my arms. Tears were rolling down my cheeks. I handed her over to the first doctor I saw. He carried her behind a curtain to an exam table. A nurse began taking her temperature and pulse while the doctor ran his hands all over her body.

He moved her arms and legs and turned her over checking her back. Carol Lee was smiling and blowing some bubbles with her saliva. She thought the doctor and nurses were playing with her.

"She's fine. Check her temperature several times through the night. If there's any change bring her back. But, her vital signs are good and I don't believe there's anything to worry about at this time." With relief I took a deep sigh. I picked her up and held her close to my chest. When I got home she ate her baby food and that evening drank part of her bottle. Russ and I got up several times during the night. Her temperature was 99 and she fussed some when I inserted the thermometer. I managed to doze off near daylight. The moment I awakened I went straight to her crib. Her little face was hot, she was burning up with fever. Russ had already left for work. I threw a bath blanket over her and ran to Mr. Steiger's to call Dr. Mattis. He agreed to come right away to our house. He arrived in less than an hour.

"I got her fever down but she doesn't seem as playful." Dr. Mattis did a thorough examination, "I think she might have pneumonia. We need to keep the fever down. Only time will tell. Keep bathing her with tepid water and rub her arms and legs with rubbing alcohol if she has a temperature. Grind up these baby aspirin and give her one with her baby food every four hours as needed. Take her temperature every hour. If her fever is still high by supper time call and I'll come back. Otherwise, I will stop in and see how she's doing tomorrow." Carol Lee wasn't her usual self but didn't cry or fuss much. Russ and I took turns holding her and sponging her down with a cool wash cloth. Her fever went down and she was peaceful—it was after midnight when I put her down in her crib and Russ and I went to our room to get some rest.

I woke up startled. I had slept longer than I thought. It was day break when I ran into Carol Lee's room. She looked pale and her eyes were rolled back in her head. I took hold of her little shoulders and shook her, "Carol Lee, Carol Lee, its' Mommy." There was no response. I picked her up and held her face next to mine. She was cold and lifeless. I ran into our bedroom, "Russ, wake up. Help me! Carol Lee isn't right. She's not breathing! "Oh, God, please don't take her from me." Russ took her from my arms. I struggled not wanting to let go.

"Please God, save her!" Russ held her head against his chest, "Run next door and call the doctor!" I reached for her.

"No, go call the doctor. Did you hear me, woman? Be quick about it—get Dr. Mattis." He turned away from me; "I'll take care of her. Go now, hurry, as fast as you can." I ran next door and pounded my fists on Mr. Steiger's front screen door. Mrs. Steiger appeared in her night gown. "Mrs. Steiger, please help, I need to use your phone. It's my Carol Lee." I was crying hysterically.

"Oh, my, sure, Naomi go right ahead?"

"Mrs. Steiger can you go over and help Russ with my baby. Wait, help me find Dr. Mattis's number. Please, I can't find the number. Hurry, I need him to come quick. My baby, she isn't right."

"What's wrong, Naomi, here sit down and let me call him for you. Dad, go over and help Russ with the baby while I wait on the line for the doctor. I need to speak with Dr. Mattis. It's an emergency!" Mrs. Steiger spoke with a raised voice.

"Tell him, it's my Carol Lee. She is...Oh, It's an emergency. I need him to come right away!"

"Dr. Mattis, I'm calling for Mrs. Bryar. It's her baby, Carol Lee. The baby is worse and not responding. Mrs. Bryar wants you to come. It's urgent! Yes doctor, Naomi is here with me. Her husband is with the baby next door. Okay, I'll tell her."

"Naomi, he's on his way." C'mon Naomi, let's go over and see what we can do to help. Russ and Mr. Steiger were standing beside the crib with Jan and Les tugging at their pant legs.

They were still sleepy and asking all kinds of questions. Mr. Steiger took them by the hand and led them down stairs. Mrs. Steiger stood beside me. As I reached to pick Carol Lee up from her crib, Russ took hold of my arms and led me a few steps away. I looked over my shoulder at my dear sweet angel lying there in her crib, like she was asleep. I began to pound his chest with my fists, screaming, "Why God, Why did you take her from me."

"Shh, try to pull yourself together. Jan and Les will hear you, they don't know what's happening." I went to pieces, and don't remember much of what happened for weeks afterward. I do remember the open casket in our parlor for three days. My little Carol Lee all dressed up in a pink silk dress, bonnet, and booties to match lying there in a pure white satin lined box. I sat staring at the casket stunned as people came with all kinds of casseroles and food, and spoke their kind words which I couldn't really comprehend. Vases of flowers kept coming. The sweet smell perfumed the entire house.

Les was quiet and stared at his sister not sure what was happening, but Jan wanted to pick Carol Lee up and wondered why she was so still. After her funeral, I began blaming myself for what happened. I asked myself over and over, why did I take the basinet up to the attic? I should have left her in her crib while I went back and forth with loads of clothes. She was sleeping when I left her. I was away only long enough to run the clothes through the ringer into the basket before running up to the attic. She must have crawled over to the edge of the basinet—enough to tip it and fell to the floor. I couldn't get Carol Lee's image from my mind as she lay there smiling at me from the linoleum floor. I saved some of her clothes, rattles, and things in a trunk in the attic.

I go to the attic often and sort through her things. I hold her little sweater up to my cheek and long for her. Jan keeps asking, "Where's Carol Lee?" The tears come to my eyes and I always answer, "She's with God in heaven."

"Why did she go?" Jan asks.

"Because God needs and wants her with him. She's happy and safe now. That's enough, you go on now, and play with your brother." After she runs along, I sit and cry. I wake up in the middle of the night and sob until my chest aches. I cry until I think I've no more tears left. Russ takes me in his arms until I fall asleep. Somehow we get by. One day runs into the next. As Russ and I look into each other's eyes across the table we know our thoughts are of our dear Carol Lee. No words are spoken, we know each other's grief.

Jan and Les coaxed Russ and me for weeks about getting a puppy. Russ brought the cutest little black and white ball of fur home. It was a 47 variety not to grow larger than a medium size poodle. Les named him Spot. Russ made it clear to the kids they'd have to help feed and clean up after the pup. They were fast to agree. When they forgot, Russ scolded them. He tried to explain that puppies have to be fed and watered and the importance of caring for Spot. It became clear it was Russ's dog and followed him everywhere. Caring for a dog did help me focus more on the day to day happenings. Spot chewed the kids' socks, shoes and got into the chocolate candy dish and chewed pieces covered the rug. Anywhere Russ went by car Spot was in the seat beside him.

CHAPTER 6

Just a few months after we buried our Carol Lee Mom burst into the kitchen unexpectedly. "Come, Noan, we've got to get to the hospital right away. It's your father. I guess it's his heart."

"Oh, Mom! Is he going to be okay?" I reached my arms out to grab hers.

"They just called from the hospital. He was taken by ambulance. I don't know what to do. He's just... I mean, your Pop is...gone!" The tears began streaming down her cheeks as she spoke.

"What? You mean he's gone? No, it can't be, not my Pop! There must be a mistake. What did they say? Couldn't they have done something to save him?" I cried out and tears flowed down my cheeks.

"Your father has been struggling for months and steadily getting worse, not only with his leg, but having difficulty swallowing, and talking. You probably didn't notice much with your short visits. He struggled to control and cover up his nervousness when anyone was around. When he reached for his glass of water half the time he spilled it or knocked over something else reaching for it. The doctor began to think he had developed St. Vitus Dance."

"What's that? I don't understand. We need some explanations!" I looked at Mom and realized I had to calm down for her sake. We hugged each other and our tears ran down our cheeks. I wanted to yell and scream and smash something, but I knew I couldn't.

"They're holding him at the hospital. I thought you would want to go down with me and your sisters to say goodbye. I called Bern and she and Ray are on their way."

"Oh, Mom, I'll get my coat and grab the kids." I turned and went sobbing to Les and Jan.

"Mother, what's wrong?" Les, asked. Jan looked up and ran to me.

"Get your coats, we have to go see Grandpap at the hospital."

"Jan grabbed her coat, "Why is he in the hospital, Mother?"

"He's real sick and we must go see him. Hurry up now, Mom's waiting." I went next door, and Mr. Steiger drove us to the hospital. Mom was wiping away her tears with her handkerchief. "Andy was engraving a watch at the Brent Building and they found him slumped over his desk. The police pounded on my door. The way they talked, I believe he was gone before the ambulance arrived." I thought I was in the middle of a nightmare. I heard Mom asking where they put Pop. I fell into an empty chair and was unable to hold back any longer-bawling out of control.

Jan started crying, "Mommy, Mommy," pulling on my arm.

Mr. Steiger led her and Les away, "C'mon, let's go get some ice cream. Your Mother needs to be with grandma now."

"God, help me!" I cried out loud.

"Naomi, Pop's in here. Mom whispered and motioned for me to enter behind a closed curtain. I got up and staggered to Pop's side. I took hold of his hand and placed it to my cheek. His hand was cold. He looked at peace.

Mom kissed his forehead, sat down at the head of his bed taking hold of his other hand. Our eyes met and no words were spoken.

A male nurse entered, "Take as long as you like."

I don't remember how long I remained.

Bern and Ray came and we sobbed and clung to each other. Mom's hands were shaking when she stood up. I remember hugging her before I left. I could hear Jan and Les asking questions out in the hallway. When I entered the waiting area Jan and Les came running. I took their hands and told them to be quiet for Pop was sleeping. I couldn't handle their questions at this time. I was thankful for Mr. Steiger interventions and he drove us home. Bern and Ray took Mom home and stayed with her and my sisters that night. Russ fixed supper for Les and Jan and put them to bed. Bern and Ray helped Mom with the funeral and church services. I remained in a state of shock for days and during the funeral. I wasn't of help to Mom other than showing up. My heart ached for Pop. I felt guilt for not being there when he needed me the most. Mom never said anything at church about Pop going downhill. He loved his grandchildren and it had been weeks since we stopped by. And to think I was his favorite, he called me his "Little Princess." If only Mom would have warned me. I went through daily motions but remained numb. Pop was my best friend and confidant. I believe he favored me above my sisters and suffered when he couldn't make good his promise to send me to college. I think he died more from a broken heart than any heart attack. Ever since the stock crash Pop had not been himself. Every day he went downtown and waited for work at his old desk. But little or no work came in. He had to watch Mom work twice as hard doing other peoples dirty laundry. It's no wonder he died at fifty. Oh, how I miss my Pop!

After the funeral I made it a point to take the kids up the street to Mom's more often. How I wished I had made more of an effort before.

"How are things, Mom?"

"It's hard when I look over at Pop's chair and it's empty. It isn't easy. The girls bicker more with each other and more neighbors are requesting I do their laundry and ironing. It's an effort to keep up with it all, but it keeps me busy. Lord knows I need the money. What I miss most is talking with your Dad before bed. There are always questions about your sister's homework. And trying to explain to Viola or Genevieve that I can't afford to buy them clothes in the department stores—they have to wear each other's. There's nothing wrong with the hand me downs from Aunt Grace or Aunt Minnie. The girls fuss and complain. I do my best to change the hem lines and shorten sleeves for them."

"For heaven's sake, Mom, do you want Russ and I to have a serious talk with Viola and Shirley?" Genevieve had taken a job and was dating Edgar.

"Oh, I don't know. The problem is when I used to put my foot down and say "No" your dad would find a way to get whatever it was. He would ask at the church, get an old scooter, roller skates, or tricycle and fix them up behind my back."

"It's worse on the weekends. They don't know what to do with themselves after church. You, Russ, and your kids are never home on weekends. You're always down at the river. You don't even bring your kids to church like you should. I worry about Les and Jan being bitten by a snake, drowning in the river, or overcome with ivy poison."

"Mom, it's not as wild as you think. I'm so tired of hearing this. Please, why don't you let Uncle Herman and Aunt Ted drive you down to their cottage. Their place is fixed up like a home with a screened in front porch. It's only an acre up the lane from us. Why won't you come?"

"I don't like all those bugs and mosquitoes. The girls might get hurt and I don't want them falling into the river. I don't know why my sister, Ted, likes it. I guess you both have a lot in common."

"Well, you complain about me taking the kids to the cottage and don't know how beautiful the country is with all the fir trees along the river. If you come for a visit you might just fall in love with it like we have."

Russ and Edgar built an insulated ice box for 50 or 75 pounds of ice to keep things cold for a week. Russ brings more ice on the weekends from the ice house about twenty miles away from the cottage. Some melts away in route, but there's enough left of the block to keep milk and meat until Russ gets down the next weekend with more ice. I thought the only thing that really bothers me is the narrow windy dirt road leading into the cottage. It's only one lane and carves along the mountain ridge with the river flowing about 100 feet below. In some places the road winds along the mountain about 300 hundred feet above the river. When Russ meets a milk truck or an occasional car, he has to drive right to the edge of the road to pass. When we pull over on the side closest to the river, I try not to look down. There is only a foot of clearance, or less, between the wheels of the car and a bank leading straight down to the river.

Not too long ago, Uncle Herman and Aunt Ted went too close the edge going around a bend in the road and Uncle Herman lost control. Their car went down the embankment. Lucky for them trees stopped the car before it plunged into the river. Uncle Herman suffered broken ribs and Aunt Ted had a broken collar bone. My cousins were in the back seat and had black and blue marks from being thrown around the back seat. Mom was aware of the accident and knows Uncle Herman drives too fast. No wonder she's hesitant to ride with him.

It was the middle of the summer when I talked with Aunt Ted and got the surprise of my life. Mom agreed to ride with them to their cottage for the day. They were driving down on Saturday, and for some reason had to come back the same night. Mom didn't say anything to me about it. I guess she and my sisters were going to surprise me. I didn't say a word and prepared meat loaf, macaroni salad, and Russ picked up two cantaloupes. We stopped for ice and headed for our cottage. I looked over at Russ, "Do you think we could speed up a little. I have to get there before Mom arrives. I want the picnic table and food ready."

"You don't even know if she's really coming. She may have told

Aunt Ted she would ride along and backed out at the last minute."

"I don't think so. I want to surprise her with how civilized and beautiful it is along our river."

"Well, I don't want you to build up your hopes and be disappointed when she doesn't show up." He directed his attention to Jan and Les in the back seat, "We can make good eating out of the picnic food can't we kids?" Jan and Les spoke in unison, "Yeh."

I glanced at the river when Russ pulled in the driveway. It wasn't high and we would be able to take the boat out. The kids ran to see if our row boat was full of water from recent rain. Russ and I unpacked the car. I started arranging paper plates and casseroles to carry to the picnic table. I yelled to the kids, "Come in here and help. Take this tablecloth to your Dad."

Les and Jan carried the oilcloth table cloth from our large kitchen table to the picnic table at the river bank. I had another linen cloth for the other end. I heard a car coming up the lane and ran to the back of our property to see if it was Uncle Herman's green Chevrolet. As the car approached, Aunt Ted rolled down the window. I could see Mom in the back seat with my sisters. "Mom, I can't believe it! You finally came to visit, I can hardly believe my eyes." I pretended to be totally surprised. Aunt Ted winked and smiled when I said, "Come down after you unpack the car. I'm fixing a picnic lunch."

"Sure, sounds great. I have a few things I brought special and will bring them along, Noan." (she always called me, "Noan", like many of my relatives did.)

"I should have everything set up in about half an hour, see you then." I was excited and hoped this visit would convince Mom this was a healthy place for Jan and Les to be raised and not this wild, dangerous place she was led to believe. Pop never did see our cottage, of course. It hadn't been finished very long before he died. He was familiar with the area, but had not come down mainly because Mom was so negative. She was always scolding me about exposing her grandchildren to unknown dangers at the river and not going to church on Sunday.

I placed a jar of pickles and the cantaloupes at the corners of the linen table cloth to hold it down in case of a breeze. Jan and Les helped with several trips back and forth with paper plates, silverware, meatloaf, macaroni salad, and a thermos of Kool aid. I heard voices, looked up, and saw Mom and my sisters coming down the lane with Aunt Ted and Uncle Herman. Jan, Les, and I walked back to greet them. Aunt Ted and Uncle Herman had been at our cottage numerous times. In fact, Uncle Herman helped Russ put up the frame. "Mom, let me show you inside the cottage." My sisters, Viola and Shirley followed in tow. Aunt Ted and Uncle Herman headed for the picnic table to join Russ.

"Mom what do you think of this old table Aunt Minnie gave me? I found these odd chairs and painted them to match."

"Yes, I see, but why did you paint over the straw and leather seats-they were antiques?"

"I didn't think about it. I'm proud of myself being able to paint. I had paint all over me. I'm learning I can do a lot more than I thought. C'mon, let me show you upstairs the way we have all the beds arranged in a big circle. Jan and Russ made this handrail out of a slender tree. Jan helped sand and varnish it."

"It looks nice and serves the purpose. So, Jan takes after Russ?"

"Yes, now that she's in second grade she isn't afraid to try anything with Russ at her side."

"Mom, Shirley and I want see what Jan and Les are doing down by the river, Viola said."

"Don't go any farther than the picnic table. I don't want you falling in that river."

"It's okay, Mom. Russ and Uncle Herman are sitting at the table with Aunt Ted. They will be fine."

"All right but don't go down the bank to the river."

"We won't." Viola and Shirley said in unison.

Mom followed me up the steep wooden stairs and looked around the large room.

"It was Russ's idea to put in four windows, two large dormer windows facing Uncle Herman's, one facing the river and the other toward the lane for light. I like the one overlooking the river the best." Mom's expression said it all. She didn't like seeing the river flowing by.

"I wouldn't want to worry about that river flooding into my front yard, nor about water snakes." Mom said.

"Don't be ridiculous. The river will never reach our front yard. It isn't possible with our high embankment. This is the reason Russ chose this lot over the others." I kept to myself, the fact about the Johnstown flood of 1936. It did reach this far down river and overflowed all the banks along here. When we bought the land from the farmer he showed us some driftwood stuck in a tree as high as our cottage roof. However, that was the worse flood since 1889 and took place two years before we bought the lot. Chances were remote a flood like those would happen again in our lifetime.

"How do you manage to undress up here with five beds and no partitions? There's no privacy."

"This is how it works, Mom. We women go up and get ready for bed first. We yell downstairs to the men when we are all settled in. The men and boys sleeping up here use lanterns and flashlights to find the right bed. They undress in the dark and crawl into bed. Sometimes when all of Russ's relatives visit we have to put three of the kids in one bed. Jan was upset about one of her young cousins wetting the bed a couple of different times when he was sleeping with her. Without partitions we have room for more beds. We place cots downstairs and on the front porch when we have big reunions. It's funny at times when Aunt Betty or Aunt Dot start joking in the dark to speak up to ensure their husbands find the right bed before crawling in."

"For heaven's sake, what do you do in the morning when it's daylight?"

"Well, the men tell us when they are ready to get up and we women turn our heads while they slip into their trousers at the bedside."

"Well, I don't think this is the best arrangement for Jan and Les to witness, for that matter, any of your nieces or nephews."

"Mom, believe me it's harmless and the kids get a big kick out of coming to the cottage and all sleeping in one big room. It's like going to a Boy Scout Camp. They laugh and carry on back and forth at night until it's hard to get them to quiet down and go to sleep." I could tell by Mom's raised eyebrows and stern look she didn't see any humor in my comments.

"I see, well it may seem like fun for you, but I don't think it's the best arrangement."

"Mom followed me downstairs, and down the steps to the picnic table where Russ was cutting the meat loaf. Thank heavens it turned out to be a cloudy day, no rain. I hate when we plan a picnic and have to hold it inside. Aunt Ted was cutting the watermelon she'd brought, and Mom went to sit by her. Russ looked over at Uncle Herman, "Do you want a beer?"

"Sure, I'll have one, if you are." Mom was laughing with Aunt Ted as they batted at a couple of yellow jackets diving after the macaroni salad. That was the first time in weeks I heard Mom really have a good hearty laugh. I was glad she was occupied and not paying too much attention to Russ and Uncle Herman having a beer. Pop didn't drink alcohol, and Mom disapproved of anyone drinking alcohol. Aunt Ted and I told Mom how we play cards by a kerosene lamp and tell stories in the evening. When we're lucky with getting reception on our shortwave radio we listen to the *'Green Hornet'* or *'The Shadow'* with Jan and Les. The kids share a bottle of Pepsi on Saturday and Sunday nights. They pour their Pepsi into single shot whiskey glasses and drink one shot at a time. They take turns pretending to be bartenders while playing poker.

"Mom do you want me to take you and the kids for a ride in our new row boat after lunch? Russ got the farmer to build us a good sturdy one."

"I want to go." Viola said, with her mouth full of potato chips.

"No, I don't think so. Neither of you have ever been around water. It's too dangerous for you and Shirley. You might fall overboard." Mom said.

"Mom we won't take them out in deep water. I'll have them sit on the seat with me while Russ rows. Jan and Les row me around the river all the time and they are younger than Viola or Shirley. They each take an oar and bait my hook when we go fishing. I usually read a book while we're fishing. I guess one sees my bait floating on top of the water and grabs it. The kids yell at me when a fish is after my bait. Much to my amazement, I grab my rod and pull in a rock bass or sun fish. Jan or Les remove my prize from the hook for me, too. If it's big enough we keep it for our pond, or clean it for a fry later. Don't worry about the girls, it's safe, I promise."

"Well, I guess it's all right, but stay close to the bank where I can see you." I took Shirley by the hand and Viola walked along side of me down the river bank to the boat. Russ pulled the boat part way up the bank to help them climb in. Jan and Les shoved the front of the boat away from the bank and jumped in. Russ pushed against the bank with one of the oars. We floated out and Russ put the oar back in place and began rowing up the river. I waved back at Mom and Aunt Ted. Viola and Shirley followed suit.

My sisters, our kids, Russ and I enjoyed the boat ride and when we got back Shirley couldn't wait to tell Mom about the turtles she saw on a water soaked log across from Uncle Herman's cottage. Mom still wasn't convinced life around the river is full of fun and totally safe. It would take more than one afternoon with Aunt Ted, Uncle Herman, Russ and I to show her it isn't as dangerous as she imagines. My hope is she will come again. This turned out to be one of my most memorable picnics. If only my Pop were here—that would have made it absolutely perfect.

CHAPTER 7

When World War II broke out Russ tried to enlist, but he and his brother, Don, were rejected due to a problem with their hearing. I took a secretarial job at the railroad. Many jobs were open to women because most of our men were going off to war. Russ's three younger brothers joined the Air Force and were in different parts of the country for training. Russ hated not being able to fight for his country. He continued at the railroad and became more resentful with time.

Before going to work at the railroad I sent Jan and Les up the street to Mom's house early in the morning. She made sure they had breakfast and were properly dressed for school. Mom made them comb their hair and sometimes sent them back down the street to change their clothes when what they had chosen to wear was inappropriate. Les and Jan carried their lunches, and we gave them money for soup and a drink at a mom and pop store across from Fairview School. Most of the children in our neighborhood still went home for lunch, their mom's hadn't joined the work force yet. I became one of the air raid wardens for our street. I wore a helmet and carried a flashlight with a black lens. We had black out practices in the event enemy planes were spotted. When the sirens sounded everyone had to pull down their blinds and turn out their lights.

When I wasn't on duty and we heard the air raid siren, Les would pull down the blinds, Jan turned off the lights, I grabbed a flashlight, and we ran upstairs to hide in the attic stairwell. The kids and I would huddle together on the dark attic steps until we heard the all clear siren. When the battery in our big shortwave radio was charged we tuned in for news and listened for the all clear signal. When Les and Jan heard foreign languages on the radio, they got excited and thought the Germans were close by. Our ice man was of German decent and all the neighborhood kids were afraid of him. He had a couple gold caps on his front teeth which scared them. The kids used to run behind his truck and pick up ice chips when he was delivering ice to the neighbor's. Since the war started the kids ran the other direction when he came up the street. They feared he would attack them.

I can remember Jan running into the house one day screaming, "Mother, am I really adopted?" She was teary eyed.

I said, "Where did you get such a ridiculous notion?"

"Les said the ice man is my real father, a Nazi, and I was adopted." Les came into the kitchen laughing hilariously.

"Les, stop teasing her. Look how you have upset her. Tell Jan you were kidding before this goes any further!"

"She is so stupid. She believes anything you tell her."

"Never mind, she's younger and teasing her to be afraid of Mr. Smyth isn't good. Tell her the truth or your father will deal with you when he comes home."

Les ran out the kitchen door, "Jan I can't help it if you look like the ice man."

I put my arms around Jan, "Your brother is teasing, forget what Les told you. You're not adopted and the ice man is harmless. He's been in this country for years and has nothing to do with the war." Russ worked second shift and was never home when the kids were bickering. He did help correct them on weekends.

Les and Jan went around the neighborhood gathering bolts, pieces of iron and metal to turn in for the war effort. We were rationed for silk stockings, cigarettes, butter, and gasoline. I had trouble getting margarine—even the kind you had to mix. Margarine came in a square box and looked like a pound of lard. A small orange pellet was enclosed, when mixed with this lard-like substance, it turned yellow. It looked like butter, but didn't taste like butter. Russ hated his meals without real butter. He would nag at mealtime because all we had was margarine, and there were times when there was none of that either. When I snagged a pair of nylon stockings we used fingernail polish to stop a run. Sometimes I just had to go to work with a run or snag in my stockings. About this time women began to wear slacks or pants to work. I refused to wear pants and continued to have my hair and nails done at the beauty parlor. If Russ could spend money on beer I could have my hair and nails done. But Russ didn't seem to notice. I received compliments at work for the way I dressed and acted around the railroad men.

Russ began drinking more beer and the more he drank the more we got into disagreements. He would upset me until I lost control of my temper. I threw anything within reach especially when he headed for the door. He would slam the screen door on his way out and head for the local tavern. I knew he was bitter not being able to join his brothers who went to war. Russ hated working for the railroad. Everyone had to make sacrifices during the war, but he lost his patience. It was upsetting to see him this way.

Even more difficult was seeing another flag appearing in one of our neighbors' windows with a star in the center indicating they had lost one of their boys in the war. Russ and I were concerned about his three brothers, my brother-in-law, and the neighborhood boys who stopped frequently to visit Mom for pie or cake. They were all gone. It was a big celebration when one of them came home on leave. They all flocked to Mom's like the old days. Mom never stopped baking. She baked something special for each one on leave and continued to bake for the neighbors in order to make ends meet—there was always something in the oven even on the hottest of days. My sisters came to our house for their Saturday bath, and continued to baby sit our kids.

Mom's old house was creaking worse than when I lived there. Rats were scurrying up the walls between the partitions from the unfinished dirt cellar. Mom would remove her shoe and tap against the wall to scare them. A few seconds of silence would occur. Then, you could hear them running back and forth behind the plastered wall. She was lucky they didn't chew through the walls and get into the main house and cupboards. Mom set traps around the cellar and caught some. It got to be funny. My sisters would yell, "Mom there goes one!" Then off came one of Mom's shoes. Les and Jan, my sisters, and I laughed as she went after them with such vengeance.

When I took the kids to a movie on Saturdays the newsreels were scary. They showed Hitler and his troops marching and seizing more countries. Usually a long clip of the bombings in England, people rushing into bomb shelters and speeches by Winston Churchill were shown. Large billboards around town depicted Hitler's bayonet stabbed through the belly of a baby. No wonder the kids were scared when they thought the Germans were coming.

When Russ provoked me I blurted out, "You son of a bitch, God dammit."

Russ, would have a half smile when I didn't repeat the slang words exactly as I had heard men and women yell back and forth at the railroad. Russ smoked and I began smoking too. He rolled his own cigarettes, they were clumsy, and fell apart. I bought a cigarette roller and tobacco to make our cigarettes more uniform. I only smoked at home, at the cottage, and in restaurants. I liked a cigarette or two along with my coffee. It was frowned upon for a woman to smoke on the street, or on the streetcars like men did.

With Russ and I both working we could afford to buy a house two doors down from the one we had been renting. I enrolled the kids for dancing lessons. Jan took ballet, toe, tap and acrobatics. Les danced with her at times and took piano, oboe, and later saxophone lessons. When Jan entered Keith Junior High School, our house, cottage, and car were paid for. But, life in the city fragmented our family. We were all going different directions during the week, except for church in the school months, and gathering the family together for dinner on Sundays. I rarely got Russ to church, unless the kids were giving a speech or singing. I would still have to coax him into it. The kids and I did manage to eat suppers together.

Russ continued to work the 3 p.m. to midnight shift and he made stopping at the local tavern a regular habit after work. I could smell alcohol on his breath when he crawled along side of me in bed around 1:30 or 2:00 a.m. On Saturdays during winter months he always cleaned up and went to Danny's Tavern. On Sundays he frequented the Moose or Elk's Club. He used to invite me on a Saturday or Sunday night. I liked an occasional drink, but mostly it was fun to go out to socialize and coax Russ into a dance or two—which I enjoyed. It had been weeks since he invited me to go along. He would get cleaned up and head for the back door without a word.

"I guess you're going out drinking again, Russ. Don't you think you are over doing it lately?" This wasn't the first time I confronted him about his drinking. With a mean ugly stare he snarled, "It's the only way I can relax. Don't you understand woman what I go through at the railroad shops all week?"

"Well, it seems to me drinking is all you want to do on the weekends. There are things you could be doing around our house. I'd like to re-do the hardwood floors in the dining room and parlor."

"All you do is nag, woman, Don't you see I'm tired. I just want to relax."

"I think if you took more of an interest in our house you could get your mind off drinking. It's not a good influence for the kids either."

"That's enough! I don't want to hear anymore. If it weren't for you and the kids I wouldn't have to go near those shops."

"So, it's our fault you have to go to work? Why don't you bid on some other job if you hate it so much!"

"You don't know what you're talking about. We're having lay offs in different departments and you know it. I probably will get bumped into a worse job as it is because there are guys with more seniority. I'm sick and tired of hearing you tell me what I should or shouldn't do!" He walked past me and went out the kitchen door, slamming the screen door behind him. It does no good to confront him about anything anymore. Thank heavens he's in better spirits when we're at the cottage.

Les was writing little poems and trying to write short stories. I encouraged him and read everything he wrote. I worried about Les because of his rheumatic heart, and I insisted Russ not make him do strenuous work around the cottage. There were always weeds to be cut due to all the rain. We had a large garden and our well had gone dry. Russ began digging deeper. Jan helped Russ with any project he undertook. Les stayed in the background because he knew he could not keep up with Jan, nor was he interested in physical labor. He always went along when there was fishing and swimming, but didn't have the stamina for heavy work. He did a lot of reading and writing on the front porch facing the river. Les tried to help Russ, but it never seemed to suit. Russ would work with him a short while, sensing his disinterest. Several times I overheard him say, "Go on in and help your mother with the dishes." Of course, Jan was delighted when Les was told to do the dishes, or come indoors to help me with the cooking. Jan would do anything to avoid doing the dishes or working indoors. She was at Russ's side every chance she got.

Russ and Jan removed smooth flat bottom stones from the river, loaded them into the row boat, and made steps up the steep embankment. She helped re-dig the well. Jan would stand in a large 10 gallon bucket attached by rope to a pulley on top a tripod Russ had built. Russ lowered the rope and eased Jan down into a 14 foot well. She would dig and fill the bucket with wet dirt and small rocks. I would hear her yell, "Dad, the bucket is full. You can pull it up now."

"Stand aside, honey," Russ would call down to her as he yanked on the rope and dragged the bucket off to the side to empty it.

This went on for hours, weekend after weekend, as they alternated digging trying to get deep enough to fill the well with water. When Jan got tired, Russ would holler, "Get in the bucket, honey and I'll pull you up." Jan would stand in the bucket and Russ would raise her to ground level and swing her over to safety. I felt the work was too heavy, but Russ insisted he was making sure she didn't work too hard. One nice thing- when we were at the cottage I could talk with Russ without ending up in an argument.

After Less had a few poems published in the local newspaper he kept talking about becoming a writer. It was exciting for Les, Jan, and me to see his name in print. The women at church remarked about reading his poems in the paper. I was so proud of Les and called attention to Mom and all the relatives about it. Russ would barely acknowledge his poetry, certainly not praise him for his accomplishment.

"Boy you've got to think about a trade and get your head out of the sand. You'll not be able to make a living writing, so forget it!" Like his father and brothers, Russ's hate for the Railroad grew stronger. Everyone seemed to condemn the railroad. But Russ insisted it was the only way to make a living. As Les continued his writing, Russ and he grew further apart. Jan became his favorite, although he would deny it. He spent more time with her in target practice, hunting, and fishing. Les continued to do his best to tag along.

When the war was over I quit my job at the railroad. My asthma got worse and I had to stop going to the cottage in August. The fields were loaded with ragweed and got the best of me—I could barely breathe. The doctor had me wear a black rubber mask resembling the protective gas mask used during the war. It was annoying and cumbersome. The adrenalin did help, but made my heart race. I wheezed until I wasn't sure I would make it through the night. I prayed for the first frost to come early and kill the ragweed.

Les and Jan helped me by cooking simple meals and doing household chores. Jan did the washing and ironing. They took turns dusting and scrubbing. After a heavy frost, it was like a miracle. In a day or two I could breathe normal again. But, for some reason, I began stumbling and falling over the least little bump in the sidewalk, or over the curb. I tore my silk stockings and ended up with bloody knees. I shrugged it off to inattention. My mind was always wandering, rather than concentrating on the imperfections of the streets or brick sidewalks.

Russ's drinking increased to several six-packs over a weekend at the cottage. We drifted further apart. I admit he was easier to get along with after a few drinks. This led to his taking straight shots of vodka with beer chasers, I'd try to reason with him. "Russ I don't think you should drink before going to work. What if your boss smells alcohol on your breath?"

"You let me worry about it. I need a drink or two to muster the courage to go down there and face another eight hours."

"Russ, if you hate your job that much, please bid on something else."

"How many times do I have to tell you, woman? I don't have the seniority to bid on better jobs—I've no choice. Let me alone. All you do is nag!"

I couldn't discuss his drinking without ending in a fight. "Russ, will you unclog the drain in the bathroom sink? I can't get the water to go down." He turned and walked away from me. That night, I used a plunger and the sink was filled with dirty water and large black pieces of gunk floating about. When he went to shave the next morning, I finally got his attention, "You made a worse mess. You don't know what you're doing, woman."

"At least I tried a plunger on it. Damn you, Russ. You aren't lifting a finger to fix anything around here."

"There you go again. Nag, nag, all you ever do is nag."

I may have made it worse, but at least he took the drain apart and cleaned it out. I surprised myself with how many things I could accomplish when I had to. The sink just wasn't one of them. Almost daily I heard him say, "I would rather take a beating than go to work." On Saturday evening, just like every other Saturday, he shaved, put on a pair of gabardine slacks and a nice dress shirt. "Where are you going?" I asked. Even though I knew his pattern.

"I'm going down to Danny's Tavern for a beer."

"Can I go along for a change?"

"There's nothing going on down there tonight. You'd be bored."

"No, I wouldn't. I want to get out of the house. Russ, we used to go out Saturday evenings. Now you leave me here and most of the time you don't even tell me where you're going."

"I've told you time and again I want some peace. There is nothing going on and no reason for you to tag along."

"Please. C'mon take me along. You can bring me home early and go back out if you want."

"No, I need to be by myself. I've got to go." He opened the back door. I got up from my chair, and grabbed his arm. "Wait, Russ, please. I really want to go."

"Let go of my arm, woman." He pulled away and kept right on going.

"You son of a bitch," I yelled as he walked out the back door. "God dammit," I cursed to myself. I wanted to throw a plate at him but I'd have to clean up the mess. My anger led to tears. I sat down at the kitchen table and cried. What happened to the man I married? It's as if he doesn't want me around. Oh, I'm good enough to wash his greasy overalls, iron his white shirts, shop for groceries, cook, and clean up after him. Well, it's time we have a serious talk. So, I'm not working at the railroad anymore and bringing in a paycheck. I've plenty of work to keep this house in order. Of course, house work isn't real work according to him. I should be entitled to go out at least on a Saturday night. If it were proper I would show him.

I can imagine the expression on Russ's face if I walked into Danny's Tavern, sat at the bar and pretended I don't know him. I know women who go looking in bars for their husbands. Why not?

CHAPTER 8

A few rays of light came through a small slit of a window in the heavy metal door behind me. It had been hours since the nurses dragged me here. I don't know how long I'd been day dreaming and must have dozed off. I sobbed and cried out until I was hoarse- nobody came. Desperate and frightened I wondered what would come next. My life lately was like a puzzle. The pieces didn't fit. I struggled to stand several times but with my arms bound in this damn garment I couldn't get my balance.

I heard footsteps in the hallway. I cried out, "Get me out of here! Why are you torturing me?" My voice was louder and shrill since I had stopped sobbing.

Keys rattled, the door opened and there stood nurse Claney.

"Mrs. Claney, where have you been? Help me get out of this thing! I can't get my breath."

"Not now, Naomi. We will. But Dr. Dixon wants to see you first."

"Can't you at least loosen these straps? They're cutting off my circulation."

"Yes I know, however you're late for your appointment. She leaned over, yanked me to my feet by the straps at my back and I was able to keep my balance. Claney held onto the straps and led me down a long dark narrow hallway to a set of floor to ceiling metal doors. A male nurse with a large ring of keys unlocked the door and nodded for Claney to lead me through. She steered me into a room that looked familiar. It was cluttered with stainless steel cabinets filled with medical instruments. A black leather examining table with white paper stretched down the middle took up most of the room. A black leather stool with chrome swivel wheels and a goose necked lamp were pushed to one side.

Claney led me to a gray metal straight backed chair and let go of the straps. I flopped onto the seat. I noticed a large black recliner on the opposite side of the room by a window screened with heavy black twisted wire.

Through the doorway entered a short stubby man in a long white coat leafing through a manila folder, "Well, Naomi, the head nurse told me you acted out again this morning? You're making it more difficult on yourself and frightening the nurses with this type of behavior. What do you have to say for yourself?"

"Dammit to Hell what kind of a place is this? Did the head nurse tell you she and her nurses forced me into this thing, dragged me to a dark room and locked me up?" I took a closer look at him. He was bald except for a rim of reddish hair leading from his temples around the back of his head. A few thin strands of longer red hair swept across his freckled crown. Reddish hairs protruded from his nostrils and his neck was rubbed red from a heavily starched collar. His coat sleeves were soiled and turned inside out at the ends. There were ink marks around his lapel and side pockets. I've seen him before. Perhaps it was yesterday or the day before. Why can't I remember?

He peered at me over his dark rimmed glasses, "You brought all this on yourself, Naomi."

"I did? How so? Is this how you treat a person who doesn't do exactly as they're told? Why are you holding me against my will? Where's my doctor?"

"Now, Now, Naomi, you know very well I'm your doctor now, Dr. Dixon."

"There's got to be a mistake. Dr. Hill's my doctor."

"My, Oh my, we're forgetful today." And with a discouraged grin he continued with, "You've been under my care for weeks."

"What?" I snapped back, "No, you're wrong, doctor. I've only been here a few days." I remembered seeing those black oxford shoes with thick rubber soles resembling the tread on snow tires. But when was this?

"If you're my doctor, as you say, what am I here for?" My arms were throbbing in unison with my heart beat. I could feel my pulse at my wrists.

"Let's start again, Naomi! You're in the Pennsylvania State Hospital." He hesitated, "And...," He paused and reopened the folder and shuffled papers. It was as though he was unsure himself how long I'd been here. By the disgusted look on his face I thought I'd better soften my tone of voice.

"Naomi, we're doing our best to help you. But we need your cooperation. You're condition has improved but I can't release you yet."

"What is this so called 'condition' I have?"

"To call it by name isn't important, you're just not yourself. Let's leave it there for now," he said.

"You're right." I tried to lower my voice, "I'm not myself but who could be when we're kept locked and bound up! I can barely breathe in this tight thing."

Our eyes met and his brows lowered. I saw a look of concern as he walked to the doorway, "Nurse please remove Naomi's strait jacket, it will no longer be necessary."

"Doctor, are you sure? You want her out of the restraint?"

"Yes, let's make Naomi more comfortable."

Mrs. Claney untied the ties at my back and unwound the straps around my body. She acted coy and avoided eye contact as usual and pulled the jacket over my head. I rubbed one arm and then the other. What a relief! I had imprints from the seams imbedded in my skin like long deep cuts. Oh, how I wanted to throw that garment over her head and then his to see how they liked it! I glared at her but held my tongue. She got my message. I was furious. She wasn't concerned about me or would have helped me get out of that contraption sooner.

"Thank you, nurse, that'll be all for now."

"Shall I wait outside Doctor?"

"No, it won't be necessary." He closed the door behind her.

"Look at these grooves in my arms Doctor. Why do you allow this type of treatment by these nurses?"

"Naomi trying to escape puts the staff on edge and leads to consequences just like you've experienced. Kicking and screaming will not get you home sooner," he scolded.

"But, doctor, I can't stand it in a room with a bunch of women who are crazy."

"I realize a few women are annoying." He sounded apologetic, "We have to learn to get along with one another, Naomi. Have a seat in the recliner by the window. You'll be more comfortable."

He rolled himself on the swivel stool right behind me. I got a whiff of his after shave. It reminded me of my Pop who always wore "Old Spice."

"Is that better?" he asked.

"Yes, Doctor Dix…What did you say your name was?"

"Dixon, Dr. Dixon. I want us to become friends, Naomi. In order to get to know one another better I need to ask you a few questions. Lean back and get comfortable. I'll put on some soft music. Close your eyes and try to block out any noise from the hallway."

"Okay." It had been a long while since I heard one of my favorites, "September Song." I sensed somehow he knew it.

CHAPTER 9

"Naomi, picture your favorite place and describe it to me."

"I'm sitting in my row boat and the sun is warming my back. I've drifted away from the rocks protruding in the middle of the river."

"Where is this river you describe?"

"It's near Groundhog Valley in the Pennsylvania Mountains. Russ built our cottage along the Juniata River. The river winds through the mountains of tall dark evergreen trees reflecting their shadow onto the water. I named our cottage 'Shangrila'—it's hidden from the sky under the shade of tall oak and fir trees. It's my hidden paradise."

"Sounds like you're at peace when there. I take it your husband likes it too?"

"Yes, he comes down on weekends and loves to fish in the summer."

"Your husband claims you're upset with him? Is that so, Naomi?"

"Upset? You've got it right. I can't wait till I get my hands on him. He moved a strange woman in our house as my care giver. She was disgusting and a liar. She convinced Russ and my kids I was imagining things and confused. I was bedridden for a year and my doctor couldn't explain why. I believe those pills she insisted I take made me worse. She was syrupy sweet when Russ or my kids were around."

"Was her name Maggie?"

"Yes. And I hated her calling me 'Nomi.' The way she talked down to me as if speaking to a child."

"I heard you lost your temper with her. What did she do to provoke you?"

"As soon as the kids and Russ were gone, she would brag about taking care of the cooking and house work. I resented her having to change my bed because I couldn't make it to the bathroom in time. She complained but it was obvious she was in charge of me, my husband, kids and there was nothing I could do about it."

"How did that make you feel, Naomi?"

I opened my eyes and blurted out, "I wanted to get out of bed and smack her when I heard her bragging to Russ and the kids about her stew or all the house work she had done. I wanted my house and family back. But I was too weak and could barely walk across the hall to the bathroom. I struggled with the thoughts of remaining bedfast and decided to give up. I refused some of her food and didn't want to swallow the pills. I thought it was time for me to join Carol Lee and Pop in heaven."

Maggie, staring down at me insisted, "Take these pills, Nomi." I was sick of her ordering me about and making me take those pills. I began to pretend to swallow until she left the room. I spit the pills into a sock and hid them in my dresser drawer. I prayed for the Lord to take me home.

I remember one day I asked, "Maggie will you bring me some crackers, or bread to keep at my bedside. I won't have to call on you when I feel sick to my stomach."

"Nomi, if you eat your meals there is no need for crackers or anything else."

"Dammit. Bring me some crackers or I'll tell Russ you're refusing." The next morning I found crackers on my bedside table.

After a few days of snacking and no pills I began to feel stronger. My energy slowly improved. I began to walk around upstairs every day and look out the window. When I heard her coming I'd crawl back into bed and pretend to be as weak as before.

About two weeks later I felt strong enough to take my home and family back. I went downstairs got the broom from the cellar way and screamed, "Get out of my house you son of a bitch!" I chased her out the front door and down the porch steps.

"That's when you hit her, right?"

"No! I tried but missed. I kept swinging my metal boom wildly with all my strength. She threw her arms over her head and backed away. Lord knows I wanted to strike her. I'd had enough of her lying and trying to take my house and kids away from me."

"What did your husband say about your chasing the housekeeper away?"

"Russ was furious but the kids thought it was great. They were happy I got rid of her."

"Could you be mistaken and really bruised her badly?"

"No. There was no blood I just kept swinging and she backed away. I wish I had hit her, it would have served her right."

"Your husband said you have an uncontrollable temper. Is this true?"

"No. Well, sometimes I lose my temper, but who doesn't. I had a whole year or her hovering over me and telling me what to do. If I hadn't been so sick, I would have chased her out sooner."

Dr. Dixon paused and shuffled through papers in a folder on his lap, he reviewed her vital signs and blood tests, all except her blood pressure were normal. She weighed in at 135 pounds and was 64 inches tall. He thought, *she's attractive and an intelligent woman at 43. He noticed her coal black hair as it lay in natural waves pressed perfectly into place emphasizing her pure marshmallow white skin. Her morning outburst made me think her diagnosis of 'behavioral disorder' might include a touch of schizophrenia.*

"Naomi, what kind of relationship do you and your husband have?"

"As good as any, I guess. The old man is drinking a lot and has lost interest in the house. He never did get along with our son. Ever since Les was diagnosed with a rheumatic heart Russ was impatient with him. I intervened when I thought Russ was being too rough or wanted him to do heavy work around the cottage. When Les started saying he wanted to be a writer when he grew up, Russ would raise his voice and preach to him about finding a trade of some kind—being a mechanic. I encouraged Les to write poems and saw nothing wrong with it. I didn't want to see my son working for the railroad."

"What about your daughter, Jan. Does your husband get along with her?"

"Oh, yes, he thinks the sun rises and sets with her. They are always together."

"Has your husband ever hit you, Naomi?"

"Yes, when he had too much to drink. Only a couple times he lost his temper and hit me across the side of the head. I was scared. The kids started screaming and ran down from upstairs to protect me. When they appeared he calmed down. Russ didn't mean to hurt me he just lost his temper."

"Did you ever hit him during a fight?"

"No, but I threw pans, and anything within reach over the years. One or two may have grazed him."

"Do you still love your husband, Naomi?"

"Well, it's not the same. He and I used to get together and went through the motions on Sunday afternoons when the kids were gone. He smelled of alcohol and cigarettes and always fell asleep afterward. It's my duty as a wife, you know. I didn't refuse him but there wasn't much in it for me."

"Is there another man in your life?"

"Yes. He is a kind and patient man, a lot different than Russ."

"Tell me, Naomi, who is this other love in your life?"

"Dr. Hill, he was supposed to meet me here. What happened to him?"

"Are you sure this love is reciprocal?"

"Of course, I'm positive about him. He used to call me all the time."

"Maybe it's out of concern. Don't you think that's it, Naomi?"

"No! You're wrong he really loves me."

"The old man hates me now because he probably found out about Dr. Hill. Isn't that why I'm here? I'll get even with him and whoever else is responsible for putting me here! God knows I gave Russ plenty of chances to change things, but he's set in his ways. I would have liked him to be more romantic, take me out to supper and dancing from time to time. Like when we were first married. For years he took me out dancing on New Year's Eve. I miss getting dressed up to go out. The only time I dressed up lately was to go to church, or for an appointment with Dr. Hill. He always appreciated and commented on the way I looked."

"So you think Russ is jealous and this is the reason why you're here?"

"He brought me here. I'm not sure if others were involved, but I'll find out and when I do they will pay the price!"

"What do you mean by, 'pay the price'?"

"It depends upon the time and the place, and who is responsible. They will get their due, I can assure you. Wait till Dr. Hill finds out where I am. My son will get to the bottom of all this!"

"Well, for now, Naomi I want to assure you I'll do everything for you to have the best of care. Let's take one day at a time. And we'll talk soon again."

"We've had a nice chat today. Let me get the nurse and she'll take you back to your ward."

"Is that it! When can I go home? I can't stand much more of this."

"Not just yet, Naomi. We have to get you completely well and back to normal."

"I don't understand. Why won't you release me?"

There was a pause and with a puzzled look he scribbled something in the manila folder with my last name on it. He got up, opened the door and called for a nurse. Who should appear but nurse Claney. She looked at me rather sheepishly and walked over to the recliner where I was sitting.

"Nurse, please take Naomi back to the ward. We're finished for today."

"Yes, doctor. Should we increase her medicine or did you write a new order?"

"No, there are no changes for now. Naomi, I'll be seeing you again soon."

Nurse Claney took hold of my arm, "The sooner you release me the better. Let go of me. I don't need to be led!" I walked beside her into the hallway and glanced around to see where this room was in relation to where I had been before I tried to escape. There were double doors and nurse Claney had keys this time to open them.

"Are you feeling better now?" Claney asked.

"Yes, better than when I had that contraption around me cutting off my circulation. Where were you while I was stuck in that room?" She ignored my question and changed the subject.

"We've got to get back dinner trays will be coming soon." Mrs. Claney chatters on with the usual tone of pleasantries. Dinner was the last thing I had on my mind. Another nurse walked up, "Naomi, your daughter is here. Mrs. Claney, will you take Naomi downstairs? Her daughter is waiting." Mrs. Claney nodded, and we headed for the elevator.

I was thinking as we rode in the elevator Jan may have news about me getting out of this place. And, she always brings me something good to eat. Jan was waiting by the elevator door as it opened. Jan always looks nice. Her dark brown almost black hair in place, she's all grown up although still in her teens. I think those tap and ballet dancing lessons helped her have a nice figure. She's a good dancer and I hope one day she will be a dancer or in show business. I named her Joan, after Joan Crawford, my favorite actress, but we nicknamed her Jan. She's attractive and takes after my side of the family. We are about the same height, have the same dark eyes—her hair isn't quite as dark and curly as mine. She wanted braces for her upper teeth, but we couldn't afford it. I can't imagine Jan without a slight protrusion of her upper teeth. I don't understand why she hasn't been able to persuade Russ to let me come home.

"Mother, how are you feeling today? I brought you a peanut butter sundae." She led me to a table in the visiting area.

"Fine, but you've got to get me out of here! Most of the women here are crazy."

"Yes, I know, Mother, but you're undergoing treatment. I can't take you home yet. Eat your sundae. It's already melting."

"If your brother were here he would find a way to get me out of this place."

"Mother you know Les is overseas and it will be some time before he can get home on leave. Even if he were here, there isn't anything he can do till the doctor releases you."

"Jan, why am I here of all places? I'm not sick."

"Mother, I've told you before, Dad said this was the only place being able to provide you with the type of treatment you need."

"What treatment? I don't see any special treatment except talking with that Dr. Dixon and occasionally a pill or two. Oh, yes, I guess you could call what I get from these nurses treatment. They treat me like a criminal. What have I done? Is there something I don't know?"

"No, Mother, you've not done anything except lose your temper and seem confused while you were bedfast. I don't fully understand this whole business myself." Jan had a worried look as she spoke.

"Where's your Dad? I can't wait to get my hands on him. Why doesn't he come here and face me?"

"Mother, I try to get him to come, but he won't. He's drinking more than ever. When I ask him to come he flatly refuses. I suppose he's afraid of how you would react."

"I'd react, all right! I would like to lay my hands on him, one more time."

"Mother, please don't go getting yourself upset. Do you like your sundae?"

"Yes, it's my favorite."

"How are the meals here? Are you getting enough to eat?"

"No, I'm always hungry. The food is horrible and tasteless. I can barely get it down."

"I'll talk with the nurse when she comes and see what can be done."

"Jan, I don't have any of my own clothes. I'm sick of these old house dresses."

"I marked your clothes, even your socks with a black marking pen. I don't know what happens to everything. I was taking your clothes home and washing them myself, but it wasn't working out. I can't come to visit on the same days during the week due to my irregular hours at work."

"I can't understand what they do with my personal things. Someone has to be stealing them."

"Mother, I don't believe anyone is taking your clothes. I think they're losing them in the laundry. I'm sorry, but I can't stay long today. I wanted to check on you and bring you a sundae. I'm due at work within the hour. I'll get the nurse to take you back upstairs." Jan went to the reception desk while I waited at the table. I noticed there was only one other person visiting a woman in the visiting area. Jan walked back slowly to the table, "Promise me you will do what you can to get me out of here."

"Mother, I have never stopped trying and will continue until you're home, I promise." Jan took hold of my arm and led me over to the elevator. I grabbed her arm with both hands.

"Jan, don't forget your promise." The elevator door opened. A different nurse appeared and took hold of my left arm.

"Nurse, will you see if Mother can get some snacks from time to time between meals. She says she's always hungry." Jan asked politely.

"Naomi doesn't eat all her food at meal times. It's no wonder she gets hungry," the nurse replied sharply.

"Still, I would appreciate you looking into some snacks for her. Is it a problem to offer her snacks between meals, or do I need to call her doctor?"

"No, you needn't call her doctor. I'll see to it," she said with authority.

"Bye, Mother, take care, I'll be back soon." Jan waved goodbye as the nurse led me into the elevator. I waved to Jan as the elevator door closed between us.

CHAPTER 10

I'm the concerned daughter, the only one visiting Mother often enough to see what is happening. I began to think about when Mother first started having trouble getting around. It was at the beginning of my junior year in high school. My brother, Les, was in his first year of college at Penn State Undergraduate Center. He continued to work at the ice cream factory while going to college. Mother was falling down even in our kitchen in which she was familiar. It began to be a struggle for her to get up and down the stairs at the house. Her energy was gone. She never was much of a cook, but when she put her mind to it her meals were fine.

Lately, her meals consisted opening a can of soup or making a sandwich. She loved to read and went from cover to cover very quickly. Mother joined several book clubs and my Aunt Genevieve, we called her "Beb," exchanged books every week. Routinely I found her reading at the kitchen table. I noticed her feet shuffling constantly under the table, and the last two fingers on her right hand were always in motion. Les and I were doing almost all the house work which gave us little time to study. Mother began staying in bed longer and came down stairs for meals. We thought this was temporary like when she had her asthma attacks. However, days went into weeks and she was getting weaker.

Dad was concerned and telephoned Dr. Hill. He took Mother for an examination and blood tests. Dad said, "Dr. Hill thinks your Mother is anemic but some blood tests had to be sent out."

A few days later Dr. Hill telephoned Dad with the test results. I heard Dad say, "Surely doctor there has to be a reason for her weakness." Dad barely hung up the phone when I asked, "What does she have?"

"Dr. Hill isn't sure, but thinks her immune system is down based on her asthma history. He said it will take time for her to regain strength," Dad explained.

I knew she was worse when she no longer had her eyes glued to a book. She was resting in bed more than she was up and about. Dad prepared breakfast and lunch, and Les or I put together a supper. If Mother didn't come down to the kitchen we took her meal upstairs to her bedroom. Les worked most evenings after college and I took on the task making supper. Mother gave me instructions on what and how to cook. We didn't get a chance to talk to Dad much except on weekends. It was a Saturday when Dad caught us both together.

"Something has got to be done to keep things organized around here."

"I think we're doing a pretty good job taking care of things," I interrupted. Les followed with, "I don't think things are any worse than when she has her asthma attacks."

"You kids need help, and so do I. This is getting to be difficult making meals and doing the house work," Dad snapped back.

"So, what are you saying, Dad?" Les asked.

"Well, I've got to come up with some kind of solution to keep things running smoothly." I blurted back, "She will snap out of this quickly as she does her asthma when the first frost comes, you'll see."

A few weeks later, a Blatchford's furniture truck delivered a green couch that made into a bed. Dad directed the drivers to place it our dining room.

"Kids, I'm glad you're both here. I've hired a housekeeper to take over the responsibilities for your Mother till she's back on her feet. I'm sure your Mother and both of you will agree this is best for now." Les and I were speechless. We were surprised he did this without discussing it beforehand.

"Maggie will move in tomorrow and I'm sure you'll like her. She has agreed to do the cooking and cleaning in exchange for a place to live. I was lucky to find someone willing to do this without costing me a fortune." Our dining room was right off the kitchen and this was to become the new housekeeper's bedroom. Oh brother!

I will never forget the day I first laid eyes on Maggie. She stood, about five by five on the fat side. I would guess she was in her fifties, but looked every bit in her sixties. Her hair was a dull grayish white with unkempt stray wisps. Thick gold rimmed glasses with magnifying lenses gave her eyes a tired look and deep dark circles lay beneath. She had loads of rouge on her cheeks and bright red lipstick on her lips in a cupids bow fashion. She had splashed too much of a nauseating cheap perfume. It smelled like "Evening in Paris". White curly whiskers hung from her double chin. I guess she couldn't see them with those thick glasses. She's was quite a sight.

I observed her closely those first few weeks. Maggie wore cotton print dresses bra less which hung loose, not unlike her pendulous breasts hanging down to her waist. The jar she kept by the sofa/bed was disgusting with both sets of her teeth usually soaking. She called Mother, "Nomi" I wasn't sure if she could even pronounce Naomi correctly.

When Les and I came home late in the evening, she scurried out of the dining room to tell us what she'd cooked for dinner, and how to heat it up. Maggie always added how bad Mother was, and described her diarrhea, "I bathed her up real good." Les always brought home a pint or two of hand packed ice cream from the ice cream factory. We liked to sit at the kitchen table and visit together without her butting in. The moment Les started dishing out ice cream Maggie would appear in the dining room doorway. We were stuck with sharing our ice cream and Maggie smacking her gums together without her teeth. We didn't like the intrusion, but felt it necessary since Mother needed care.

Les and I would make faces at each other when her back was turned or she headed into her bedroom, our dining room. Maggie bragged in detail about the work she did around the house. When I saw her on her knees, I wasn't impressed with her small pan of clear water, and no scrub brush. I referred to it as, "Wiping Up." I'll give her credit for her cooking. She was a pretty good cook and did make a lot of roasts and stews. Dad was relieved knowing Maggie was there during our absence.

A year went by and Mother was weaker than before Maggie arrived. Doctor Hill shook his head each time he made a house visit. He didn't have an answer for her condition. Mother rarely got out of bed. I took her tea and toast when I got home. One evening Maggie stood in the doorway of the kitchen in her usual see through nightgown, "I gave your Mother tea and toast an hour ago!"

"Mother said she's hungry and wants tea and toast," I snapped back. I walked past her and went up to Mother's room.

"Maggie claims you had tea and toast a short time ago?"

"No, I haven't!" Mother answered trying to raise her voice. I went back downstairs to the kitchen. Maggie watched me put on the kettle and prepare toast. She told Dad the next day I wouldn't listen to her.

"Jan, I want to make it perfectly clear. You're to pay attention to what Maggie says. Your Mother is sick and confused. Maggie is trying her best to help her and I need you and Les both to cooperate. If Maggie says your Mother had tea and toast, you're not to prepare another tray. It's no wonder she has loose bowels all the time. Do you understand?"

"Yes, but Mother claimed she had nothing since supper."

"I don't care what your Mother says. You listen to Maggie."

I didn't know who to believe, but Dad was emphatic. I began to think maybe Mother did make a mistake about the time. I didn't feel right about convincing Mother she was mistaken when I wasn't sure. There was no way for me to make tea without Maggie hearing me.

From then on, when mother asked for something to eat, I would check first with Maggie. Otherwise, I would convince Mother she had forgotten and try to get her to go back to sleep. Mother would look at me with those dark brown pitiful eyes, insisting it wasn't so, but too weak to argue. I didn't feel comfortable taking Maggie's word before my own Mother's. Mother always accepted my explanation, but I went to bed with a question as to whether or not Maggie always told the absolute truth.

I started my senior year, realizing I wouldn't be going to college. I dropped French to make my school schedule easier. I took daily gym, cooking, harmony, chorus, and English. I didn't need many credits to graduate. I decided to have some fun my last year of school. It was Indian summer—a beautiful warm day. After school I went straight home, walked through the parlor, threw my books on the cocktail table and proceeded to the kitchen. "Mother, you scared me. How did you get down here? At first, I thought you were Maggie. What's going on?" She looked up from her book with a devilish grin. I peered through the dining room doorway to see if Maggie was there, "Mother, where's Maggie?"

"She's gone, I chased her out of the house," Mother proudly pointed to the maroon metal broom with plastic bristles leaning against the kitchen wall. Her eyes sparkled with excitement.

"You what? No, you're kidding? Wow! Tell me what happened?" Before she could answer, I put my arms around her and we hugged. It was like old times, her sitting and reading in the kitchen. The excitement and joy diminished as I began thinking how Dad would react.

"Mother, what will you tell Dad? And how did you get the strength to chase her out?" It was like a miracle and I couldn't wait for the answer to come before I had more questions.

"Well, for the past couple of weeks I had more energy. I walked around upstairs building it up. The stronger I got the more I resented Maggie hovering over me and acting like this was her house. Until a few weeks ago, I had to put up with her bragging about how Russ and the kids liked her stew and how hard it was scrubbing and caring for this house. She brought my meals and pills and I accepted the way things were. I was too weak to do much else. The horrible part was her having to change my bedding when I had an accident—it was humiliating. She lied about a lot of things, especially when she brought me tea and toast after supper. Her tone of voice was entirely different when any of you were around."

It was hard for me to imagine all this was taking place and Les and I didn't suspect it. I was happy Mother was back on her own two feet.

"What shall we have for supper?" Mother got up from her chair and opened the freezer for ideas. It was like this year never happened.

Mother removed some vegetable stew and I got a pan from the cupboard and we heated it up. Les came home two hours later. His face lit up like a Christmas tree when he saw Mother and me side by side at the kitchen table.

He threw the bag of ice cream on the table, "I don't believe it! What's going on?" He leaned over and kissed Mother on the cheek, took hold of both her hands and with teary eyes didn't bother putting the ice cream in the freezer. He got three bowls from the cupboard and the ice cream dipper and began scooping.

"Les, Mother chased Maggie out of the house. Wait till you hear what has been going on around here."

"What are you saying, Jan. I want to hear every word from the beginning. Do you want butterscotch royal or chocolate fudge, Mother?"

"I'll have butterscotch," Mother replied.

"What about you, Jan?"

"I'll take some of each, let's celebrate!"

"Mother, tell me how in the world you got Maggie to leave?" Les looked at Mother with his silly grin as she began to explain.

"She was scared of me once I began questioning what the medicines were for and why I wasn't as weak. I waited till I had built up my strength and courage. It took several weeks without diarrhea and weakness. I began to see through her and what she was up to. It started with my refusing some of the food she brought me. I began asking for cheese and bread, or soup. I requested she bring me a box of crackers too. She argued, but finally brought some saltines. I ate them in between meals. Those pills she laid on my tray each day I stopped taking. I hid them in a sock in my dresser drawer. I never was sure what they were for to begin with. As I lay there so weak I decided the pills didn't agree with me. The clearer my mind got, the more I noticed her syrupy sweet attitude around Russ and you kids. It was disgusting. You've no idea how her voice and mannerisms changed once you were out of the house."

Les and I could hardly believe what Mother told us. Neither Les nor I were fond of Maggie and weren't sorry she was gone. It was wonderful to have Mother downstairs once again. Les and I laughed hysterically, as she repeated the story again.

"I got out of bed, went downstairs, picked up the metal broom out of the cellar stairwell, and charged into the dining room. Maggie was sitting on her bed and I yelled, 'Get out!' Her false teeth practically fell out of her mouth. I repeated, 'Get out of my house, and take your purse with you!' Maggie threw her arms up in front of her face, ducked, and tried to grab the broom by the bristles and pull it away from me. She dropped her purse, scrambled to pick it up, and ran into the screen door trying to get away. I chased her out onto the porch and down the steps to the sidewalk." Mother continued with, "Maggie yelled back, 'Nomi you're a sick woman and you'll be sorry.'"

Thank heavens Mother thought to hook both front and back screen doors once Maggie was out of the house. She couldn't get back in.

"Your father will have to change the locks on the doors. I never want to see her near this house again!"

Dad worked till mid-night and didn't hear Mother's story until the next morning. To his amazement, too, Mother was in the kitchen like old times when he went down for breakfast. Mother said he took a double take and started scolding her. She gave him a brief description of the events of the day before, as she fried him a couple of eggs and bacon. That evening Mother gave me an account of Dad's remarks.

Your Dad said, "I hope you know what you're doing, woman, because there will be no help for you. How long do you think this strength will last?"

I answered him with, "For years. I feel the best I've felt in a long time."

"There will be no getting Maggie back, if a need should arise. Maggie worked for board and keep and I gave her a few dollars now and then, we're lucky to have had her," Your Dad answered abruptly.

I was fast to respond with, "I'm better now, I don't know why, any more than the doctor does. I'll make another appointment to see Dr. Hill. Let's see what he thinks about my recovery."

I wish I could have been there to hear the two of them. I was looking forward to the weekend when I would see and hear from Dad directly. It will be great to be together once again as a family.

CHAPTER 11

Things got back to normal. Mother gathered up the dirty clothes, did most of the cooking, and helped me dust the furniture. I did the washing, ironing, and scrubbing. I was happy Mother was feeling stronger. I took a job at the candy counter at the theatre from five in the afternoon until ten o'clock. With the money I earned I was able to buy most of my own clothes. I liked to wear what the rest of my friends were wearing at school. I bought a pair of white buck shoes, argyle socks, some wool skirts, and sweaters.

I was determined not to go to work at a factory or a five and dime store after high school. The Bell Telephone Company was offering new graduates a job in Philadelphia. The first two weeks were with all expenses paid—even the trip by train. It was over 200 miles from home. I talked with Dad about going to Philadelphia after I graduated. He thought it was a good opportunity for a better job, but said Mother wouldn't approve.

The next afternoon when I came home from school Mother was sitting at the kitchen table reading.

"Mother, you know how much I wanted to go to college. I took all the college preparatory classes. But I don't see how I can work and go to college like Les does. My closest friends are going to Philadelphia after graduation. Bell Telephone is hiring, paying Betty and Nancy's way to Philly by train and two week's salary in advance."

"That's too far away, and you know it!" Mother said. "I'm sure you can find a good job around here. Les is working his way through college—you'll find a way." She had her head buried in a book and barely glanced up as she spoke.

"But, Mother, this is a guarantee for a stable job with good wages and a chance for a future. You tell me where I can get a job here in town?"

"They make good money at Sylvania. What's wrong with working where your aunt Viola and Shirley work. If it's good enough for them it's good enough for you. Now, I have heard enough. I said, No, and that's final!"

Over the weeks, I tried buttering her up. I shared the fact Betty and Nancy mother's were letting them go and now our other friend Sonja was given permission to go.

"I don't care what your friend's mother's think, or say. I need you here, and you will find a job here in Altoona. I'm sure of it."

"Mother, I didn't go through high school and graduate to work in some God forsaken factory. I don't want to work at Sylvania on an assembly line." I raised my voice in desperation. She went back to her reading, as though we had settled the matter. I was determined not to be stuck at some menial factory job. I coaxed Dad into letting me go. He agreed to sign the papers without Mother knowing it. He knew there would be hell to pay when Mother found out. I hid the train tickets from Mother and tried to warn her in advance that I was really going.

"You are **NOT** going, Jan, let's not get into another argument over this." I just couldn't get her to listen and understand what was about to happen. The day before I was to leave, I tried one more time to get her attention. "Mother, I'm taking a job in Philadelphia. I have the train tickets. I leave tomorrow." She got up from the kitchen table, slammed her book down, and ran upstairs. I followed her to my room. Mother started going through my dresser drawers and throwing my clothes on the floor. She leafed through the books in my book case at the head of my bed.

"Mother, Stop it! You won't find the tickets. Please, don't do this, Mother. I just want a chance for a decent job." I gathered up everything as she went and straightened up my books.

"I'll find the tickets, and when I do they will be ripped up. You're not going." She began crying hysterically, ran to her room and threw herself across her bed. I hadn't seen Mother this upset in some time and feared for her health. I wanted to go to her, but knew it was better to let her alone. I started downstairs and could hear her sobbing. I had the tickets hidden in a pair of shoes in the back of my clothes closet. I packed my suitcase after dark and hid it in the attic stairwell.

The next day I heard her rustling around in different rooms in the house looking for my tickets. I kept my bedroom door shut. My heart ached, and I didn't know what to do, except to keep out of her sight. As I was walked down the stairs with my suitcase the next morning, she screamed, "Your father has signed you away! How could he do this to me?" She came out of the kitchen with red eyes, bags underneath and tears rolling down her cheeks. She must have been crying all night. I felt horrible to leave her this way. Mother grabbed at my arm and took hold of my suitcase as I stepped toward the door. "Jan, please don't go. I beg you."

Dad walked out of the kitchen, "Woman, let her go. This is what she wants to do. Give her a chance." Dad had to take hold of both her arms and hold her back from the door. I looked over my shoulder, and wanted to go back and hug them good bye. It was one of the most horrible experiences of my life. I could feel my heart racing and pounding at my temples. The taxi was waiting. The driver opened the door, I threw my suitcase and purse across the back seat and slid onto the seat beside them. As the taxi pulled away from the house, I took one more look out the back window. There was Dad still holding Mother's arms standing in the doorway. This should have been a happy time filled with excitement. Instead, it was one of the saddest days of my life.

Les telephoned a few days later. "Mother is still crying on and off and furious at Dad. She keeps saying, You signed our daughter away and I'll never forgive you, Russ." I couldn't have gone had it not been for Les and Dad saying they would help her with the house work. At the time, I didn't think of Les, how he could carry a full load at college, hold a full time job and still find time to help mother. I was preoccupied with having graduated from high school, moving to a big city with my closest friends, and starting a new job.

CHAPTER 12

I rode the train home every two or three months. Mother was happy to see me and did forgive me. She was coping, thanks to Les, and Dad. Every time I left for Philadelphia it got harder to leave Mother. Her eyes were glassy and she was sad when I packed up to leave. I found Philadelphia exciting and I was making good money. I saw a future with the Bell Telephone Company. Dad promised if I saved at least $500.00, he would help me find a used car, so I could come home more often. He held to his promise. I came home with $500.00 and we found a 1949 Plymouth with 50,000 miles on it. I saw a yellow and black Chevy convertible I fell in love with.

"I'll take no part in buying you a rag top. You don't have a chance in one of those if you roll over." Dad, with his dream of racing and experience as a car mechanic, ruined my chance for a convertible. I settled for the 1949 shiny black Plymouth sedan. I was happy when I drove it back to Philadelphia and showed it to my friends. I drove it to work occasionally, but parking at 17th and Arch in downtown Philadelphia was expensive. It was cheaper to ride the "L" train. I'll never forget the day Dad and Mother came to see me in West Philadelphia. They decided to take a vacation, visit me, and see our relatives who lived by The Chesapeake Bay. I was surprised Dad agreed to drive over 300 miles. He hated driving to Pittsburgh to see his brother and that was only a 100 mile trip. To think he would drive farther to see me and our relatives in Maryland was remarkable. Mother looked bright and happy that day, sitting beside Dad in the plush front seat of his Packard. It was as though she didn't have a care or problem and being bedfast for a year had never happened. I introduced Mother and Dad to the landlord of my rooming house. I was pleased and excited to see Mother and Dad together on this trip.

When I telephoned a few weeks later, she remarked, "Your dad and I had such a good time on our trip." I felt a warm tingling feeling go through my body while talking with her. I was relieved to hear everything was going well for her. I loved my job, had a nice car, and a lot of fun living in a boarding house with my three friends from high school. We went out to supper, to parties on weekends, even rode the "L" train to work together when we worked the same shift. I couldn't think of a time I was any happier. I promised Dad when he signed the permission papers for me to take this job, I would not get into trouble, or be around anyone drinking alcohol. I held my promise until one night when my roommate, Betty, fixed me up with a blind date. We went to a party at one of their friend's houses. When I got there they were serving alcohol. I panicked, and right away my promise to Dad came to the fore. I was afraid the place would be raided by police, and I would be in jail because I was under age.

"Betty, you've got to get Richard to take me home." I kept looking around expecting the police at any time. Betty laughed, "You're a silly girl. What's your problem?"

"I promised Dad, and you know it! If the police show up I've had it."

"You aren't drinking. Relax, we're having a good time. Your imagination is running away with you." Betty didn't make a move to get us out of there. I went to Richard and explained, "I made my Dad a promise I wouldn't be around alcohol. I've got to get out of here." He just stood there with a drink in his hand and laughed at me. I sensed something bad was going to happen. Without another word I left him standing there pushed my way through the crowd and went out the front door. I looked up and down the street for a taxi. I had no idea how I'd get home, but finally caught my breath outside. Thank heavens Betty realized I left. She came running down the sidewalk after me. "I didn't think you were serious. I thought you would calm down eventually. When I couldn't find you I knew you meant business. Richard is getting his coat. You're probably right we shouldn't be here. He will see we get home." Of course, Betty got a laugh from all my roommates when she described my ashen face and fear of the cops raiding the party. I took the punishment from their laughter and the claim I was too old fashioned. At least I knew I had kept my promise to Dad.

I worked hard at my job trying to get recognized for a promotion to Senior Operator. Almost a year had passed since I moved to

Philadelphia. It was right before Memorial Day when I received a phone call from Les.

"Jan, you need to come home as soon as possible to be with Mother. I've joined the Air Force, and leave in less than three weeks for basic training." he blurted out without taking a breath.

"What? I can't come home. What about my job? I'm about to be promoted."

"Mother still needs help around the house and I'll be gone. I did my best, Jan. Some of my friends joined the service and have been sent to protect South Korea. I have to report to upstate New York on the 20th of June for basic training."

"Thanks, a lot, Les. At least you could've given me some advance warning." I said abruptly, raising my voice. For the first time in years I was provoked at him. How could he expect me to drop everything and leave town?

"Jan, I'm really sorry. I decided to join and it happened so quickly. I was sworn in and I didn't realize I'd have to report so soon. My two years at college are up, and I can't afford to go down to the main campus at State College. I barely was able to afford these two years working full time and you know it! I don't think you realize with your short visits how difficult it's been this last year with you gone. You'll have to come home and take over for me."

I was furious, so mad I wanted use a few curse words and scream at him but I didn't. Instead my heart ached and tears began to form. In seconds it seemed like my whole world came apart before me. How could I leave my job, a future and my friends.

"I don't know how I can." I choked up, fighting back the tears. I wanted to refuse but knew I couldn't. "Is Mother worse?" I asked, my voice quivering.

"No, Jan, she's not worse, but someone has to be here to help her. She can't do the heavy work, the laundry, ironing and scrubbing. Oh, she tries, if I let her, but I'm afraid she'll fall down those steep cellar stairs. I hope to see you before I leave. You've got to come home!" he ordered.

"I don't know how or when I can get there. I'll check with my supervisor tomorrow. I can't get up and leave my job at a moment's notice. As hard as I've worked I will not jeopardize my job." I banged down the phone. My dreams and hopes were shattered. I felt tightness in my chest and tears poured down both cheeks thinking about returning home. Sadly, the next morning I advised my supervisor of my resignation. She said, "Why don't you try for a hardship transfer upstate near your hometown?" I was somewhat relieved to find out a transfer might be possible and put in the paperwork.

I finished my shift and rode the subway home alone that evening. I looked out at the Philadelphia skyline as the "L" train climbed up from underground, crossed the Schuylkill River, and headed to the west side of the city. This was the first time in a long while my attention was glued to the tall buildings and how beautiful the lights flicker their sparkling reflection back at me from the stillness of the dark river. I knew I had no choice but to return home for Mother's sake. My friend, Sonja at our rooming house told me farm towns were closing their small telephone offices. That was where switchboard operators remained all night for fire and rescue. Altoona was going to expand telephone service to surrounding communities.

This was encouraging news. I thought a transfer might be possible after all. As the days flew by I thought of all the places I wanted to see before leaving Philly. I hadn't been to the Liberty Bell or the Betsy Ross House. I dragged myself back and forth to work hating the thoughts of leaving. Mrs. Norris called me into her office, "Jan, they accepted your transfer to Altoona. You start there in one week."

"Oh, thank God, I was worried sick about having to go back home without a job. It's bad enough to leave but without a job would be horrible."

"You're a good employee, Jan, and we're sorry to lose you. I want to wish you the best of luck. I'm going on vacation tomorrow and need to say goodbye and good luck. She shook my hand, then pulled me close and gave me a big hug. I pushed back the tears and said, "I'll miss you and Philadelphia. Thanks for your help." The rest of the night I could barely concentrate on the calls coming in on my callboard. I was so sad, but glad at the same time I had a job waiting for me. It was ironic I'd leave Philadelphia a couple days short of one year after I arrived. I hugged my friends at the rooming house goodbye. my Plymouth was packed and I headed for the turnpike.

Seven hours later, I drove up in front of my house. I ran up the porch steps, the door was open so I rushed through the parlor to the kitchen. Mother practically knocked the chair over getting up.

"Thank God you've come home, honey."

We hugged. She was excited and happy to see me. I took a good look at her and realized how much I loved her. I felt a warm feeling radiate throughout my body, much like when I was a kid and she hugged me because I got hurt. I knew instantly I had done the right thing, and how fortunate I was to be able to get a transfer.

I had bitter feelings toward Les, since the day he ordered me to come home. The moment our eyes met my bitterness and hurt were set aside. Throughout our entire lives, all we had to do was look into each other's eyes and we understood one another.

"Welcome, home, Sis." He stretched his arms out to hug me. We hugged for a long time and I felt a feeling of being safe and secure. It was only a matter of a couple days until I felt Philadelphia seemed a dream or in a previous life time. It felt as though I had never left home. There were things around the house two men wouldn't think about. Oh, they helped with the laundry and minor house work, but a general house cleaning hadn't been done since I left. It was evident Les had a real struggle this past year. How he went to college, worked full time, and helped Mother, I'll never know. His determination must have kept him going. I realized he did need a break from it all. Whether the Air Force was the right move remained to be seen.

The next day Dad got up early and met me in the kitchen.

"Jan, it's good to have you home. We missed you." He put his arms around me and gave me a little hug. He never was much for hugging. I don't remember him ever kissing me. I looked into his eyes. He looked tired and worried. We were all together once again as a family, but not for long. One bit of happiness for Mother, but a bit of sadness too with Les leaving.

I drove us down to the railroad station to see Les off. We all hugged him goodbye and waved as he boarded the train. He waved out the window at us and we waved back as we walked along the side of the train as it moved slowly, but it picked up speed and Les was out of sight. It was sad as we walked to the car. Mother, Dad, and I drove home realizing it would be some time before we would see him again.

CHAPTER 13

I adjusted quickly to my new job, but did miss my friends and Philadelphia. As part of my benefits, I got a kick out of installing telephones with chimes on all the floors of our house. A princess phone which lit up was by my bed, a desk set in the living room and a wall telephone in the cellar by the washing machine. I noticed after a few days, a lot of calls were coming in. When I answered, there was click and no response. I questioned Mother, "I don't know why, but when I run to the phone and say 'Hello' no one answers. I watched Mother at times and she almost fell trying to get to the telephone. Sometimes I could hear heavy breathing on the other end of the line, but no one spoke. As the weeks went by, Mother started talking about her doctor and how he was falling in love with her. I felt it was her imagination.

"Oh, he calls when you two are not home," she remarked. There was no way I could validate this. Mother seemed obsessed with this notion about Dr. Hill. When we were in the kitchen together she would say, "My honey and I will be together soon." Mother pointed out Dr. Hill's home on our way to the store and inferred she would probably end up there. I tried to convince her he was just interested in her well-being.

"Mother, please don't misconstrue his concern for you as a patient to be anything more than that."

"Jan, you don't know what you're talking about. You're rarely around here in the afternoon."

On my days off, especially when I was standing between the kitchen and dining room ironing, she would talk incessantly about his good looks, and their plans to be together.

"Mother, I know him, I can't imagine anything going on here. You need to stop imagining this type of thing." I heard her talk about him to the point I began to think maybe she was right after all. If Dad heard about it there would be big trouble. It was beginning to get on my nerves. I continued to try to discourage her, but it wasn't working.

It was apparent Dad and Mother had drifted apart. He was drinking more, especially on the weekends. Things went on much the same for months. We drove to the cottage on weekends when I wasn't working. Mother and Dad got along much better at the cottage. When home Mother sat reading, at the kitchen table and Dad went in and out to get a beer or two from the refrigerator before work. They barely spoke and when they did, it ended in an argument. I could hear them yelling back and forth. Something would smash, followed with a door slam. Dad always left the house when she started throwing things. I had seen him duck on occasion on my way into the kitchen during a brawl. When they were at peace he would plop down in his easy chair and watch T.V. till time to get ready for work. They didn't discuss much except what to get at the grocery store, or argued over the household bills. I was busy learning my new job, resuming bowling, doing the washing and ironing, and catching up with the housework. Mother cooked and helped with the dusting and dishes. I did most of the housework between split shifts, or on days off.

Before I knew it, summer was gone and fall was around the corner. Mother's hay fever kicked up and we went through the asthma attacks. It was another trying time with Mother's wheezing keeping me awake. It was a scary time and asthma seemed to take an even greater toll on her this year. Thank heavens, the first frost came early and she snapped out of it.

Deer season rolled around. I was excited about going out with Dad the first day of buck season. On Saturday we left before day break for the mountains. It was snowing which made for a great first day being able to track deer in the snow. I positioned myself on a high mound and leaned back against a tree. I could see a panoramic view of thick woods beneath me. I had perfect visibility to look for deer coming in and out of the brush. I didn't have a scope on my rifle so I had to scan the woods carefully for horns. Dad went down the trail to another of his favorite spots. We met for lunch by the path where we parted ways with flashlights.

"Dad, I saw about ten doe but no bucks. They were milling and snorting below me as the fog rose from the ground."

"Yep, they're all around us, but the bucks are hiding in the thickest of brush." We agreed to meet at five o'clock unless we heard shots. Shots would mean one of us bagged a deer. The plan was to walk in the direction of the shot and help track or gut out the deer, if it were down. Dad told me he would hike a mile and walk toward me to chase any bucks my way before going back to his favorite spot. Five o'clock arrived, and I walked back to the place we had lunch. "Did you see any bucks, Dad?"

"No, not one set of horns today," It was dark already and about six o'clock when we pulled up in front of our house. Mrs. Steiger, our neighbor, came running over to greet us at the curb, "Your wife was taken by ambulance to the hospital about an hour ago." Dad and I gazed at each other with a worried look.

"What happened?" Dad followed with, "Did she hurt herself?" Dad looked scared.

"I don't know. All I know is, she didn't look good," Mrs. Steiger, explained.

"Thank you. Jan and I will leave right away." Dad and I jumped back into my car. The hospital was a short distance away. Mother was still in the emergency room. The doctor motioned for Dad to come behind the curtains where Mother was lying on a gurney with wheels. Dad motioned for me to stay back. I peered into a slight crack between the curtains, but I couldn't hear what they were saying. Dad's face was ashen, as he walked out from behind the curtains.

"Dad, what is it? Is Mother all right?"

"She's going to be fine. It's a mix up. Somehow she was experiencing extreme pain in the abdomen. But she told the doctor she's pregnant. He asked me if there is a possibility she is expecting. I told him it's unlikely. I don't think so. They're running tests and the report should be back any moment."

"I can't imagine Mother coming here without having severe pain, Dad. Are you sure Mother said she thinks she's pregnant? Or, was it the doctor's assumption?" I offered this because I didn't want my imagination running away with me.

Dad looked disgusted, "Where would she get such a crazy notion?"

"She seemed fine last night, Dad. She was still up reading when I came home from work. Maybe she ate something at breakfast or lunch, giving her severe pain. Could it be food poisoning? They must have confused her with another patient."

"Well, this is the last straw. She can't be left alone. One of us must be there to see what's going on."

"Let's not jump to conclusions, Dad. Most of the time one of us is around, except when I work an early shift. This is an unusual circumstance. I'm sure there's a better explanation, something we don't know at this point." I didn't want to reveal the fact that she imagined her doctor was in love with her. I hoped Mother wasn't thinking it was Dr. Hill's baby.

"Well, I'll talk to her doctor about this."

Dad and I waited for about twenty minutes before the physician came out and told us Mother was free to go. He gave Dad some pills for her stomach and said her tests were within normal range. I told Dad I would get the car and bring it around. As I left he helped the nurse put Mother into a wheelchair. I met them at the front entrance. Mother looked worn out, but was not complaining or holding her abdomen when Dad helped her into the front seat beside me. I could tell by Dad's expression he was provoked, to say the least.

"What's going on, woman? Surely you didn't think you were pregnant?"

"Russ, I was having pain like before I delivered Carol Lee," she answered pathetically.

"Couldn't it have waited till Jan and I got home? Why in heaven's name did you call an ambulance?"

"I thought I might lose the baby!"

"What baby?" Dad asked in a demanding voice.

"It felt like premature labor pains. How was I to know?" Dad leaned over the front seat, "Well, this sort of thing has got to stop! We can't afford an ambulance anytime you imagine some nonsense."

"Dad, please, Mother obviously had severe pain. I've heard of women having tubal pregnancies and it's extremely painful."

"Well, there's little chance of her being pregnant here. This is ridiculous. Surely you would've had some inclination before this? Wouldn't you, woman? Answer me!"

"I guess. I don't know, Russ." Mother's voice began to quiver and her eyes were glassy with tears.

"Dad, let's get Mother home. We can go over this later."

"You bet we'll go over it. I need an explanation from her," he scolded. Thank God he stopped hammering at Mother while I tried to remain calm driving. Mom had told me about the rough pregnancy Mother had when Carol Lee was born. And Dad said Mother never really got completely over her death. I was only four at the time and was told she died of pneumonia. I may have been young, but I think I remember her casket which remained in our parlor for days.

I pulled the car up in front of the house. I took hold of Mother's arm and lead her up the porch steps, and straight upstairs to her bedroom. I hurried her away from Dad to keep them from getting into more of an argument. I laid out Mother's nightgown while she started undressing. I heard Dad coming up the stairs. He stopped in the doorway, "Here are the pills the doctor said she should take for a few days till she's feeling better." Handing them to me, he turned and headed back downstairs. Whew, I was relieved he didn't start questioning her again. I went to the bathroom, got a glass of water, read the instructions on the packets. Each label read, take one pill every four hours as needed.

"Mother, take these and swallow them down good." She nodded and took one at a time with water. "Jan, I thought I was having labor pains. I feared I'd lose the baby." Mother explained apologetically.

"Forget it for now, Mother. I want you to rest and we can discuss the whole business tomorrow. Try to relax and get some sleep. Stop worrying." I pulled the covers up, turned out her bedside lamp and left. What a mess. If Dad heard one more word about her thinking she was pregnant, let alone, it not being his baby it would be a disaster. Perhaps by tomorrow she'd forget this whole baby business. I prayed she did. I was glad to get out of my hunting clothes. I slipped into a pair of slacks and a turtleneck sweater before going down to the kitchen to talk with Dad. He was already having a beer. I looked into the refrigerator for a bottle of root beer. Before I had the bottle cap off, he started in, "What are we going to do about your Mother now?"

"I don't understand. What do you mean?"

"We tried having someone here to help care for her and she chased her away. Maggie won't come back after what happened."

"Dad, this was a misunderstanding. She was in a lot of pain and got scared. We need to talk with her doctor and see what he thinks happened." No way was I about to tell him the change of life baby she thought she was having at 42 would not necessarily be his, certainly it wasn't Dad's in her mind.

"What will the neighbors think? I can't have her getting the Steiger's involved with her imaginations."

"I don't care what the neighbors think. They are too nosy

anyway—they have nothing else to do but gossip," I argued.

"This is no time, Jan, to get smart about our neighbors. I care what they think and I tell you something has got to be done before this happens again!" He took a big gulp of beer. Dad was still in his hunting clothes and all wound up. I knew it best to let him sit there with his beer and not discuss this any longer.

"Do you want me to make you a ham sandwich?"

"No, I can't eat right now. I'll get something later," He took his beer into the parlor and flopped down in front of the television. I hurried to eat because I knew he would be back to the refrigerator for another beer soon. I didn't want to discuss the incident further.

"Dad, I'm going up and check on Mother. I left the lettuce and everything out for you. Be sure and get yourself a bite to eat. It's been a long day." He nodded, as I turned and went up the stairs. Mother was sleeping and I didn't wake her. Thank heavens Dad had been sleeping in my brother's old room since he left and wouldn't be disturbing Mother. No wonder he was upset. I had no idea at this point if they were still getting together in bed. If so, I was sure it wasn't often. Before I went to bed, I checked on Mother again. I let her sleep even though I thought she should have something to eat.

I must have been tired because I never woke up till about 8:30 a.m. I put my robe over my pajamas, peeked in at Mother. She was beginning to roll around, and I knew she would be up soon. As I walked down the stairs into the parlor, I heard Dad talking on the phone. "I need to know what to expect with her condition doctor," I quietly opened the refrigerator door and strained to hear his side of the conversation. "Yes, that'll be all right, Tuesday at 10 a.m. then." Dad came into the kitchen and started right in with, "Well, the doctor agrees your Mother needs treatment. I told him about the hospital episode and her claiming to be pregnant. I'm meeting with him in his office on Tuesday."

"What does he think is going on, and what kind of treatment is he talking about?"

"He said it will be difficult to find a place to take your Mother."

"Take mother, what do you mean? Can't she get treatment at his office?"

"It doesn't sound like it. I'll find out more on Tuesday." Dad seemed somewhat relieved.

"Dad, I think you're jumping to conclusions. We need to talk with

Mother about the whole episode. See what she has to say today. She was in pain and out of her head when she called the ambulance. I'm sure she was scared. She'll snap out of it. All she needs is some medication to relax her."

"Jan, your Mother has been slipping for some time, and you know it. She was in bed for an entire year for no reason. The doctor can't even explain it. She's lost it. I can't hold a conversation with her without her pitching a butcher knife or something at me. Remember, I believe a couple of her uncles have similar problems. From what I hear they have been in a hospital for years. No one wants to talk about it or bring it up.

"For God's sake, Dad, what do her uncles have to do with Mother's condition?"

"We don't hear much about them and never have. It's kind of hush, hush, you understand? We have no idea what runs in her family. Heavens knows what your Mother will do next. I can't go to work worrying about which hospital she will rush off to next."

"That's not going to happen, Dad. Let me talk with her and see what's going on. I'm sure she will feel better after a good night's sleep."

"Regardless of what she says, something has to be done, Jan, and that's all there is too it!" He left me standing there, walked into the parlor and turned on the T.V. I had hot chocolate with two pieces of toast and went upstairs to see Mother. She was getting dressed, sitting on the edge of the bed putting her shoes on. I knew I needed to get to the bottom of what was going on in her mind before it was too late.

"Mother, how are you feeling? Are you still in pain?"

"No, honey, I'm feeling okay, but a little worn out. Those pills must have really taken hold. Where's your father?"

"He's watching T.V. and having a beer as usual. But he's really upset about yesterday. Mother, what's really going on?"

"Jan, I told you both I had severe pain like before I gave birth to Carol Lee. It was terrible and there was no one to call. You and your Dad were gone. I didn't want to call Genevieve or Mom and get them all upset. There wasn't time. I thought I might lose the baby," she said earnestly.

"But, Mother there is no baby. How could you think at 42 you were pregnant?"

"Never mind, it is possible, you know. I missed some of my periods and with the pain and all. Well, you don't know everything that goes on around here."

"What do you mean? What don't I know Mother?"

"I don't want to keep going over it. It's done and I want to go down and have some breakfast."

"Well, prepare yourself for Dad. He's really upset. This is no time to talk with him about yesterday. I'll go down with you to be sure the two of you don't get into it."

Lucky for both of us he wasn't in his chair. I looked out the bay window and his car was gone. Mother fixed herself a poached egg, toast, and coffee. She seemed okay. I couldn't imagine that she and Dr. Hill had an affair. Was her imagination running away with her or was there more she wasn't telling me?

Dad kept the appointment on Tuesday and I only wish I could've been a little mouse under the doctor's desk. Dad came home and was making himself a ham sandwich when I entered the kitchen.

"How did it go, Dad?" I asked.

"He's going to take care of everything and get her admitted."

"Admitted, where? For what reason?" I felt empty and chills went up and down my spine.

"Dr. Hill's going to have her come in and do more tests. He thinks she has a kind of behavior disorder. He said he doesn't want to label her at this time. However, he said, in the past months he has seen a decline in her memory and cognitive thinking. And he said something strange."

"What, Dad?"

"He said, You sure have a beautiful wife, Mr. Bryar. He said he had never seen a woman with such fine pure white skin. What a strange remark, Jan?"

"Well, it's true Dad. I believe he was paying you a compliment about Mother, in his way." I thought Oh, Boy, what's that remark all about. I didn't let on it meant something more to me. This made matters worse. I didn't know what to think.

"Dad, I've got an idea. I can change my work schedule. If I do, one of us can be here all the time with Mother. At least for now until we see how she does on this medicine."

"Jan, we can no longer care for your Mother. According to Dr. Hill she needs professional help."

"No, Dad I don't want her to go anywhere. Please, let's try some other way." I pleaded.

"There's no other way, Jan. It's beyond our control. We have done all we can. She could catch the house on fire or I don't know what. Half the time I don't know where she's coming from."

"Dad, please give her more time to work things out. She's had a rough couple of years, and you know it." I thought if only Les were here he could come up with a solution.

Dad popped the cap from another beer, "I have nothing more to say. It's already a done deed. Dr. Hill is making the arrangements."

How could I warn Mother what was about to happen? She went about her daily routine reading at the kitchen table. Her feet shuffled back and forth constantly—the linoleum worn down where she sat. I didn't bring up the hospital incident again for fear of getting her upset. I couldn't help wonder if there was something more she wasn't telling me about Dr. Hill.

Two weeks later Dad told me the doctor had a bed for her in the hospital.

"Is she going by ambulance?"

"No, I'm going to tell your Mother Dr. Hill wants her to meet him at the hospital to run some tests. I'm sure she will go along with me without a problem."

"But Dad you're tricking her, and once she finds out I'm sure there will be hell to pay."

"Let me and Dr. Hill handle this, Jan. It's for your mother's own good. You'll see."

The entire evening at work I was worried sick. How long would she be gone? I had to pretend I was okay. I wanted to bawl right there at the switchboard, but I held back the tears and drowned myself by answering, 'Operator' time after time. I arrived home after my 11 p.m. shift and ran to the kitchen then up to Mother's bedroom. She was gone and I felt cold chills go through my body, much the same as when she cut herself or showed me a bruise from falling. I felt lost and empty. Tears ran down my cheeks. I just sat on the edge of Mother's bed in the dark, sobbing. Where was she and how would she bear being in the hospital? I got ready for bed and turned in. I rolled back and forth until I heard Dad come home from work about 1 a.m. I went down to the kitchen in my pajamas. Dad had a glass of milk in front of him with a raw egg floating near the top. I was at a loss for words. I didn't know what to say—I wanted to scream at him and pound his chest with my fists. My heart ached for Mother at the same time.

He spoke before I reacted, "Jan, it went fairly well until she didn't see Dr. Hill at the entrance. Two nurses took her by both arms and led her to the elevator. She started to pull away from them, but one of them said, 'We are taking you to your doctor.' She stopped and looked back at me strangely as the elevator door closed. I stood there not knowing whether to wave goodbye. I felt sad, but I was sure I was doing the right thing. I signed the papers at the front desk. Everything went as Dr. Hill said it would." Dad took in a deep breath and sighed.

"Where is she and when can I go see her?" I asked impatiently.

"You can't see her. Not right now. No one can visit for two weeks."

"Why? Mother will think we don't want to come. Where did you take her?"

"She's in Hollidaysburg, out by the Meadows."

"Oh, no! Why is she in the state hospital? How long will she be there? I feel terrible, I miss her already."

"Calm down. She'll be fine, they can help her out there, I'm certain of it."

"What did she say in the car on the way to the hospital, Dad?"

"Not much of anything. She stared out the window. I told her about her doctor's appointment and there would be some special tests. She did ask what kind of tests. I said, darned if I know. They are supposed to help you concentrate better. I was surprised how eager she was to go. She wore her favorite red dress." Dad seemed pleased with himself. It wasn't hard for me to picture what was going on in her mind—he didn't have a clue. She thought she was going to be with her "honey," Dr. Hill. I felt sick to my stomach because Dad had tricked her.

How would she ever forgive him or trust any of us again. I was glad I had no part in the plan. I was obsessed with the whole scene in my mind as he described it. Mother must have been scared and devastated when she realized she wasn't going home after the tests. I counted the days until I could go see her. I knew it wouldn't be easy, and I really didn't know what to expect. My hope was they would find out what was wrong and cure her.

CHAPTER 14

The two weeks of the so called "adjustment period" passed. Oh, yes, it was an adjustment all right with Mother being the one making the adjustment. It must have been horrible! I will never forget the first visiting day. I drove down the same country road I'd traveled on our way to the cottage for years. I must have passed the hospital hundreds of times and never gave it a second thought. The hospital sat on a hill of neatly cropped bright green grass. I drove up the driveway, followed the sidewalk to a double glass door. Solid glass extended from the top of the door twenty feet to the eaves of a steeple-like roof. It resembled the entrance to a house of worship. I walked into a spacious vestibule surrounded with floor to ceiling windows. In any direction you had a panorama view of the long field of grass leading to the road resembling a black ribbon below. On the other side of the road was a thicket of woods leading up a mountain side. I imagined it was a copycat pattern of where the horse carriages had traveled years before.

A receptionist sat to my right at a large desk facing the elevators. I was a nervous wreck, and my voice quivered as I told her, "I'm here to visit Naomi Bryar. I'm her daughter."

"I'll call and have the nurse bring her down. Have a seat." She pointed to a seat by the windows as she picked up the telephone. I sat down and looked around. I noticed a room off to her right which consisted of cream colored glossy cubicles about four feet high. In each cubicle was a table and four chairs and no one in sight. As my eyes scanned the entire room and returned, I saw the elevator doors open and there was Mother standing beside the nurse. I rushed over to meet them as they walked out of the elevator. Mother darted away from the nurse the moment she caught a glimpse of me.

"Jan, Jan, thank God you're here!" Tears rolled down her cheeks and I started bawling too.

"Just notify the receptionist when you are ready to leave, and I'll come down for your Mother," the nurse directed. I nodded as I took hold of Mother's arm and we walked arm in arm over to a table within one of the cubicles.

"Where is your father? He should be here. I want to see him."

"Mother, I thought it best for him not to come. He wouldn't have come even if I'd coaxed him."

"Wait till I get my hands on him. What possessed him to bring me to this place? He said I was coming here for tests. There haven't been any tests, nurses drawing tubes of blood and a few doctors asking me a bunch of personal questions. I sat with a group of women and a couple of nurses asking me and other women about our home life. How we get along with our husbands and children. I want to know what's going on? Why am I here, Jan?"

"Mother, Dad said Dr. Hill arranged for you to come for special treatments. He didn't say what kind. I wanted you to be seen at his office and not have to come here. Dad said it wasn't possible."

"I asked several nurses about Dr. Hill. They insisted he isn't assigned here. Your father lied! Jan whatever scheme Russ had, I'm sure they're finished with me, and I can go home now. Some of these women are moaning and crazy out of their minds. I don't have any of my own clothes. Look at this dress. It's too big and not something I would wear and you know it!"

"I can bring some of your dresses, shoes, and underwear tomorrow or the next day."

"There is no need, Jan. Tell the nurse you're taking me home."

"Mother, I can't until they release you."

"Then, get in touch with Dr. Hill, and get me released. I'm sure he had nothing to do with me coming here. He probably doesn't know I'm here. You must call him and tell him what has happened."

A sharp chill went through my body, that same feeling I always felt when she fell or injured herself. I wanted to put my arms around her and bawl my heart out, but I knew it would only make matters worse. The whole scene was like a nightmare. I wanted to wake up and find it was—a bad dream. I expected to see her in a hospital bed with a nightgown on, not in a washed out cotton common house dress and in green stretchy sponge hospital slippers. I was glad when I looked at my watch and it was time for me to leave to get to work.

"Mother, I wish I could stay longer, but I have to be a work at 4:30 p.m. I'll be back tomorrow."

"Please, Jan, take me with you. I've got to get out of here." She held onto my arm begging.

"Mother, I can't take you today, but I'll see when you can be released, I promise. C'mon walk with me over to the receptionist." I led her out to a chair in front of the elevator.

"She's ready to go up now," I told the receptionist. I heard her call for a Nurse Claney. Tears were running down Mother's cheeks, and she looked up at me with such a desperate look in her eyes. When the elevator doors opened a nurse walked toward us.

"Is Naomi ready to go back upstairs?" She asked.

"Yes. Mother, remember what I told you. I'll be back tomorrow or the next day." The nurse helped Mother stand and held onto her arm as we walked to the elevator. Mother grabbed onto my arm and didn't want to let go. "Please, Mother, go along with the nurse. I'll try to make it back tomorrow."

"Jan, I want to go home, don't leave me," she pleaded. I had to pull my arm away with force. The nurse crossed Mother's arms and hit the elevator button with her right elbow, "It's all right, Naomi. She has to go. It's almost supper time. Your daughter will be back." The elevator doors opened and the nurse led Mother inside. The nurse changed her grip and turned Mother around facing me. I waved, but Mother was preoccupied being turned around by the nurse. She didn't see me wave. Before I knew it, she was out of sight. I took a deep breath and headed for the door. Tears came on my way out. How in God's name will I be able to handle visiting Mother? As for telephoning Dr. Hill, I wanted nothing to do with him. I looked across the lawn at a picture perfect scene as I walked to my car. I got in behind the steering wheel, leaned my head back and cried out loud for my Mother. I realized I was free and Mother was confined to a place in which she had no control.

I made it a point to visit the very next day. I took her clothes and shoes to wear. I requested her dirty clothes be brought down on future visits. I left a bag of other clean clothes with the receptionist.

"Did you call my honey, Dr. Hill?"

"Yes, He's aware of where you are, Mother," I lied. I did no such thing.

"What did he say? When is he getting me out of here?"

"I don't know what he's going to do. Dad doesn't know anything either."

"How can they leave me here? You don't know what it's like. Please, Jan take me home!"

"Mother, I want to, but I can't without your doctor's permission." Once again, it was hard to leave Mother clinging to me at the elevator when the nurse came. It was time to have a serious conversation with Dad in the morning.

Dad was sitting in the kitchen with a cup of coffee for a change when I came down for breakfast. He must have already had his morning cocktail—raw egg in milk.

"Dad, what's the plan for Mother's care? And when can we expect her to come home?"

"It's up to her doctor. She's under his care and his responsibility now."

"What did he tell you when she was admitted? Was there a time mentioned for these treatments to take place and how long her recovery will take?"

"There was no discussion about her treatment. I had to sign permission for her to be totally under their care for however long it takes."

"Didn't you get any idea about a time, weeks or a month? What kind of an agreement was this? It's my Mother's life at stake."

"No, calm down. I didn't know what to ask. These are medical people. I have no business questioning them about your Mother's care. I don't want to discuss it any further."

Days turned into weeks and Mother was losing hope. Her clothes were lost and I would find her in one of those old faded washed out house dresses, two sizes too big, a muslin wide strapped slip with no bra, although I had marked everything I took her from home with a marking pen. She did at least have her own flat oxford shoes. We went through the same tear jerking visits except for the sundaes and desserts I took her which became the ice-breakers. Dad always refused to go with me to visit. I knew in my heart it was for the best. Mother talked of getting even with him sooner or later.

Mom, (we called Mother's mother, Mom.) went to visit and so did her sisters for a while, but their visits dwindled—they didn't like what they saw. Mom had high blood pressure and was taking heart medicine and to see Mother like this was hard on her. She always telephoned and asked how Mother was. The very first thing out of her mouth was, "How is Noan doing?" After all, Mother was her oldest daughter there suffering it out. I wasn't fond of the situation either, but regardless of how tough it was to see Mother, I faithfully visited every other day.

Sometimes other women were sitting around the visiting cubicles with their loved ones. Some were talking softly, others were silent. Loud outbursts of laughter or crying, did catch me by surprise from women tied to a wheelchair with a sheet around their waist. Saliva was drooling from one side or another of their mouth. Mother wasn't one bit silent. She was always pleading with me to take her home. It was always, "I don't belong here and why did your father sign me away?" She didn't talk much about Dr. Hill anymore and I was glad. Always, promising me she would get even with Dad, one way or another.

All I could do was agree she didn't belong there. But I couldn't take her home without Dad's requesting her release and her doctor signing her out. The days she clung to me at the elevator—were the worst days. My heart ached for Mother and what was worse, Dad was convinced this was the place she would get help. It never got any better or easier to visit her. The only place I had peace of mind was at work. I drove straight to work after our visits. Work became a temporary relief from the sadness and helplessness I felt.

CHAPTER 15

On one of my routine visits Mother looked listless. She could not hold her head up, and I had a hard time even getting her to eat any ice-cream. The dress she was wearing had a purple flower pattern like a flour sack and it hung down and reached the top of her bobby socks. There were times when I was pleasantly surprised when she came down with one of her own dresses on. This wasn't one of those times. I was disgusted. She did have her own shoes on—not slippers. Her hair was awry and needed cutting. Instead of the usual complaints about her clothes and taking her home, she remained silent. When I asked her questions she barely nodded or gave no response. I took hold of her chin and held her head up, so I could look into her eyes. It was as though she wasn't really seeing me. Her eyes were milky and glassy looking, as if in a trance or another world. I knew something was radically wrong. There wasn't the usual shifting of her feet, restless movements of her arms or twitching of her fingers. I looked over my shoulder at her while I walked to the receptionist and asked to speak to her nurse.

I went back to the cubicle and sat beside her to wait for the nurse. I massaged her arms, trying to get her attention. Her head hung down resting on her upper chest. Once again, I supported her head and held it back against the top of the chair. About twenty minutes later, the elevator door opened. "Mother, there's the nurse. I'm going over to talk with her, I'll be right back." I slowly removed my hand from her chin and rested her head against her chest. She remained still and didn't respond. The nurse met me half way across the room. I kept looking back to keep an eye on Mother. I was at a safe distance and Mother couldn't hear us talk. The nurse was familiar, I had seen her before. "There's something radically wrong with Mother. She's in a daze and look at her head hanging down. It's as though she doesn't even recognize me. What's wrong with her?"

"Well, it's not unusual for patients to behave this way after treatment."

"After what kind of treatment? I don't understand."

"They gave her a shock treatment yesterday. It will take a few days for her to regain her memory," she explained coldly.

"Mother was given a shock treatment! For God's sake who authorized this? There's no reason to put her through this type of torture!" I tried to keep my voice down, but it got louder.

"The doctor ordered it as therapy to get these crazy ideas out of her head."

"What crazy ideas? I want to see her doctor immediately!"

"It isn't possible. He's in clinic this afternoon."

"Well, get him out of clinic. I need to see him, now! Do you understand?"

"That I cannot do. The clinic is in town, not here! Naomi will recover and be the better for this. This effect is only temporary."

"I don't care if it's temporary or not. I want to find out why this was done."

"All right, I'll leave Doctor Martin a note that you want to see him, but there's no need for it. Your mother will be fine." She turned abruptly, never glancing toward Mother and walked to the elevator. I hurried back to be with Mother. It was a one way conversation and I barely got a hmm or nod. I continued to stay and hold her head up for half an hour, but there was no reaction to anything I said. She didn't seem to be in any pain, totally listless and still. I put my arm around her back and gave her a kiss on the cheek. "Wait here Mother. I'm getting the nurse to take you back upstairs." Still no reaction. Her head hung down with her chin resting on her upper chest. I kept glancing back at her. She never moved as I walked to the vestibule to the receptionist desk. It took only a few minutes and the same nurse exchanged quick glances as she approached Mother and me. No words were spoken. She knew I was fuming. I helped Mother up from the chair. She was weak. The nurse took hold of Mother's other arm and between us Mother shuffled along as we led her to the elevator.

"I'll see you again soon, Mother." Mother's head hung down and she never looked up as the elevator doors closed between us. I've never seen a nurse with such a cold attitude. I didn't see her name tag, but I planned to complain about her attitude to this Dr. Martin, whoever he was. I was glad it was my day off. I wouldn't have been able to concentrate at work. I could think of nothing but my poor Mother and what she must have gone through. Also the statement the nurse made about, 'crazy ideas'. I would get to the bottom of this. This type of treatment was inhumane!

It took me three days to finally get an appointment with Dr. Martin.

"Hello, there Miss Bryar. Have a seat. I'm sorry the nurse didn't tell you ahead of time how your Mother would respond to these treatments," he offered.

"We were not aware she was to receive shock treatments. Why weren't we notified?"

"It's not common practice to notify the family in situations such as these. Your Mother is receiving excellent care and we order what's in her best interests."

"The nurse said Mother was having crazy ideas. What's she talking about? Mother seems fine when I visit."

"That may be so, but, according to Dr. Dixon, she talks about things she imagines to be quite true."

"How do you know it's just her imagination? For God's sake, doctor I need to know what you're talking about. If anyone knows my Mother, it's me. I'm the one you should be asking what's true or not true that she talks about."

"Look, Miss., er" He looked down at his notes to see my name. "That is, Miss Bryar, I'm not privy to tell you the psychiatrist's findings. And I don't believe you have the credentials to advise us how to treat your mom? Or is there something we don't know here?"

"Now, wait a minute! This is my Mother we're talking about. I have the right to know what's being done and why."

"No, I believe you are misinformed. Your Mother has been admitted to our care. This includes a full realm over what medication and treatment she is to receive." I thought to myself, what an arrogant S.O.B.

"I checked with my father. He doesn't remember signing or authorizing shock treatments."

"Your father turned over full responsibility for your Mother's care. I can assure you, in a few days your Mother will have benefitted from ECT. Now if you'll excuse me, I must make rounds on my patients." He got up, turned and opened the door motioning for me to exit. He added, "If you have further questions or concerns you can ask to speak with the administrator."

"I intend to! But, in the meantime I want nothing further done to my Mother without our permission. Have I made myself clear?" He ignored my demand and shrugged as he walked away. "Furthermore," I added, "I will request to see exactly what paper work was signed upon her admission." I raised my voice to be sure he heard me. I had to hold myself back from saying things I thought about this place from the beginning. One sure thing, I would've loved to have slapped his freckled face. I'm not going to stand by and let these people use my Mother as a guinea pig. I don't know my rights, but I'll find out. I walked down the stairs and out the side door. The clouds were dark and hanging low. A few big drops of warm rain hit my face as I quickened my steps to my car. If it had been pouring rain, I believe I would have stood there and gotten soaked. In fact, I wish I would have got soaked. I got in my car and slid behind the wheel. Large raindrops began to splatter my windshield. I sat there and looked at the dark dreary valley below. Tears began to drop on the steering wheel and I felt a prickling feeling in my nose. I'd accomplished nothing and Mother was upstairs, somewhere behind me, suffering and I couldn't make it better. When I arrived home, I found Dad in the kitchen preparing a sandwich for work.

"Dad, I saw Dr. Martin today and he was no help at all. He told me the hospital staff has full realm over Mother's care. Her treatment is up to their discretion and we have no say in the matter. Is this true? Is this your understanding?" I took a good look at Dad's face and could tell he was irritated.

"Jan, you need to let those medical people do whatever they think is necessary. You're crossing the line here. You can't be telling the doctor or nurses what they should or shouldn't do," Dad scolded.

"For God's sake, Dad, you never go see Mother. What do you know about the type of treatment she's getting? She's going through Hell. I don't like Dr. Martin's attitude."

"Jan, stop It! That's enough! She's under his care. Your Mother is not a well woman. They need to treat her accordingly. Listen to me! You really need to quit stirring up trouble and stop interfering out there!"

"Dad, have a heart. How can you let her suffer like this?" He shifted his eyes away from mine, got up from the chair, and walked away from me. I couldn't believe the way he was acting. It was like he'd given them permission to experiment with Mother. Why wouldn't he take a stand?

I went to visit Mom (my Mother's mother)and told her about Mother's shock treatment. I hated to tell her, but I had to discuss it with someone. She said suspiciously, "What's your father trying to prove? Why would he authorize this kind of torture?" My aunts, Genevieve, Viola, and Shirley were upset, too, when I repeated what happened to Mother and relayed my meeting with Dr. Martin. Here I was with no authority at nineteen and my Mother suffering unnecessarily because of Dad's unwillingness to get involved.

CHAPTER 16

A few days later my grandmother on my Dad's side fell and broke her hip. Grandpap had had a stroke about six months before. He still didn't have full strength on his left side. The doctor told Dad they couldn't set Grandma's hip until she became stronger. She was frail and would be bedridden for months. Grandpap was doing his best to care for her with a nurse coming a couple times a week.

I was shocked when I went to visit my grandparents and found Maggie our old housekeeper living there. It was all I could do to remain cordial. I tried to ignore her as much as possible, but Grandma and Grandpap were mesmerized by her offering to help them in their desperation.

After visiting Grandma, Maggie approached me in the parlor, "Your Dad called and said your grandparents needed my help." Her syrupy sweet voice was enough to turn my stomach. For my grand parents' sake I didn't respond. On the surface, I went along pretending it was okay. Mother told Les and me that Maggie wasn't a nice woman when we weren't around. I didn't trust her. I began to visit my grandparents more often to make sure everything was okay. Grandpap was so grateful and praised Maggie for her help. When they asked about Mother and Maggie was listening in, I said, "She's doing better."

"I will care for your grandparents as long as they need me and stay here till they are well," Maggie offered. I didn't respond to her and tried to avoid and ignore her during my visits. Not once in my visits to Grandma's house did she utter one word to me about Mother, or ask about Les who was overseas. I should have told her Mother was great and Les was coming home soon. But, I didn't feel comfortable lying.

Two months went by and Grandma was getting by without problems. Uncle Don drove in from Pittsburgh for a surprise visit and found them alone and in despair.

"Grandpap said, "Maggie left in the night without telling us." He went around the house looking for her. She was gone, along with all her personal effects. In addition, they had a real eye opener when their grocery bill arrived. Maggie had charged a lot of things my grandparents didn't ask for and junk food for herself. She left over $100.00 due on their bill. This was about as low as one can get. She took advantage of my sick grandparents who needed help. Maggie could have telephoned and Dad would have arranged someone to take over, not sneak out in the night. She was well aware of their small monthly income. I never did like her but was surprised she stooped this low. I saw a lot of things, nail polish, bags of candy, dried fruits, and other junk food she brought home from the store when she lived with us. I never thought about it till now. Probably at the time it ended up on Dad's grocery bill, too. He would've paid it thinking she deserved it. No wonder she never inquired about Mother. I'm sure she never liked Mother to begin with, certainly not after Mother chased her out of the house. This proved she had no compassion for my grandparents either. Maggie's behavior confirmed for me and all the relatives what a bitch she really was.

Dad's comment when he heard about the incident was, "She probably had her reasons. We don't know what goes on in this woman's life." I thought he would be furious like everyone else. Instead he was making an excuse for her. My aunt came up from Lancaster to live with Grandpap and Grandma till they were able to care for themselves.

CHAPTER 17

My heart pounded with excitement as I spotted Les coming down the stairs they had rolled across the Tarmac to the airplane at Martinsburg Airport. He looked handsome in his uniform. I could hardly wait to hug him, and take him to the hospital to see Mother. I ran over the moment he walked into the terminal. We hugged each other and went to locate his bag.

"How was the flight from Pittsburgh?"

"What a thrill when you hit an air pocket. It was fun to fly over the mountains and see the bright green rolling hills and farm land. I'd forgotten how beautiful Pennsylvania is. As the plane approached it looked as though we were going to land right in the middle of a corn field."

"One day I'll see what it's like to fly," I remarked.

"I'm sure you will before too long, Jan."

Les was full of questions about how Mother had ended up in the Hollidaysburg State Hospital. I wrote him several letters, but it wasn't the same as talking with him.

"We're driving right by the hospital on our way home, and I thought we would stop and visit Mother."

"How's Mother taking it?"

"Not good. She's furious with Dad and pleads with me to get her out of there. She's been waiting for you to come home and rescue her. My hope is with you here we can do something to get her home." I drove up the long winding road to the hospital as I was accustomed to and walked with Les into the front vestibule. I asked the receptionist to call the nurse to bring Mother down for our visit. When the elevator door opened Mother looked up. Her eyes lit up when she saw Les in uniform. They hugged a long time. We stopped on the way for Mother's favorite peanut butter sundae. She dug right into it. She was much brighter today. Les told her about visiting Paris, Spain, and North Africa and other places she had only read about. He seemed happy with his life in the Air Force, and the traveling sounded exciting. I was hoping Mother wouldn't start clinging and begging him to take her home today, especially since this was his first visit.

"Les, thank God you are here to take me home." Mother's eyes looked clear and bright as she took hold of his arm.

"Well, I wish I could, Mother, but I arrived today and need to make arrangements to meet with your doctor, discuss your condition, and see if you're well enough to come home," Les explained, with his eyes becoming watery. Quickly her smile faded, "Les, you can see for yourself. I'm better now." Les hesitated. I knew he was searching for the right words, not to disappoint her.

"Mother, I'm going to do all I can. I can't take you home without your doctor's permission. I'll make arrangements to meet with him on Monday."

Mother looked at Les so pitiful with glassy eyes, "I've waited a long time for you. Son, I can't hold out much longer in this place." Her voice quivering, you don't know what it's like to be with all these crazy people." She took hold of his hand and rubbed it, "I'm so happy to see you." God, it was sad. If only we could've taken her home, right then. I knew it was time to get the nurse. Tears began to flow. Mother was about to start crying and clinging. I had been through this many times before. I wanted this to be a good visit without much sadness. Les remained at the visitors table with her, while I walked over to the receptionist to call for a nurse. I returned to the table. Mother was holding Les's hand against her cheek. He had his other arm around her. It was great seeing them together. The elevator door opened and a nurse started walking toward us.

"Are you here to take Mother back upstairs?" I asked.

"Yes, come with me, Naomi. It's almost supper time." The nurse took hold of Mother's arm. It was difficult for Les to step aside, but he managed to get her to stand up.

"This is my son. He's come to take me home. Please don't interfere. Let me go!" The nurse tried to hold onto her arm. Mother pulled away, "Let me go, I've had enough of this place, and you call this a hospital. There's nothing wrong with me going home won't fix." Mother was getting boisterous.

"Now, Now, Naomi, why do you want to make it difficult for

everyone? You had a nice visit. Don't spoil it for your kids."

Les and I exchanged glances and he intervened, "Mother, it's all right, please be patient a little while longer. I'll see what can be done, I promise. Go along with the nurse for now. Do it for me. I know you can. I'll be out to see you again tomorrow."

Les helped lead Mother toward the elevator, and the nurse held Mother's other arm. The nurse pushed the elevator button and the doors opened. Les let go of Mother's arm. She tried to hold onto him, but the nurse grabbed her other arm and lead her into the elevator. The nurse turned Mother around to face us. Mother's head dropped down in despair as the doors began to close. I waved and turned quickly, so she couldn't see the tears running down my cheeks. As the elevator started up I heard Mother say, "My son will get me out of here. You'll see." It was a sad drive home for both of us. Neither Les nor I knew what could be done to get her discharged, or how to make it easier on all of us during our visits.

Dad and I bumped into each other in the kitchen early the next morning. It was Saturday.

"Dad, it's so hard for Les to visit Mother like this. It's sad. She's going through such a rough time. I would like to bring her home for a few days and see how she does. She's doing a lot better now."

"Bringing her home is out of the question! It will only make matters worse. She won't want to go back. It's better to leave things the way they are," he said, as he got a beer from the refrigerator.

"But, Dad, Les and I can handle her and it would be great to have her home while Les is here. It would give her hope."

"No, she's not herself, and Lord knows what she would do once home. I can't allow it, even if it's possible." He walked away from me. I wondered, does he fear her or just doesn't want to face her? She had threatened to get even with him. Later in the afternoon he asked, "Will you and Les be getting down to the cottage this weekend?"

"No, I wish I could, Dad, but I have to work tomorrow, Sunday."

"What about you, son, Will you drive down with me?"

"I'd like to, but I promised some friends I'd meet with them tomorrow afternoon. Jan and I wanted to go up the river fishing, but since she has to work, I guess it will have to wait till next weekend," Les replied, regretfully.

Dad looked disappointed. "Okay, I guess it's on hold till next weekend."

I went into work on a split shift. During the morning half of my schedule, I told the girls at the office how disappointed I was at having to work on Sunday. One of my best friends felt bad since Les was home on leave. She agreed to trade days off. I couldn't thank her enough. Les borrowed my car in the afternoon and agreed to pick me up at nine p.m. at the end of my shift.

Since I now had Sunday off Les and I decided to surprise Dad at the cottage. We packed a few clothes, picked up some groceries and soda pop at the ACME store on our way to the cottage. It was fun. We drove the country roads looking for wild life as we went along. I had time to take a close look at Les behind the wheel. He seemed much older, wiser and sure of himself. It was exciting hearing about his travels to Europe and to Casa Blanca. He explained how much fun he had seeing the Eiffel tower, the Tower of Pisa, and the Kasbah.

"Jan, one day you'll see these places. I'm sure of it, because I know you have the desire to explore." I always dreamed of traveling and doing something special in my life. I never knew what "special thing" I would end up doing. Who knows maybe I'll see Europe in the future. The school aptitude test indicated my talents were suited for a forest ranger. I was sure that wouldn't happen.

We pulled into the cottage driveway and our lights shined back at us from the small windows above the kitchen stove. I grabbed one of the bags of groceries, opened the screen door, turned the door knob and walked into the kitchen. I was anxious to see the surprise on Dad's face. Les followed carrying a bag with a couple quarts of soda pop. I placed the groceries on the kitchen table, turned toward the stairs when I heard footsteps. I looked up and screamed.

"Oh, My God!" I flung my arm around and knocked over the bag. There was Maggie, as fat as ever, in one of those see through night gowns. I ran for the door as fast as I could. Les saw what was happening and grabbed my arm trying to stop me. I pulled away. The screen door slammed behind me. Les yelled, "Jan, stop!" He followed and reached my arm as I opened the car door. He tried to pull me out of the car. I turned the key, released the emergency brake, threw the gear shift into reverse and my foot down on the accelerator. Les let the car door swing shut as I spun the car around. Shale flew in the air in the driveway behind me. Les was saying something, but I didn't hear him. I drove as fast as I could up the lane to my aunt's cottage.

A few years before Dad built our cottage Uncle Herman had built his cottage up the river. My aunt Genevieve bought it from Uncle Herman. She must have heard my car coming in her driveway and was holding the door open as I entered. "What's going on, Jan? You look like you've seen a ghost." Aunt Genevieve, had a worried look. We called her by her nickname, Aunt Beb. "It's her I replied, crying hysterically at the cottage. How could Dad do this?"

"Who? What did he do now?" Aunt Beb inquired.

"Maggie's down there with Dad."

"Maggie! I can't believe it! How could he do such a thing in front of you? Has he lost his mind hanging around with that woman?" Aunt Beb put her arm around my shoulder, led me to the kitchen table, and pulled out a chair. I couldn't stop sobbing. I was betrayed by my own father. All I could think of was Mother being in a horrible hospital while Dad was messing around. I couldn't think straight.

The door opened and there stood Les, out of breath, "Jan, I'm sorry you found them together. I don't know what Dad is thinking. Why he would bring her to the cottage is beyond me. It's one thing to have an affair with her, but to bring her here!"

"Les, it's good to see you, Aunt Beb said. Thank heavens you were with Jan. What's happened to your father? He's gone from bad to worse," Aunt Beb, went on.

"Les, you sound like you knew he was having an affair, did you?" I asked.

"Yes, in a way. I wasn't sure, but there were a couple of nights I came home early and saw Dad coming out of the dining room. He had a startled look on his face. We never exchanged words about it, but I've always suspected it."

"Why didn't you tell me?"

"Maggie was taking care of Mother, and I wasn't totally sure since I never found them embracing each other. You and Dad were inseparable. I didn't want to cause a confrontation due to suspicions. You know Dad and I never did see eye to eye, especially after I went to college. Besides, I thought it was over when Mother chased her out of the house."

"You could've at least told me after she was gone. It would have helped me sort things out in my mind."

"No, Jan, I believe I did the right thing. After all, I didn't actually catch them in bed together. I suspected they had a thing going. To destroy you and Dad's relationship was the last thing I wanted to do, especially since I was leaving for the Air Force."

"You know, I wrote you about her showing up to take care of grandma when she broke her hip. Maggie got up and left early in the morning without a warning. While she stayed there she ran up their grocery bill buying candy and junk."

"Yes, I remember. Jan, look at it this way. Maggie is a selfish lonely old woman who is obviously in love with our Dad. She would do almost anything to gain Dad's favor."

Les was making sense, as always. I shook my head, hardly believing. "How could Dad betray Mother like this? I'll never be able to look him in the eyes again, knowing what he's done. My life at the cottage is over. I'll never forgive him for this!"

"Jan, wipe your face," Aunt Beb handed me a box of tissues. "Stop crying. He isn't worth it. You need a drink to calm your nerves." Aunt Beb went to the old antique cupboard and pulled out a gallon of port wine. I blew my nose and wiped my eyes. My forehead was throbbing like during a migraine.

"He owes you an explanation and needs to promise you he will stop seeing that whore. Here drink this down." Aunt Beb poured me a water glass full of dark red port.

"Les, how about you? Want some wine? Both of you can stay here for the night."

"Yes, thanks, but give me a smaller glass, Aunt Beb."

"How could I have been this naïve. I knew there was something not right about Maggie but couldn't put my finger on it. Maggie was always telling me, 'Nomi did this or I did this for Nomi.' To think I listened to that bitch's syrupy sweet voice. She talked to me like I was a child. And I believed her over my own mother!"

"Jan quit blaming yourself. How could you have known she was lying?" Les said, gulping down some wine.

"I let Dad sway me into believing Maggie was telling the truth, and Mother was getting mixed up and forgetful. I should have listened to Mother, not her! No wonder he built her up to be the great housekeeper and brought her to the house. He had the nerve to let her care for his own parents, too. How can he live with himself? No wonder he drinks all the time."

"Well, I think we should settle this right now, Les. Let's go down and tell them a thing or two. Get her out of there once and for all." Aunt Beb was all fired up.

"No, it's hard to tell what dad's reaction will be. He surely is drinking and we don't know how much is under his belt already. I'll go down and act as though nothing is wrong. After I make a sandwich I will go upstairs to my bed, as though nothing has changed."

"How can you go down there and face the two of them?"

"I want to look him straight in the eye. Words probably will not even be necessary—he'll get the message by my being there. I believe he will back down because he knows he has gone too far. I'll bet he will be embarrassed and will round up her things and leave. If she says one word to me I will ignore her as though she were a ghost. I've nothing to say to her. One thing for sure, they won't be in the cottage alone together tonight," Les offered.

"I don't know how you can do it. But, go ahead. It will serve them right," Jan said.

"Les, have another drink before you go?" Aunt Beb began pouring more wine into his glass.

"Whoa, not so much, I think I'd better go right away. They must be down there stewing and I want to put them both on the spot." Les, took a gulp of wine and got up to leave.

"Les, are you sure you want to do this?"

"Yes, Jan, I've waited a long time to stand up to Dad, and this is the time." He smiled and gave me his devilish look as he walked out the door. I thought, what if he got into a fight with Dad, it could be a mess.

"Your Uncle Pete told me a few years back that Maggie was the Madame who ran a whore house across the tracks—in the upstairs of one of those old bars. I never told you because I thought she was long gone out of both of your lives."

"She's nothing but trash. How can Dad lay around with her? And Mother is suffering because of him. Rather than trying to help her, he got rid of her—Oh, my was that it?"

"There are a lot of questions to be answered. Let's not jump to conclusions yet. But I don't put anything past him." We stayed up for about an hour looking down through the orchard of fruit trees for any sign of lights or motion. We could see a dim light shining through the trees from the cottage windows. The moon was full, and we could see almost like we had a bright light shining across her acre. The crickets and frogs were trying to outdo each other. The lights seem to flicker from the small cottage windows in the dark shadows of the tall evergreens camouflaging it.

I peeked from the upstairs window right before crawling into bed, and the cottage lights were still on. I rolled and tossed all night. For the first time in all the years I spent at the cottage the crickets and frogs were not a welcome sound. I kept mulling over in my mind various incidents over the past with Maggie.

Mother was right after all. Maggie was trying to take over and was glad Mother was bedridden. Why was Mother so weak? Why couldn't the doctor put his finger on it? In the fall, it was obvious her weakness was due to her asthma attacks and hay fever. Lord knows what Maggie was saying to Mother each day. How far did Maggie go? How mean was she to Mother when we weren't around? What about all those bowel movements? I heard Maggie report the same story numerous times. *Nomi had diarrhea again, but I cleaned her up real good.* I prayed under my breath, "Oh, God please help me sort out the facts. Could she have been so cruel and obsessed with wanting Dad to herself that she did something to keep Mother weak and confused? Surely Maggie wouldn't have gone that far, but did she? Life will never be the same again.

When I closed my eyes I could imagine seeing Maggie hanging out the second story window of one of those old bars by the railroad tracks coaxing men up for a "quickie." I couldn't get her out of my mind. Dad had gone too far bringing a whore into our house and now to our cottage. I thought about several disagreements I had over Mother's care and how I had backed down believing it was Mother who was mixed up.

I heard Aunt Beb's screen door bang. It was early, daylight was coming in the upstairs window. I must have fallen asleep for two hours, or so. I got up and looked out the window and saw the fog rising from the river. I could hear Les talking in a low tone with Aunt Beb downstairs. I hurried down in my shorty pajamas to find out what happened. Aunt Beb was making hot chocolate and Les was seated at the kitchen table. "Did they leave?" I asked.

"Yes, they're gone. Dad packed up and left before I got up this morning. The expression on Dad's face last evening was unbelievable. As I entered Maggie scurried her fat body upstairs and out of sight. I pretended not to notice. At first no words were spoken. Dad got a beer out of the icebox and started drinking. He gulped it down so fast, I wondered if he would stop swallowing long enough to take a breath. Then, with a long silence, he asked if I wanted one."

"I said I would."

"He told me it was good to have me home. He only wished there were better circumstances. He said if he'd known we were coming this wouldn't have happened. And you told him you had to work and we weren't coming this weekend."

"I told Dad you got a friend to trade days off and you wanted to surprise him, go fishing like old times."

"He said Mother had been sick a long time and he had no excuses for his actions. But he hoped one day you'd understand. He was already slurring his words. Obviously, he had already drunk plenty before I arrived."

"I told him I understood all right, but only to a point. How could he behave like this in front of you and bring Maggie of all women to our cottage."

"His response was that I had no idea what he'd been through all these years. He said he'd done everything possible to give us a good life, the best he could. And there wasn't anyone to care for Mother nor did he have money enough to hire a nurse."

"I made it clear I wasn't here to judge him and he has his own conscious to deal with. I told him I worried for you and Mother. After all, I would only be here for a few days, then what?"

"His eyes began to tear up, and he just sat there staring at the pictures hanging over the davenport for what seemed like a long time. He stood up and drained the last drop of beer from his bottle and went to the stairs. To be certain he knew I wasn't leaving and staying for the night. I said I'd be up shortly and would turn out the lights. He stopped at the bottom of the stairs, turned, and looked at me rather surprised, then continued up to bed."

"I heard some rustling around before dawn and whispers. When it was light enough I could see his bed was empty. I walked over to the window and saw his car pull out the driveway. I believe, for the first time in years, we finally understood one another. I was always in the wrong. He wouldn't budge from his position on what I should do with my life. I always wanted to be able to tell him he was wrong, but I never could. He was my father and overpowered me. Do you remember his old saying, Jan, 'As long as you live in this house you will do as I say.' We always tried to speak up for ourselves but ended up doing everything his way."

Aunt Beb had a look of disgust and practically choked on her hot chocolate, "Where did he get the idea he was so righteous? I remember when he dated your Mother, and you know he got her pregnant before they were married. Boy, would I like to tell him a thing or two," Aunt Beb was livid. Your Mother was popular with all the boys in the neighborhood. She could have had anyone she wanted. The guys were always trying to get her to go out on dates. When she went to high school, I'd see a different boy walk her to school and another guy would drop her home in his dad's car. I was jealous because she was more attractive with that coal black curly hair and nice figure. And she had to fall for your dad! She was Pop's favorite, too. I guess because she was smart and his first born." With that, Aunt Beb took a big sip of hot chocolate and ran to the sink.

"Are you okay?"

"Damn, I burned the inside of my mouth!" She got a glass of cold water and rinsed her mouth, "Watch the hot chocolate!"

I had looked forward to wading up the river with Les to my favorite bass hole. The excitement about fishing was gone. In a few hours my whole world had changed. How could I go home and face Dad, knowing he had been sneaking around with that whore.

"Les, I'll need you to help me face Dad tonight. I don't know what I'll do when I see him. I want to pound him with my fists and tell him how much I hate him for what he has done to Mother."

"Jan, I know how you feel, but after seeing Dad last night I realize he's no longer the father we knew. He's an alcoholic and a shamed man. He's down right pathetic."

"Since you've been gone I couldn't figure out why he was more negative and pessimistic about everything. His drinking is out of control. Now I think I've finally got it! He hates himself for what he has done, he can't rectify it, and has to live in shame—no wonder he drinks."

"Somebody needs to knock sense into him. I'm the one who can tell him a thing or too, if I get the chance," Aunt Beb blurted out.

Les nodded. "Jan he always was pessimistic and down in the dumps. Maybe, after last night he'll realize he's about to lose his daughter. If this doesn't bring him to his senses, nothing ever will."

Aunt Beb made us oatmeal and toast for breakfast. Les and I went down to the river bank to dig for fishing worms. We rowed up the river and spent a couple hours fishing. The crappies, sun fish, and fall fish were biting, but I didn't feel like cleaning them. We held them underwater to remove the fish hook and let them swim away. I always hate it when they swallow the bait. We always kept those, but not today. Most will die after the hook penetrates their little stomachs. It was great to fish with Les again, but I couldn't get Maggie and Dad out of my mind.

The river was calm under a cloudy fall sky. Dark storm clouds began to appear. When the sun was out my arms were warm, but when the sun disappeared—I was getting goose bumps. The trees were bright colors of yellow, red, brown and gold reflecting onto the river's edge. This is the time of year people flock from all around to see Pennsylvania. The river today had a clear greenish cast. When the clouds covered the sun the river became a dark green. Bugs began to swarm around Les's white T-shirt—especially those black and yellow striped flies. Bugs usually are a sign of a thunderstorm. The river began to ripple as the wind picked up. I wished it were summer and we could have waded up the river and maybe taken a swim in our old swimming hole. More dark clouds appeared and rain seemed imminent.

"We'd better wrap it up, Jan. It's getting chilly and we don't want to be out here in the rain." I noticed he had goose bumps on his arms too. I rowed us down the river to the cottage. We pulled the boat up the bank as far as we could and locked it to the chain. As we closed the kitchen door I wondered when, or if, I would ever be back again. It was sad. I rolled down the window of the car and looked at the river as Les drove up the lane to say goodbye to Aunt Beb.

"Did yah catch anything?" Aunt Beb asked, as she walked out to greet us.

"A few crappies and sun fish, but we threw them back." I answered, as Les and I got out of the car.

"Aunt Beb, I wanted to drop by and say goodbye for now, but, I'll see you again before I leave, won't I? Will you be driving up to the city next week?" Les, asked.

"Yes, we're ready to close down the cottage for the winter. Your Uncle Pete may come down to hunt over Thanksgiving and that will be it for this year."

"I'm sure I'll see you next week, then." Les gave her a hug and got in behind the wheel. He rolled down his window and added, "I don't know how things will play out. Dad sure made a mess of things."

"He sure has his gall, I can't understand how he can do such a thing with your Mother as sick as she is in the hospital."

"We'll see you later, Aunt Beb." Les drove slowly down the lane.

I looked out the back window and could see Aunt Beb waving. As we got closer to the city, I kept thinking what to say, if anything. Les said, "Don't say a word at first. Let him start the conversation. You'll know how to respond." My heart was pounding as I followed Les across the living room. I hesitated by the cellar door, listening for Dad's voice.

"Jan, he's not here, you can relax." Les looked out the back door. "His car's gone." I walked over and verified for myself. I was all worked up and he was not home. "Damn him! He probably is scared to face me and is staying with Maggie."

I didn't get much sleep and was in a bad mood when I got out of bed. It was about nine thirty when I went down stairs to the kitchen thinking I was ready to confront him—at least I thought I was. There he was holding a tall glass of milk with a raw egg floating on top. I glanced over at him as I opened the refrigerator to reach for the milk to make hot chocolate. He sat there speechless. I waited as Les suggested with anger swelling in my chest.

He started stirring his milk rapidly with a fixed stare at the glass. I poured the milk in a pan and turned on the gas. Finally, he spoke, "Jan, I know I can't make this right. I've made mistakes in my life and this is one of them. You kids have no idea what I've been going through."

"What you've been going through! What about Mother and me? How could you sneak around with that woman? What kind of father do I have? I guess I don't know my own father. Of all the women why did it have to be her?" Tears began to flow down my cheeks and yet I'd never been this angry and hurt in my heart. I wanted to pound him with my fists, or smash something—I didn't know what to do.

"Your Mother needed a nurse. I couldn't afford one. I was in a bind. What else could I do? I did the best I knew how." he explained.

"You could have talked with Les and me before bringing Maggie into our house. Les and I could have helped find someone who needed a place to stay. There surely was someone who would have cared for Mother in exchange for a home. Maggie was a liar! She tore our family apart. Mother must have known something was wrong. To think I doubted my own Mother's word. I blame you and Maggie for Mother's illness! I'm going to tell Mother the truth."

"Jan, grow up! I'm still your father and that's the wrong thing to do. It will not help your Mother, only make her worse. She is getting treatment. Make no mistake here. Don't do it!" Dad was pleading with me. I started bawling and lost control. "I hate you for what you've done." I ran out of the kitchen and upstairs. Dad ran after me and yelled from the bottom of the stairs, "Jan, don't do something you'll regret the rest of your life." Les came out of his bedroom and met me in the hallway. He put his arm around me and led me to the side of my bed, "I couldn't help hearing some of what was said down there. Jan, pull yourself together. He just isn't worth it!" He smoothed my hair back away from my face. I grabbed a couple tissues and blew my nose. I couldn't stop crying.

"I'll get you a wash cloth. He went to the bathroom and brought back a folded wet washcloth and placed it on my forehead. I held it in place. "Close the door, Les, I don't want Dad to hear what we're saying."

"Should I get you some aspirin? Maybe it will help you get some rest." I nodded. "I'm going to take a drive over to visit Bob, Jan. Will you be all right?"

"Yes, I need to calm my nerves. You go ahead I'll stay away from Dad while you're gone." I spoke in a low voice but wanted to scream and smash something.

"I'll go out the front, to avoid Dad." I lay there thinking, I can get through this with Les around, but what about after his furlough is over. He can leave, but I'm stuck here. I was awakened by Les shaking my shoulder. "What time is it?"

"It's 15:55."

"What did you say?"

"It's almost four in military time. How do you feel? Relax, Dad's gone. C'mon, I'll make us some tomato soup and a salad for supper. I picked up some Hires root beer your favorite." I followed him down to the kitchen and sat at the table where Mother used to sit. Les made supper and the root beer really hit the spot. I was scheduled for six to midnight and would have to pull myself together fast. We had planned to visit Mother that afternoon, but I fell asleep and I guess it was for the best. I couldn't wait to tell Mother about Maggie.

"Les, you heard Dad pleading, actually ordering me not to tell Mother about him and Maggie. What do you think?"

"Jan he's been wrong about a lot lately, but I'm inclined to agree with him about not wanting to upset Mother more than she already is. She's furious with Dad already. We don't know how she'll react." Les looked worried, "I fear it might make her go over the edge. On one hand it may help her and on the other it could be detrimental"

Our eyes met. Les knew I was in a quandary and placed his hand on my shoulder. My voice began to quiver, "What am I going to do after you're gone and I've got to make these decisions on my own?"

I stood up and Les hugged me. I buried my head against his chest. He changed his voice to one of assurance, "Jan you're strong and you can do whatever you make your mind up to do. Don't let this ruin your life. Things will get easier, I promise. It will take time for you to sort things out."

I felt better and stepped back, "I hope you're right." It made sense to talk with Dr. Martin first whether or not to share Dad's affair with Mother. "Les, you wanted to meet her doctor so I'll make an appointment. His professional opinion could help us make a decision."

CHAPTER 18

I heard the telephone ring at about 8:00 o'clock in the morning. I was waking up after working a late shift. Gently I picked up the receiver of my princess phone. I overheard Dad saying, "Give me another chance, I won't let it happen again." The voice on the other end said, "Look, Russ you have gone too far this time. Drinking on the job is against company rules. We have discussed this before and you know it."

"You know how rough it's been with the wife in the hospital and all. My whole world is falling apart. Please give me another chance. I've always been a good worker. Doesn't twenty five years count for something?"

"Your quality of work isn't the issue. Bringing vodka into work in your thermos and getting tipsy is dangerous around this heavy equipment. You know what I'm talking about."

I had no choice but to stay on the line. Obviously it was his boss at the railroad.

"I'm going to do you a favor. I could have you fired, but I'm going to recommend you retire on disability. In this way, you will not lose your railroad retirement benefits."

"Tom, you and I have known each other for years. Don't do this. Let me continue to work. It's all I have! I promise I will never drink on the job again." Dad choked up.

"I'm sorry, Russ, but this is final. It's over! Come into the office tomorrow and I'll start the paperwork. I'll see you then."

"Tom please don't do this to me." Dad was begging.

"That's it, Russ. There's nothing more to say." I heard a click—his boss hung up. I waited till Dad hung up the phone downstairs before I laid my receiver down. He was lucky he had a boss willing to let him retire and not fire him. I wouldn't say a word and see if he mentions the conversation. I had made up my mind to avoid him wherever possible. I had nothing more to say to him. What a dilemma. A few days ago I would've been devastated if he told me he was retiring. It's as though I had grown up in two days and was no longer daddy's little girl. I couldn't feel sorry for him—not after what he's done.

Our appointment with Dr. Martin was set for 2:00 p.m. at the state hospital. On the way, I told Les what I heard over the telephone.

"Oh brother, this is going to make matters worse." Les said.

"Whatever we do we can't let Dad be aware we know what's going on."

"You're right, Jan, we'll see what he tells us in the next few days." We arrived a little early. I told the receptionist we had an appointment with Dr. Martin. I heard her tell someone over the phone we were there. She gave me an odd look, "Have a seat. The doctor will be down." We sat on a bench close to the front desk. After about ten minutes the elevator doors opened and Dr. Martin walked over to meet us. "Dr. Martin, this is my brother, Les. He's home on leave."

"How nice it is to meet you. How long are you home for?" Dr. Martin asked.

"Three weeks all together and the time sure is flying by." Les responded.

"Doctor we're here about the incident I told your nurse briefly about over the telephone. We need help in deciding whether to tell Mother our Dad had an affair with another woman. Since it's the same woman, our former housekeeper, the one Mother ended up chasing out of the house, we thought it might help her to know she was right all along about Maggie. To think we thought Mother was imagining Maggie wasn't a nice person. We know now, Maggie was there with an ulterior motive. You're probably already aware of the incident, right?"

"Yes, I'm well aware there was an altercation between Naomi and her housekeeper. I've not been able to establish the extent of the housekeeper's injuries."

"I beg your pardon, as far as we know she never hit Maggie. She only scared her half to death."

"Let's move out of the hallway." He led us through the visiting area and unlocked a door I hadn't noticed before when visiting.

"Have a seat. We can talk more privately here." He sat on the other side of a desk facing Les and me, "You mean there was no physical harm? I thought this was an assault case and one of the reasons for Naomi's admission." He looked puzzled.

"There must be some mistake, Dr. Martin, there was no assault. I don't know where you got your information, but it's wrong! Mother was getting forgetful and imagining things. At least we thought so, until now."

Les looked surprised and interrupted, "Who told you Mother injured Maggie?"

"I can't divulge medical information on our patients and Dr. Dixon has been assigned as the attending physician."

"This is our Mother we're talking about." Les raised his voice, leaned forward and looked straight at Dr. Martin, "Surely we have a right to know?"

"No. I'm sorry but this is confidential information." Dr. Martin quickly closed the folder in front of him.

"Doctor, let me start from the beginning. It was after you joined the Air Force, Les. Mother ended up in the hospital Emergency Room when Dad and I were out deer hunting. She complained of severe pain and thought it was labor pains. They did a pregnancy test and she wasn't pregnant. Dad was so upset about Mother going to the hospital he met with her physician, Dr. Hill who said she needed further evaluation and treatment. As far as we know he made the arrangements for Mother to be admitted here."

"Yes, I vaguely recall something about an E.R. visit, but my impression was a physical assault really landed her here."

"What assault?" I edged my chair closer to the desk, "Again, there was no physical contact. Mother chased the housekeeper out of the house with a broom. I don't understand this assault business, doctor. What am I missing here?" I glanced over at Les. I could tell by Dr. Martin's expression he was getting irritated as I spoke.

"Well, perhaps," Dr. Martin hesitated. "I may be wrong. I have many cases with varied reasons for admissions. I can't remember every detail. But to get on with your question, I do not believe it's in Naomi's best interest to tell her about an affair your father is having, at least, not at this time. We are just beginning to make some progress according to Dr. Dixon. This could be damaging information."

"But, doctor if she knew he was having an affair with Maggie when she was her care giver, housekeeper, wouldn't this prove in her mind she was right about Maggie. Her actions were justified? I know she doesn't regret chasing her out of the house because we discussed it at length at the time."

"I'm not sure this information would be of help to her mentally." Dr. Martin offered.

"Well, it was like this. Mother would tell Les and I how mean Maggie was to her when we were gone. We didn't believe her. Maggie convinced us our Mother was confused and losing her memory."

"Dr. Martin, let me make this clearer. Maggie would say Mother had been fed and Mother would say she hadn't eaten anything for hours." Les, explained.

"Are you saying this is a case of neglect, then?" Dr. Martin questioned.

"Yes, and probably more than that. It got to the point we believed what Maggie told us and not what our own Mother said. She was weak and bedridden for almost a year. We thought she was confused and losing it. Les and I are beginning to realize there may be other reasons we can't explain at this time." I said, as Les glanced over at me as if to say hang it up.

"I still do not believe this information would be therapeutic. Just because your father had an extra marital relationship with this woman does not imply she treated your mother poorly."

"Your advice, then, is to keep this information from Mother. And, you believe this would not help her to get well any sooner. We'd like her to be able to return home. Do you have an idea at this time when she will be well enough to be released?" Les asked.

"It's hard to say. Dr. Dixon is her therapist and would be able to address her overall progress. However, it's my opinion sharing the information about your father's affair could be detrimental. This is how I see it for now. You will have to excuse me as I must get back to my appointments—you understand." Dr. Martin got up from the desk and shook Les's hand, "I'm glad I met you and best of luck." He opened the door and we lagged behind. I spoke softly so he couldn't hear me, "Les, do you agree with what he said?"

"I'm not sure, but I guess we have to go along with it for now."

"What about this assault business? Where do you suppose this came from? This clinches it for me, Les. One way or another I'm going to find out if that bitch Maggie claimed Mother hit her."

"Now, exactly how are you going to go about that, Jan?"

"I'll find out where she lives and get information out of her one way or another."

"Jan, don't go getting yourself into trouble. Maggie isn't worth it. She's a liar and we can't take her at her word."

We walked over to the receptionist's desk and asked to see Mother. The elevator door opened about fifteen minutes later. There stood the nurse holding onto her arm. Her hair was a mess, the old house dress she wore was way too big and food stuff was spilled down the front. Les shook his head and rolled his eyes toward me. I knew that look. It was one of disbelief that this was our Mother.

"Mother, how do you feel today?" I asked. Les and I got on opposite sides each holding onto an arm and led her to the visiting area.

"Okay, Thank God you're here to take me home son."

"No, Mother, I can't today, but I hope it will be soon." Les said, sadly.

"I've been counting on you to get me out of here. Did Jan tell you how crazy these women are here?"

"Yes, I know Mother, but we met with Dr. Martin today and he said you are making progress."

"He did, did he? Then, why doesn't he get me out of here? Dr. Dixon says the same thing. What's wrong with me? I feel fine and why am I kept hostage? I want to go home. I don't belong in this place. Why doesn't your father come and see for himself what goes on here. Where is he anyway? He's a coward and can't face me. Isn't that it?"

"Mother, he doesn't go anywhere except to work. I've seen a big change in him since I was gone. He's drinking heavily and isn't the same." Les, explained.

"Mother let me comb your hair. You don't like it this way do you?"

"No, Jan. I like it pulled back and they just comb it any old way. Tell your Dad I'm waiting!"

"That looks much better, Mother. Thanksgiving is coming up and I want to take you home for the weekend. I'm going to talk with Dad and your doctor about it."

"What does the old man have to do with whether I'm well enough to come home? I want it to be for good. Do you understand? You tell him I want out of here now! I'm not waiting till Thanksgiving. I want to see him face to face! He doesn't understand what he's done to me. Please, son, take me home?" She took hold of Les's hand and looked up at him with those pleading dark brown eyes. It was pathetic, my heart ached as I watched her.

"Mother we're trying to get you home, but Dad and your doctor have to sign some papers in agreement that you're better. We can't sign you out. Please try to be patient," Les, replied.

"I've been waiting for you to come home. Your Dad has no idea what I'm going through. I'm doing everything they ask me to do now. You've got to get me out of here before it's too late!" Tears started running down her cheeks.

"Mother, don't cry, Jan and I will continue to work on Dad. It's a slow process—we need to get a lot more information on how to circumvent the system."

"Son, these doctors won't pay attention to Jan, she's only twenty. I've prayed that you could find a way to have me released—I know you can. You don't know what it's like, day after day in this God forsaken place." She was sobbing.

I took some Kleenex from my purse and wiped her face. It was hard to see her this way. Mother, leaned over and said she wanted to go to the restroom. I took hold of her arm, helped her to her feet and we walked together into the women's room. I guided her to the toilet and stepped outside with the door half shut thinking about Maggie and Dad. At that moment, I wished I could blurt out the whole story to Mother. I walked with her to the sink and took a wet paper towel and wiped the food stuff from the front of her dress. She rinsed her hands and I handed her a couple of paper towels. From the ladies room I led her toward the vestibule and motioned for Les to join us. Mother seemed like her old self to me.

"Mother, let's go over and look out the window. It's a clear day. Look at the autumn leaves. They're beginning to fall from the trees. Les, stay with Mother while I have the receptionist call for Mrs. Claney to come down. I'm sure it's getting close to supper time."

"I don't care about supper," she said raising her voice. "Please son, take me out of here!"

"Believe me Mother. I wish I could. We're trying to figure out exactly how to go about it." Les put his arm around her at the window as I turned and went to the receptionist.

"Mother's ready to go back now." The receptionist picked up the phone and I walked back over to the window. Mother was fired up and I hoped she wouldn't make a scene.

Les spoke up, "Mother look at those cows grazing across the road." He was trying to change the subject. Mother showed no interest. In the distance we could see the same road we used to take to the cottage since we were kids. I felt the ribs in my left chest wall begin to throb. They always did when I was getting upset. How sad it was to see Mother like this. I heard the elevator door open. I turned around and saw a nurse coming toward us. It was not Mrs. Claney.

"Naomi, come along now, it's almost supper time." The nurse took hold of her arm rather abruptly. Mother pulled away from her for a moment. I thought we were headed for a problem. "Mother, it's okay I gently took her other arm and walked along with the nurse to the elevator. Les followed and as I let go of Mother's arm Les reached over and kissed her on the cheek. The elevator door opened and the nurse escorted her in. The nurse pushed the button and the door began to close.

"Kids, don't leave me like this!"

"Naomi, they'll be back again. Wave to them goodbye," she urged. Mother threw her right arm up in an attempt to wave. Les and I waved back. We both said "Bye Mother" at the same time as the elevator door closed. I could hear Les sigh as we walked to the exit. It was always a relief to get out of there and take a deep breath of fresh air. Les looked at me strangely as we headed for the car. We both knew this hospital was no place for Mother.

"What can we do to get her out of here, Jan? I can see how hard it has been for you to visit Mother day after day," Les said.

"Believe me, I've tried to get Dad to intervene in Mother's care—he won't take a stand. I'm beginning to know why. There's no way I can take care of Mother on my own without living at home with Dad. I'm anxious to see if he will agree to let me have her home for Thanksgiving. With you here, I think he might. In that way he can see for himself she's better. If he doesn't I don't know how I'll be able to face Mother. After all, I do pay a lot of the bills at the house. I should have some say in the matter. He doesn't lift a finger around the house. Mother will be expecting to come home. It will give her a ray of hope. Can I keep her home is another story. I think she will be fine and cause no problems as long as I keep her away from any confrontations with Dad."

"He will probably let you bring her home but will leave the house not wanting to face her. If you think he will sit across from her at the dining room table for a Thanksgiving dinner, forget it. I can't believe he really wants her to suffer, but I'm not sure what goes through his mind. I think he drinks to block his guilt. He will probably hit the bottle even more now that we know about his affair."

"Les, I think he is numb most of the time due to the vodka and beer. I believe it's the way he wants it. Or, maybe it's not the way he wants it, but the only way he can live with himself. He complains about his arthritis, and I'm sure he has discomfort, but arthritis isn't the real reason for his drinking. Dad insists he has to drink to dull his pain. He promised me many times he would quit. For short times I was encouraged when I didn't find any bottles of vodka in his clothes closet. Then a few weeks later I would find another hiding place—the coal bin. I guess he knows I rarely ever go in there. Each time I confront him he says, he knows he has a drinking problem, but he can quit."

"You'll see," Dad always says. He sounds sincere. He doesn't even try to hide the bottles anymore. I see them in the regular trash barrel."

"Jan, let me talk with him. I think it will be easier since we have begun to see one another eye to eye for the first time."

"That's a good idea. I've nothing more to say to him since I found out about Maggie. I wonder how long it will take for him to tell us he has to retire. As for the reason, I'm sure he will never tell us the truth."

"Perhaps seeing Mother after these months will make him realize the wrong choices he made, and he will try to make up for it." Les went further to say, "One thing for sure he has lost your respect, Jan, and it has been extremely important to him. I think he's finally seeing me for who I really am. Is it because I wear the uniform and he never could? He was so proud of his brothers all serving in the Air Force and resented the fact he was stuck with his job at the railroad."

"I can see it in his eyes when he sees you in your uniform. He looks up and his eyes light up. I can tell he's proud of you. I'm sure part of it's because you're serving your country, but he always thought you were a dreamer and had your head in the clouds. In his mind college was a waste of time. He sincerely felt you had to have a trade, be a mechanic, machinist or carpenter. You've proved him wrong, and he finally realizes it. When he's not at work, he just drinks and sits in front of the T.V. half asleep. Believe me, I'm thoroughly disgusted with him."

CHAPTER 19

Les was sleeping in Mother's room since Dad has been using Leslie's room. I went over to wake him for breakfast. Dad was still asleep across the hall. "Les, come down and have breakfast with me before Dad gets up," I said softly.

"Okay, let me go to the john, brush my teeth and I'll be down. Heat the milk for hot chocolate," he added. I ran downstairs in my robe and started breakfast. I kept hoping Dad wouldn't get up early and come to the kitchen. The milk was boiling and I had two pieces of toast buttered when Les joined me.

"I want to avoid Dad as much as possible, Les. I can't face him. Since you agreed to ask Dad about bringing Mother home, I'll stay out of it. Here's the plan, I'll stay in the hallway upstairs till I hear you ask him. Then, I'll tiptoe half way downstairs if I can't hear him clearly. What do you think?"

"Well, okay, but you'll have to be extra careful he does not hear you listening in. If he catches you it may change his mind and the whole thing will blow up."

"I'll be real careful." We finished breakfast. The moment I heard Dad in the bathroom I rushed up and slipped into my bedroom and closed the door. Les was to read the paper and pretend not to be waiting for him in the kitchen. I heard Dad go down the stairs. He always went straight to the refrigerator for an egg and milk.

"Dad, Jan wants to bring Mother home for Thanksgiving. Mother seems to be doing great and deserves to be able to come home for a visit. What do you think?" Les paused.

"What brings this idea up all of a sudden? No, I think Jan is asking for trouble. Your Mother will not want to go back after a day or two at home. You kids think you know best, but I'm the one who will have to deal with it. You won't even be here then, will you son?"

"That's right Dad, but Jan can handle it. She wants her home and considering the circumstance between you and her lately. I think it would help matters if you let her bring Mother home. Let her be the judge in this case. You haven't even seen Mother since she was hospitalized and don't really know how she is. This will give you a chance to reconcile with Jan."

"It sounds good, son, but Jan and I don't agree when it comes to your Mother. I'll have to think about it. You forget your Mother has an uncontrollable bad temper."

"Dad, Jan needs to know right away because arrangements have to be made in advance to get Mother a pass. The doctor wouldn't give her a pass if he thought she wasn't well enough to come home. Give Jan some credit. After all, she's the one who goes to visit her all the time. Mother seems calm to me, and I don't see where she will be any trouble."

"All right, son. Jan can bring your Mother home on one condition. She has to take full responsibility. I'll have no part in it!"

"Okay, that's good enough for me, Dad. I'll tell Jan. You won't be sorry, I'm certain of it."

"I'm not so sure, but let Jan know exactly where I stand in this matter."

I was so excited. Thank God, he finally agreed to let Mother come home. It will be wonderful to have her here. I'll cook a turkey, make dressing, fruit salad, and Mother's favorite date and nut cake. I'm sorry Les won't still be here to enjoy it. All of sudden, my mind shifted to getting her room ready. I left the hallway and tip-toed to her room. I sat down on the edge of Mother's bed thinking of all I'd have to do before her visit. The linen would need changing after Les leaves and I'd have to sort out her favorite clothes. Her silk underwear, nightgowns and stockings were in her top dresser drawer. I didn't take them to the hospital since I knew they would get lost or ruined in the laundry. I probably should wash her robe to make it smell fresh—it's been hanging in her closet. Since I'm washing clothes I might as well take a look in her closet and see what else needs washing. Her dresses were in plastic clothes bags and hanging right where she left them. I grabbed her robe and decided to check her dresser for her newer nightgowns and underwear.

Her second dresser drawer was sticking and I had to yank to get it open. Pills were spilled out between her underwear and stockings. I looked further and found a sock filled with more medicine. I removed the sock and emptied it out onto the bedspread. Different shapes and colors of pills rolled out. I remembered Mother saying something about hiding pills she didn't want to take any longer. And how she pretended to swallow them to satisfy Maggie and spit them out once Maggie left the room.

It was a few weeks later, I believe Mother said she began feeling stronger and had less trouble with her bowels. It wasn't too long after that when she chased Maggie out of the house. These pills weren't her vitamins or iron pills. There were two distinct types. I wondered if Les remembered what Mother said that night when we found her sitting in the kitchen after a year being bedfast? I yelled down the steps, "Les, can you come up here?. I want to show you something."

"Jan, what is it?" I grabbed his arm and yanked him from the hallway into Mother's room, "Shh, I have something that will interest you." I closed the door behind him.

"What's the matter, Jan?" Les looked excited. "Didn't you hear? Dad agreed to let you bring Mother home."

"Yes, it's great! But look what I've found!"

"What now, I swear Jan you're driving yourself crazy with all these things." I pointed to the pills scattered over the top of the bedspread."

"So, what's this all about?" He asked, with a puzzled look.

"Remember the night you came home from work and found Mother sitting in the kitchen after chasing Maggie out? Do you recall what Mother said about her pills?

"Jan, I don't know what you're talking about. Sure, I remember her telling us how she got rid of Maggie, but I can't remember anything about her pills. Do you realize how long ago it was?" Les asked.

"Well, if my memory hasn't failed me I remember her saying she stopped taking her pills and hid them."

"Jan, I don't get it. Why would Mother hide her pills?"

"Don't you see? She didn't want Maggie to know she wasn't taking the pills she was given." My heart started racing and I could feel the blood rush to my face. "Don't you remember her saying different times she didn't think the pills she was taking were helping her? Then, the night we found her at the kitchen table she said she quit taking them and hid them in a sock in her dresser drawer. There's got to be a connection between stopping the pills and Mother regaining her strength. I'm sure of it!"

"Oh, I see where you're going. A few weeks after Mother stopped the pills she became strong enough to chase Maggie out of the house. What do you suppose went on between the two of them that day? I'm sure there must have been some nasty words exchanged. I wish I could have seen Mother running after her with the broom." Les, chuckled.

"Knowing what I know today about Maggie, here's what I think. When mother discontinued the pills her dizziness and weakness began to fade. I think the pills were causing her illness rather than curing it. If my memory serves me well it was only about two weeks after she stopped the pills that she chased Maggie out. That's significant! Think about it. Mother's mind was clear when I came home from work that evening. She was looking in the refrigerator for something to put together for supper. You were as surprised as I was to see her sitting at the kitchen table—do you remember?"

"Oh, Yes, I remember. I was shocked! It was as though a whole year of being bedridden never occurred."

"Even before this, I never was sure Maggie liked caring for Mother. She always talked to me, like I was a child, and bragged about all she did for Mother, the cooking and house cleaning. We've no idea what went on in our absence or how bad she treated Mother. You were in college and working full time. I was working six nights a week after school."

"Wait just a minute, Jan. He gathered up the pills and put them back into the sock. Since we don't really know what went on. Let's slow down and not jump to conclusions yet."

"Well, Maggie always acted so sweet and innocent in front of Dad or either of us. Mother may have been putting up with God knows what. She was so weak and sick she probably accepted whatever Maggie dished out, feeling there was little she could do about it. To think I let Maggie influence me and didn't take my own Mother's word about when she had her last cup of tea."

"Jan quit beating yourself up. Where's all this leading?" There's nothing we can do about it now. We can't prove there was any wrong doing. We've got to forget this and work on getting Mother home."

"I'm looking for the truth. Also, I remember Mother saying she began to refuse Maggie's food and ask for soup and toast mostly. Even Dr. Hill couldn't explain why Mother was bedridden. Exactly what miracle happened to give her the strength not only to get out of bed, but to chase Maggie out? Don't you see what I'm saying?"

"Ah, Jan, you've got yourself all worked up. Your blood pressure is probably high as red as your face is. I don't know where you're going with this, but I think you're headed for trouble." Les, warned.

"I may be jumping ahead of myself. But I believe Maggie was giving Mother something to that kept her weak and confused. The question is can we prove it?" I grabbed the sock from Les and shook it as I spoke, "Here's the proof! I need to know what these are for and why they were given to Mother. Now where can we get someone to analyze these pills?"

"Oh, boy, I'd think pharmacists have a way of identifying them. Some pills are numbered and some can be identified by their shape, size, and color. The pharmacists have a large reference book to identify the classification. There are at least several dozen. But, Jan I think you're carrying this idea too far." Les had a worried look, but I knew I had his attention. Les took the sock, removed a pill and turned it over, "I don't see any numbers. I wonder what these funny shaped ones are for and what about these capsules?" Les had that funny smile of his, like when we were kids and he had a crazy idea.

"That's it! We need to find a pharmacist to identify them. Les, I've heard stories about people losing their written prescriptions. They take a couple of pills down to the drug store and ask for refills. Our druggist surely can identify them. Can you can come up with an idea of what to say?"

"Jan your already thinking there was foul play here. Let's slow down a bit and go about this in the right way. I don't know what it is, Jan. But all our lives I somehow get involved with whatever devilment you're up to. You got me in trouble with Dad a number of times with your ideas. We could show the druggist a couple of each kind of pills and say our grandmother ran out of her pills, and her doctor is out of town. Could he identify them and tell us if she can do without them till her doctor returns. The main thing is the druggist needs to tell us what they were prescribed for and whether she can do without these for a few days. This will give us the information we need."

"Les, that's brilliant! I knew you would come up with a plan. Now I'm beginning to get scared. For what condition do you think they were prescribed?"

"I've no clue. I don't want to believe the worst, Jan. These may be harmless. I know what you're thinking. You don't suppose Maggie would....surely she wouldn't have......."

"Yes, I believe she would have done almost anything to stay in our house and be carrying on with Dad each chance she got. Les, I think in order to pull this off at the drug store, you would be more convincing if you dressed in uniform to make a visit to Smith's Drug Store. They will see it as more urgent when you tell them the story about our sick grandmother. After all, Mr. Smith will be glad to see you home on leave and think nothing of it. He probably will fuss all over you about being in the service. He's known you forever."

"Remember how we used to go down to his store with a soda pop bottle worth two cents, and ponder for five minutes over his candy counter. He used to get impatient with us because we took too long to make up our minds for two cents worth. We usually ended up buying the same old thing, B-B-Bats, or licorice." Les started laughing. "Oh, yeah, how could I forget." I busted out laughing too. This was the first we had a belly laugh together since he came home.

"Okay, but I'm going to be rather nervous trying to pull this one off. But it has to be done. You're right we need to find out the truth for Mother's sake."

"I'll get an envelope for you to carry the pills down to Mr. Smith. Can you go tomorrow?" I asked, anxiously.

"Yes, Jan I'll go tomorrow after breakfast. Dad will probably wonder why I'm wearing my uniform, so I'll tell him some of the guys wanted to see how I looked in my class A's."

"Les, I'm sure Dad will believe whatever you tell him. It also gives him another chance to feel proud of you. I know you don't want to go around in uniform while on leave, but everyone likes seeing men and women in uniform. I'm sure the neighbors and Mr. Smith won't think a thing of it."

CHAPTER 20

"Jan, I did as we planned. You were right, Mr. Smith was glad to see me and full of questions about North Africa and everywhere I was stationed. I mulled this scenario over and over in my mind before I got there. I wanted to blurt out the real reason but we needed proof Maggie was a criminal. It reminded me of high school when I used to memorize the words for a part in a play. I got more nervous when I walked in and up to the counter. Mr. Smith took the pills back behind the counter, and I saw him get a big book from the shelf. I walked around the store and pretended to look at various items and was beginning to perspire in my armpits. It seemed a long time before he called me back to the counter, He told me the pink one is Docusate Sodium and the other is Tagamet. Mr. Smith gave me a 14 day supply for grandmother."

"I asked if they were for her blood pressure. He said no. They are for constipation and G.I. disturbance." He agreed to mark each packet and how to take them accordingly. Then he asked if the pills were for Jennie, I had to correct him and say it was for my other grandmother on my father's side. He asked for her full name. I stuttered around, getting more nervous by the minute. I couldn't think of grandma's first name for a moment—'Bessie Bryar,' I said. It didn't seem to bother him I was stammering about. He was busy counting the pills and typed up a label."

"Les, let me see what Mr. Smith gave you. You know darn well Mother was not having problems with her stomach and constipation. What in God's name was Maggie doing giving Mother these?"

"Are you sure, Mother wasn't prescribed these?" Les asked.

"I never saw the name of these two drugs anywhere before. Dr. Hill may have ordered something for Mother's nerves, but not Docusate

Sodium and Tagamet. I never saw any pill packets with these names. The question is what kind of reaction would they cause?"

"We can look them up in the library. They have reference books with lists of medications and even pictures of different pills to identify, the librarian can help us find what we are looking for," Les said.

"Can we get over to the library tomorrow before I go to work," I asked.

"Sure, I don't see any reason why not. Let's plan on it."

At work I was so excited I could hardly concentrate on what the customer's were saying. I picked up signal after signal, "Long Distance", and somehow got them connected to their parties. I went straight to bed when I got home after the evening shift. Worried about what we would find out at the library the next day I couldn't sleep. Les and I had breakfast together and discussed what to tell the librarian. I knew the library wouldn't be open until 10 a.m.

"Les, I'm going to let you talk with the librarian because I might say the wrong thing."

"Calm down, we could even tell her the truth. As a result she might be more helpful. We don't have to mention names and it's unlikely we'll know her. I'll ask her where the drug identification books are and we can research the pills."

I drove cross the railroad tracks to the other side of town near where we both went to high school. Les remarked, as we passed Vince's Pizza shop, "Remember when we picked up hoagie sandwiches there? They were the best." My palms were sweating as we approached the library parking lot. I felt like a detective doing private investigating and I had to act somehow different. Les seemed calm and I was glad he was going to do the talking. He approached the desk and asked, "Where do I find the reference book to identify drugs?"

"The Physician's Desk References are in the back of the library," She pointed to small tables and chairs as she spoke.

"Thank you." Les answered, politely. I practically knocked Les out of the way to get to the tables and started looking for a book titled *The Physician's Desk Reference*. There were several volumes on the shelves. Some were red and some were blue with the year on the front. I picked up one marked 1956 and began thumbing through. Les leaned over, "Let's see, Docusate Sodium. Here it is. Turn to the page it's listed on." I leafed quickly to the page number.

"Here's the description, but where does it list the side effects?"

"Keep going, Jan, it's got to be here somewhere. How about under the contraindications? There on the next column is the heading, *Side Effects*."

"Listed here are abdominal pain, headache, nausea, and joint pain. Mother never complained much about pain. I know she was sick to her stomach at times. This doesn't add up."

"Jan, it says less common, dizziness, fatigue and muscle aches and not to be used longer than one week."

"Where does it say that? Let me see! Oh, My God, I knew we were right. Remember she was weak and could hardly get out of bed. It wasn't like she didn't want to get up. She complained about being woozy all the time and held onto the wall when she walked across the hall to the bathroom. I can't believe it! Maggie must have given this to Mother for months!"

"Jan, are you sure? Do you realize what you're saying? This is criminal." Les's face was ashen.

"Why didn't we suspect something was wrong when the doctor said he couldn't find a reason for her weakness. He was puzzled about her condition. Les, look under the T's for Tagamet."

"Jan, you need to slow down and take a deep breath. You're getting yourself all worked up. Here it is, Tagamet. Side effects are agitation, anxiety, confusion, depression, disorientation, hallucinations, low blood pressure and mild diarrhea."

"Maggie's passion drove her to this end. Think of the implications. She could've killed, Mother. Les, look here where it lists some rare symptoms--dizziness and muscle pain. That bitch! She's going to pay for this. Wait till I get my hands on her."

"Jan, you can't take this into your own hands. What are you thinking?"

"Put the books up. We're finished." I started for the front door and Les had to run to catch up with me. Tears were streaming down my face and I pushed them away with the back of my hand. I was bawling out loud when I reached the car. Les caught up with me and put his arm around me.

"Jan, it's not your fault. There's no way you could have known what was going on. Pull yourself together." I got behind the steering wheel and lay my head on the back of my hands, gripping tight.

Les tapped me on the shoulder, "C'mon slide over, I'll drive."

"If only I had listened to Mother. She was trying to tell me things about Maggie, and I would cut her off and change the conversation.

All because Dad scolded me, he said I was to pay attention to what Maggie told me because Mother was exaggerating and mixed up. For example, Mother wanted tea and toast and Maggie said she just had some. I began to shrug off Mother's comments and believed Maggie's side of the story. It's a wonder Mother made sense about anything with all those drugs in her system. Oh, God, how can I ever forgive myself for being stupid?"

"Stop it! You're torturing yourself for something you had no control over. We need to figure out how to handle this information and where to go with it."

"To the police, that's where! I want her in jail to pay for what she has done. She practically killed our Mother, and she's responsible for where Mother is today. Maggie has ruined our family and she's going to jail. I won't rest till I have her behind bars."

"Jan, we need more than this to go to the police. It's our suspicion she gave these drugs to Mother. But how do we prove it?"

"Les, it's simple. Mother told me she stopped taking the pills Maggie was giving her and put them in her sock. They were there, as she said. Remember not too long afterwards she chased Maggie out of the house. Where do you suppose Mother got the energy and strength all of a sudden? The facts are clear and they add up!"

"Do you think the police are going to believe us when Mother has been admitted and remains in a state hospital for some condition we don't even understand?"

"Well, Les, once we get this information to her doctor, this will throw a different light onto Mother's situation."

"I'm not sure her doctor will even listen to us after we questioned him about her care the other day. He isn't too fond of us after our last encounter." Les said.

"I don't care what he thinks! You don't think Dad was in on this pill business, do you? I'm beginning to question my own father's integrity. You don't think he would stoop that low and be part of Maggie's scheme?"

"No, Jan, I can't for one second believe he knows anything about how far Maggie went in her warped state of mind. He may have played around with her, but he wouldn't try to harm our own Mother, I'm certain of it!"

"Les, I'm not sure of anything anymore. I thought I knew Dad, but to find him sneaking around with Maggie, I'm not sure what he's capable of. I'm so mad at him, I can't even look him straight in the eyes or I start crying. How can we get at the truth without finding Maggie and accusing her?"

"She'll never own up to giving Mother those pills. If we put her on the defensive it will be her calling the cops on us. For all we know, she may have friends in high places. Ones who frequented her whorehouse in the past. If so, they will defend her as their former prostitute. I heard she was friendly with one of the judges in town when she ran her whore house. She may be uneducated, but cagey enough to know exactly what she was doing at the time." What Les said made sense, "Wait, I've got an idea. Let's come up with a way to trick her into a confession."

I looked over at Les, he had that look about him, the same as when we were kids and he came up with a story or scene he was writing for a play. We used to act out different scenes for the neighbor kids under our back porch.

"How about telling her we found some pills in a prescription envelope with her name on them. They were stuck between the two drawers in the night stand by her bed when she lived with us. And these pills have been identified as the medicines she gave our Mother for months. Fortunately, our Mother pretended to take them in front of you and later threw them in her dresser drawer. These pills were never prescribed for our Mother. This is a criminal act and she could have killed our Mother!"

"That's brilliant, Les! Do we hide a tape recorder under your coat, or what? The police won't take our word against hers unless we get a witness, or record her confession."

"Jan, you are getting ahead of me with your imagination. How do we find her? Do you know where she lives?" Les, asked.

"No, but we could follow Dad and see where he goes. He knows where she lives. Probably it would be easier to come up with some reason we've got to get hold of her. We could ask Dad for her address."

"As worked up as you are with Dad, Jan, he's not about to give you her address. He'd be afraid of what you might do to her when you found her."

"You're right, I didn't think about him doubting my reason for wanting to see her, regardless, of how convincing my story could be." As we drove back across the tracks my mind was working overtime to come up with a way to find Maggie. Never before this did I ever want to see that woman more than I did now. Realizing Dad would be at work by now, I could enter the house without my blood pressure rising. I went straight to the kitchen and prepared lunch. I made some sandwiches and Les added root beer and potato chips.

The next morning I tiptoed down the hallway to wake Les. I was careful not to wake Dad across the hall. I shook Les's shoulder and whispered, "Les I think I know a way to find Maggie. Get dressed and come downstairs." Les entered the kitchen in his pajama bottoms and a T-shirt, "Jan, you don't have to whisper. Dad isn't here."

"What? I can't believe he stayed out all night with that bitch after all that's happened." I looked out the back door window. Dad's car wasn't there.

"I was watching television last night till about mid-night. In fact, I was waiting up for you, but got too sleepy. In the middle of the night, I had to make a trip to the bathroom and with the full moon could see Dad's car was not parked out back. He didn't come home from work last night. It doesn't leave much to my imagination as to where he spent the night."

"Damn, him! How can he continue to do this?"

"Jan, he probably figures there's no use hiding it any longer."

"You would think he would try to make amends. Doesn't he have one shred of decency left?" I got the milk, poured right from the carton into the sauce pan and lit the gas burner with a match.

"Jan watch it! The gas is too high."

I turned the flame down and prepared our usual breakfast.

"What's the latest on your plan to find Maggie." Les asked?

"Well, I think if you go down in uniform to the Brown Derby and ask for her..."

Les interrupted me, "What? How did I get into another episode?"

"I figure the bar tender wouldn't pay much attention to me. But if you go, have a drink at the bar, and say, "Would any of you happen to know where I can reach Maggie Horner?" Then, you could follow up with, "She used to be our housekeeper, I've lost touch and wanted to visit her while on leave."

"I believe if anyone knows her whereabouts they will. According to Uncle Glen she used to go in there all the time. In fact, I bet she met Dad there."

"Oh, brother, here I go again. It's kind of like when I went to see Mr. Smith at the drug store, right?"

"Les, I'm not afraid to do it, but I'm sure you can pull it off easier than I can."

"What makes you think they'll give me her address?"

"You'll be in uniform, and who wouldn't want to help a serviceman find a lost friend. If they know her, you'll get a straight answer. Maybe they'll think you're more than a friend."

"Oh, brother, I hope they don't get that impression. She's no friend of mine. Jan, it turns my stomach to even pretend. Are we going a bit too far? What do you plan to do if you do find her?"

"I'm going to put her on the spot and scare the living shit out of her."

"Jan, you can't take the law into your own hands. We can't prove she gave those pills to Mother in a vicious way. Suppose Mother said she had a sick stomach, or other symptoms and Maggie was only trying to help her by giving her what she had been prescribed herself for a similar complaint."

"Surely, you don't believe that. Do you?"

"No, but we really don't know the entire story of what went down," Les, offered.

"This is our only chance to find out the truth. The pieces are beginning to come together. We've got to do this for Mother's sake."

"So, I've got to dress up in my uniform again. I'm beginning to feel like an imposter in uniform."

"C'mon, Les, You'll do it, won't you? Think, of how close we are to getting enough information to go to the police."

"I never did like the Brown Derby. Yes, of course, I'll do it. But you'll owe me big time."

"When do you think you can go down to the Brown Derby?" I asked, anxiously.

"Probably tomorrow evening, after we're sure Dad's gone to work. Running into Dad at the bar is the last thing I want to do."

"Gee, I didn't think about the possibility of you running into Dad. It's a good thing you thought this through. He stops there after work, around mid-night."

To make his promise good, the next evening, Les put the uniform on and headed to The Brown Derby. I waited anxiously for his return.

Les returned after dark and said the sign hanging out front was dim and read *'The Brown Der'*. The B and Y were gone. He laughed as he described the smoky room with older men in coveralls sitting at the bar smoking. After ordering a Fort Pitt beer he practically choked on, he asked if anyone knew Maggie Horner. He told them she used to be his housekeeper and wanted to look her up while on leave. The bartender said she used to come in now and then but he hadn't seen her lately. Les asked if he knew where she lived.

"It was like we figured, Jan. He said, she had an apartment on the other side of the railroad tracks by the Eighth Street Bridge."

"You did good brother. Did you notice how close The Brown Derby bar is to the shop gates?"

"Yes, and it was as dark and dingy as I remembered. The same old mirror hung behind the bar. There was no reflection due to dirt and smoke. I was a nervous wreck expecting Dad to barge in at any moment. The whole gang turned their heads in my direction when I thanked the bartender, gulped the rest of my beer and went for the door. Tomorrow let's take a drive across town and take a look."

After breakfast Les and I drove over the bridge and found an access road running parallel to the railroad tracks. The bartender was right. There stood an old three story apartment building covered with red brick shingles facing the tracks. There were boarded up windows on the street level from stores having gone out of business. I don't remember ever driving down a street that close to the tracks. If I did, it would have been a long time ago when businesses were operating there.

"It's probably where she wants to be. Who knows she may still be doing tricks over here like she used to on 10th street, according to Uncle Pete. What do you plan to do if she still lives there?" Les asked.

"I'm going to confront her with the facts we already have and threaten to go to the police."

"Are you prepared for her reaction? She's not going to welcome you with open arms, like an old friend you know, especially when you start accusing her of poisoning our Mother." Les warned.

"I can't wait until I see the expression on her face when I tell her I know what she was up to. The satisfaction of seeing her squirm after what she did to Mother and our grandparents will be worth a million! She wrecked our family. But what I really want is to see her go to jail for what she's done."

"Jan this is risky and your plan may backfire. When are you planning to go inside?"

"Tomorrow. I want to do a dry run before work. I'll check to see if her name is listed inside the building with an apartment number."

"I better go with you. You're not going to rap on her door tomorrow if her name is listed, are you?"

"No, I want to see where she lives and get a feel of the surroundings before I confront her."

"Okay, Jan, we'll plan on coming back then."

That evening when I got home after work I rolled my pillow in a ball, tried every position to get to sleep, but I couldn't, I decided to get up—it wasn't daylight yet. I pictured in my mind different scenarios at Maggie's apartment. I wondered if I should go to an attorney first, and ask him for advice about recording our conversation. I decided to record our conversation anyway, because it would be her word against mine in court. I needed other evidence besides Mother's sock full of pills and the side effects we found listed at the library. Could I get a confession out of her, a slip of the tongue of how she hated Mother, or even worse wanted to kill her.

Dad's bedroom door was shut. I wondered why I didn't hear him come upstairs, I must have fallen off to sleep at some point. I tiptoed downstairs to the kitchen. I felt hungry and put the milk on to boil and started spreading crackers with peanut butter. Then, I heard the third step creak. Oh, it better not be Dad, I'm not in the mood to face him.

"Jan, I'm glad it's you down here. I couldn't sleep worth a darn and I'm starved. I ate supper too early yesterday." I was relieved, "Les, I'm making some hot chocolate and peanut butter crackers. Do you want crackers or what?"

"Hot chocolate is fine. I'll make toast. You know, Jan, I've thought this whole thing over and I believe we should drop this idea of confronting Maggie. I'm afraid this whole thing may get out of hand. I don't want you to get hurt. We can't trust her and what she may do."

"Don't be ridiculous. I'm not afraid of her. She's nothing but a big bag of blubber. She doesn't scare me. If she tried to lay a hand on me I'd floor her. She doesn't stand a chance against me."

"That's what I'm talking about. If you both get into it, one of you may get hurt. I know you can handle yourself, but there are many emotions involved. It could turn out different than we expect. It could ruin our day in court." Les, warned.

"Les, I'm shocked. Do you think we should let Maggie get away with what she's done? If you don't want to go with me, you don't have to. I can handle everything from here myself!"

"Shh, Watch, your voice is getting loud. All we need is for Dad to hear what you're planning. I know you only too well. When you make up your mind there's no changing it. I wasn't saying I wouldn't go with you. But don't go knocking on her door, at least not until we decide exactly what you're going to say and do."

"I need to trick her into a confession. I'll have a tape recorder running the entire time. How about something like this, *Maggie we're trying to find out what Mother is allergic too and wondered if you could help. During the year you took care of her what medicines were you giving her? The doctor believes there are certain pills she's been taking all along making her confused and weak. Do you remember the names of what you were giving her?* If she doesn't tell us, I will add, can you identify the color or shape of the pills you gave her? This will prevent her from getting the wrong medicine again."

"Jan, she's not a smart woman, but if she's guilty and we believe she is, I don't think she will cooperate. What if she says she never gave any pills to Mother? Then what? Is the milk boiling yet?"

"Yes, hand me your cup. I'll tell her she's a liar and I have proof that she poisoned our Mother. And that I'm going to the police with the information."

"This is what I'm talking about, Jan. You will lose it and Lord knows what will happen from there," Les, scolded.

"I'll rehearse exactly what I plan to say. I'll catch her at her own game. She's deceitful and I will trick her into telling us the truth, you'll see." We had a mini breakfast. I realized my brother was right. I could lose it, but I didn't want him to know I had any doubts, or he would be totally against the plan. Les and I left the house. We were surprised Dad didn't come out of his room when he heard us in and out of the bathroom. In the past, he used to tie up the bathroom with his sitting on the toilet smoking. I was nervous when we started out, and by the time we got to the Eighth Street Bridge my heart was pounding with excitement. Les parked a block down the street from the apartment building. We walked up to the front entrance. The door was in need of paint and warped at the bottom. Les had to give it a kick with his foot to get it open. We peered into a dark corridor. There were no windows for light so we left the door ajar. Near the stairs was a list of names next to apartment numbers, many were written in pencil or crossed out.

"Here it is, Les." I pointed to her name, barely legible, across from the number 301.

"Who goes there?" A gruff voice yelled down from an upstairs hallway. Les and my eyes met. We didn't want to spoil the surprise of our visit. We ducked back away from the stairs and headed for the door we had left open. We ran down the street as fast as we could. Hoping whoever was yelling at us couldn't see us from an upstairs window. We were out of breath when we reached my car. Les started the engine and floored the pedal. He spun the tires of my old Plymouth around the corner and down the street. I looked over at Les, and we both started laughing hysterically. He steered the car over to the curb, and with the engine still running, pulled on the emergency brake. He used the back of his right hand to wipe the tears from his eyes—he was laughing, tears running down his cheeks. He glanced at me and we laughed harder. Not only was my heart racing with excitement, my abdomen was getting sore from laughing. It was scary and funny at the same time. It was like when Les and I were kids. We laughed until it hurt and had to catch our breath.

Nervously, I kept looking over my shoulder expecting to be shot at, like in a detective movie. Les and I were half scared and yet there was nothing to be frightened of, or was there? After Les got his composure, he said out of breath, "Now, that's a taste of what you're up against. Do you still want to confront her face to face?"

"Yes, we've gone this far and can't quit now for Mother's sake."

"You realize I only have a few days left till I have to go back to Louisiana. I promised Aunt Beb I would visit with her again. Time is running short."

"You're right. How about the day after tomorrow at this same time? I hope we find her home. Otherwise, I'll be going it alone."

"Jan, promise me you won't go over there alone if we don't find her home. The old building looks creepy, and what about the old man from upstairs?"

"I wasn't scared. It only startled me."

"Oh, Yeah, we were both scared and you know it."

"Well, I guess I was, but I didn't want her to see us. It has got to be a surprise and besides I have to rehearse exactly what I'm going to say." Les released the emergency brake and headed for home. At work between each call light I answered, 'Operator' I mulled over in my mind what I was going to say and in what order.

CHAPTER 21

Les and I decided to go out to a restaurant for breakfast. We wouldn't have to whisper and worry about Dad hearing us.

Les parked around the corner, out of sight from the entrance to Maggie's apartment building. I walked up the stairs and Les followed close behind. The brown paint was worn from the center of the stairs and many creaked as we tried to avoid making noise. I took hold of the banister. It was loose and not worth holding onto. My heart beat faster with each flight we took. The third floor was darker and more dismal than the first two. I was out of breath at the top. Les could probably hear my heart beat as we walked down the hallway to number 301—in the middle.

I pounded on the door with my fist. I was more determined than ever. It was seconds until the door opened a crack, but it seemed like a long wait. All I could see was a tight chain keeping the door from swinging open and a ray of light coming through. "Maggie is that you? It's me Jan, Jan Bryar. I need to talk with you right away. It's an emergency." My voice was quivering by the time I got out the word emer-gen-cy. I reached into my pocket and turned on my tape recorder.

"Oh, it's you, Jan? What is it? Has something happened to Russ?" She inquired with a worried voice.

"Open the door! I can't talk to you from out here in the hallway." I said, raising my voice. I heard the chain release and there she stood braless in a shear see through loose night gown. The light from the window behind helped show everything transparently down to her black silk underwear. At least she had her teeth in for a change. There was enough light to see her uncombed thin white straggled strands of hair. I stepped into the room onto a worn out rag rug. I noticed a maroon couch behind her with two sagging cushions and an end table with a glass lamp. The square dark red cardboard shade made it difficult to see around the room. There were gray looking gauze curtains, tied back at the window sill.

Several picture frames were on top of a console television in the corner. I strained my eyes to see if any were of Dad, but it was too far for me to tell. A doorway led to a small efficiency type kitchen. Two large closet doors were on the other wall. I believe it contained one of those hide-a-way beds.

"What's wrong? Why are you here? Is it Russ?" She ran one question into another. It was that same syrupy sweet patronizing voice I remembered well.

"No, I'm not here about Dad! I need to talk to you about Mother. This is ex-treme-ly important. My voice was quivering and I had to strain to keep from faltering. The doctor needs to know what medicines you gave her during the year she was bed fast. He believes her pills caused serious allergic reactions. If he can identify which ones caused the weakness and confusion he can avoid prescribing drugs of the same family." It was hard to keep from stumbling over my words even though I had practiced beforehand.

"Why are you coming to me about this? Go talk to the doctor she claimed was in love with her. He knows what she was taking. I don't remember anything about her pills, and it's none of my business."

"Oh, but it was your business! Who are you talking about?

What doctor did she think was in love with her?"

"All she talked about during the day was her honey this and her honey that. Whoever her regular doctor was, I don't remember his name. You don't know the half of what I had to put up with your Mother. All I got done was wiping her ass after she messed herself, changing her bed, cooking, and cleaning." She blurted out bitterly.

"I don't want to hear this nonsense! I came here to inquire about her pills to help her get well. All I hear from you is a bunch of complaining. Give me a straight answer. Are these the pills you were giving her?" I held out a hand full from the sock for her to see. "Look, tell me, are these the ones?"

"How do I know? I don't remember." She looked away and started shaking her head like a nervous tic back and forward. For a moment, I thought she was going to pass out.

"Answer me! Tell the truth for once in your life!"

"No, No. Get away from me. I don't have to answer you. Get out of here! I'm not going to be a part of your scheme. You're up to something, and I'll not be a part of it."

"Oh, you're not are you? Well, you're going to tell me, all right. I came here to get answers and you're going to tell me which of these pills you gave to Mother and why, or I'll go to the police. Do you understand me?" I moved closer and held the pills right under her nose.

"Stop it! What kind of bull shit is this? You're crazy, like your mother. I should have known better than to let you two in. Get out, both of you!"

"No, I'm not going until you tell me the truth, you bitch! You know very well you gave these pills to Mother to keep her weak and confused. They were your pills, weren't they? Answer me! You gave them to Mother knowing full well what you were doing. Didn't you? Here, take a good look and tell me which ones you fed her?" She backed away and fell onto the davenport.

"Get away from me or I'll, I'll call the manager. You can't barge in here like this. Her face blushed red as she turned, grabbed the phone, and started dialing. Les stepped forward out of the doorway shadow, "C'mon Maggie for once in your life, come clean and tell the truth. If you don't, you will be facing a court battle you cannot win," Les said, moving closer.

"Both of you are nuts. You don't know the first thing about what you're talking about. Wait till your father hears about this. How dare you barge in here and threaten me."

On impulse, I grabbed the telephone receiver from her hand. At that moment, I could feel a rage within me, an urge to slap her right across the face with it. This anger had been brewing inside of me for a long time. As our eyes met, I saw a frightened and pathetic old woman. Something stopped me before I let her have it. I never saw her move so quickly.

She ran toward the doorway and began screaming, "John, John, come quick! Call the police." Les moved out of her way and within seconds I heard someone coming down the hallway. Les stepped forward and grabbed hold of my arm. I dropped the phone, and Les pulled me out into the hallway. I looked back over my shoulder and said, "Damn you Maggie. I should've known we were wasting our time coming here. You need to go to jail for what you've done and I hope they throw away the key!" As we reached the top step a rough looking guy with no shirt joined Maggie in the center of the hallway.

"What's going on, Maggie? Are you hurt?" The man said.

"John, go after them. They threatened me. She was going to hit me."

"They, forced their way in. Be my witness. Get a good look at them. They are up to something." By that time, Maggie and this, John, were at the top of the stairs leaning over the banister. Les and I were on the second floor landing. Maggie raised her syrupy voice, "Both of them are crazy like their Mother. She's the one I told you about, 'Nomi', remember?" She yelled down the stairwell, "I'm going to call Judge Cummings and tell him how you barged in here and threatened me." Les and I were skipping steps and ran out the door we left partly open. We ran trying to avoid tripping over the broken and uneven bricks in the sidewalk. As we rounded the corner, I looked back and didn't see him coming after us. I jumped in the car on the passenger side and Les slid behind the wheel, "Les, hurry let's get out of here." Les started the engine, let the clutch out too fast and the wheels spun leaving more rubber behind than before. I could feel my heart beating up the sides of my neck. The warmth I felt over my body was as if I had just come out from under a sun lamp. My blouse was soaked at the armpits. I kept looking out the rear view window to see if anyone was charging after us.

"Whew, it was a close call. Not that I couldn't have handled the old man, but all I need is to get into a fight and end up in jail. The military does not take well to airmen getting into brawls while on leave. Jan, you can relax. No one is behind us." Les said, with a sigh of relief.

"I came close to hitting her. I don't know what came over me. I stopped in the nick of time."

"Jan, I wasn't sure what you were going to do when you grabbed the receiver. I couldn't imagine you would actually hit her with it. What came over you? Boy, was I glad you didn't lay a hand on her, or we could be in real trouble. I've seen you lose your temper when we were kids, but not like this. I thought for a moment I would have to step in between the two of you."

"I lost it! I was outside of myself, as if it wasn't really me until our eyes met. It was weird. I guess what they call, "a flight fight response" came over me. Thank God, I saw her for who she really is. She's nothing more than a cheap, sloppy fat, whore, who would stop at nothing to get what she wants. She took advantage of all of us. Going to jail for hitting her would not be worth it. At least now she knows, I'm aware of what she was up to and not afraid of her. Did you hear what she said about calling Judge Cummings? He was the one Aunt Beb talked about. He must have got free service from her when she ran the whore house?"

"Probably, Maggie raised her voice to be sure we heard every word, as we ran down the stairs. A scare tactic, Les said. "Who knows, maybe she will telephone him. But I seriously doubt it. I watched her face as you and she went at it. I've no doubt in my mind she recognized those pills. The way she stared at your hand, and began shaking her head nervously, I'm certain of it."

"The question is what do I do next? I tried to get her to cooperate without knowing why. First by being nice and trying to bait her, but she's cunning enough to realize it was a trap. It backfired and I exploded accusing her out right. I can't wait to hear all this on tape when we get a chance." I reached in my pocket and stopped the tape recorder.

"It was obvious she hated caring for Mother. I wasn't sure how she would react to your accusation. I did hope she would be stupid enough to trip herself up and give us something to work on. But, I guess it was too much to ask for." Les offered.

"Well, I think I should bring charges against her. Mother is where she is because of her. I'm sure of it! I'll contact George, my attorney friend. Do you remember George Le Mott? He married Dee Burns."

"No, I don't. But, I think you should hold off a day or two to see if Maggie does anything. Most likely she will tell Dad. That's something else we will both have to deal with. I seriously doubt she will call the judge. If she does, what would she tell him? We were trying to help our Mother in knowing what pills may have caused a serious reaction of diarrhea, weakness, and confusion? The fact you grabbed the phone, backed her up against the couch, and flatly accused her really took guts. I must admit I began to worry when you grabbed the phone." Les had a stern look which broke into a big smile of approval.

"You're right, as usual. I need to be prepared for a real bawling out when Dad finds out. I've been avoiding him as much as possible. We barely exchange words." Les parked the car in front of the house and we both walked from the front door straight to the kitchen to get lunch. Dad startled me as I entered the kitchen. He was sitting back against the wall having a cigarette with his coffee. "Les and I are going to make a sandwich. Did you have lunch yet?" I asked, without looking at him.

"Yes, I had a couple of scrambled eggs and ham." Les came to the rescue with, "Dad I'm glad you're here. I wanted to tell you my leave is up in a couple of days. I've been busy running around. It seems like we're always missing each other."

"It's okay, son. I know you're busy with your friends. I want you to have a good time. I would like to sit down and have a drink with you before you leave."

"Sure, how about on Saturday? I have to catch the train on Sunday," Les said.

"That's fine. While the two of you are here I have bad news."

Right away I got nervous. I thought maybe Maggie had telephoned him before we got home. I remained silent. I tried to think quickly how I would explain my actions with Maggie.

Boy was I relieved when he said, "I've been bumped off my job and they want me to retire. I hadn't planned on retiring yet, but it's probably for the best. I'm sick of the railroad and being bumped around. I guess seniority isn't worth a damn anymore."

I responded quickly with, "Well, Dad, maybe you can start the antique shop you always talked about." I acted surprised, but I knew the real reason. Maybe this would be enough of a shock to his ego that he would get serious about another career and stop drinking.

"Dad, I don't think it's bad news. You've complained about the railroad for years. This gives you an opportunity to do what you want for once in your life," Les offered.

"We'll see. I can't believe it's really happening." He took a long drag on his cigarette. I could see he was really depressed and trying not to let on. Exactly how he would put in his days would remain to be seen. Even though I was furious at him and disgusted with his behavior, I couldn't help but feel for him. "When is the big day?" I asked.

"I have to go in tomorrow to sign the papers, and Friday will be my last day."

"I didn't expect you'd have to retire that soon. Will they have a party for you?" I asked.

"I declined. But some of the guys and I are going to get together an evening next week," he answered, looking a little brighter as he spoke.

"Here, son, take my chair." He got up carrying his cup of coffee and cigarette, and headed for his easy chair in the parlor. Les looked over at me and I made a funny face and motioned with my hands palms upward. As much as to say, what a relief, he didn't know where we had been. Les got out a can of chicken noodle soup from the cupboard and the can opener. I opened the refrigerator to see what we could use for sandwiches. I peered around the door to check on dad. I could hear the news on the television. I was hoping he would go upstairs so we could talk, but he didn't. We had lunch and talked small talk about Les going back on Sunday. The reality of Les leaving was beginning to set in.

That evening when I sat at the switchboard I grabbed every light appearing on my board. I reached over and answered lights in front of the girls sitting beside me.

It was a busy night and I said "Operator" as I dialed up one number after another. I thought about the events of the day. I knew I needed professional advice before contacting the police. I telephoned George the next morning from the phone in the cellar. Dad was still in bed and Les was upstairs. "Can I speak with Attorney Le Mott?" I asked. I could hear the girl leaving her desk to get him.

"This is George, who am I speaking with?"

"George, this Jan how are you doing? I haven't seen you or your wife since the night I saw you at the movies. I need some legal advice and would like to make an appointment."

"Jan, how about noon tomorrow?" I agreed and hung up the phone. I went up the cellar steps and met Les in the kitchen heating milk for cocoa.

"Les, my appointment with George is at noon tomorrow can you go with me?"

"Gee, Jan if I had known ahead of time I wouldn't have made plans to meet Charlie and Catherine for lunch. I promised Aunt Beb I would drop by and see her afterwards."

"It's okay, I know you're running out of time. If you're still up when I get home after work tonight I'll let you know what he says." After breakfast, I did ironing, let Les take his bath, before I tied up the bathroom. Dad must have got in late because his bedroom door was still closed when I hurried into the bathroom. The last thing I wanted was to run into him. He came out of his room just as I opened the bathroom door, "I'm finished." I said in haste as I ran across the hallway with a towel wrapped around my head. I put a few curlers in my hair, turned on my dryer, after placing the pink plastic cover over my head.

I arrived at George's office shortly before noon, I was anxious to tell him what was going on with Maggie. George was not familiar with what had happened to Mother. I didn't know exactly where to begin as he stepped out into the waiting room, "Jan, it's good to see you, come on in. He held the door for me as I walked by his secretary and into his office. George closed the door behind me and motioned for me to sit down in front of his large mahogany desk.

"What brings you here today, Jan? Hope you're not in any serious trouble," he said jokingly, and leaned back in his leather chair.

"Not really, George. But I need advice. As you probably know, Mother is in the state hospital. It appears that Maggie, our house keeper, during the year prior to Mother's being hospitalized, was giving her drugs that were not prescribed for her."

"Hold on, let me get this straight. You believe your Mother was given drugs by the housekeeper. What happened?"

"She became weak and confused and remained bedfast for an entire year."

"That's awful. Who would do such a horrible thing? It's hard to believe. Are you sure? What kind of proof do you have?" He looked concerned, leaned forward in his chair and picked up his pipe from the ashtray.

"It's a long story, but I found these pills in a sock in Mother's dresser drawer. I showed George the different pills I had found. Mother told me Maggie gave her pills at mealtimes. She thought they were doing no good and pretended to swallow them in front of her. But after Maggie left the room she spit them out and hid them."

"I don't quite get it. How did your Mother know they were not prescribed for her? What made her suspicious?" He looked puzzled.

"Well, she really didn't. She was weak and discouraged and thought the Lord was calling her home, so she stopped swallowing the pills. To her surprise after a few days of not taking the pills she began to feel stronger and less confused. Without telling us she walked around upstairs gaining more strength each day. When she was strong enough she went downstairs on her own. I came home from work, and there she was sitting in the kitchen—it was like a miracle."

"That's a remarkable story. You believe this woman was purposely giving drugs to keep your Mother bedfast?" He asked.

"Yes. I confronted her, but she denies it. I could tell she was scared and lying through her teeth. The pharmacist identified the pills for me which were never prescribed for my Mother. The side effects were exactly what Mother was experiencing. Maggie gave her large doses to keep her confused, weak and with profuse diarrhea. Do you see what I'm getting at?"

"Oh my, that's a serious accusation. I'm not sure I can be of help, though. This is a matter for the police, but I don't know how you will prove Maggie really gave these pills to your Mother. Or can you?"

"I can explain what Mother told me and show the pills to the police. My problem is, will they believe me?"

"I think they will believe you, but proving it is another matter. I doubt if they would interrogate Maggie just on your word. Since your Mother only suffered weakness and confusion, I hate to say it, but she did not die or end up paralyzed as a result. It's one person's word against another and how to get a judgment against this housekeeper remains to be seen."

"Well, as a result Mother was committed to the state hospital. It confused her to the point she imagined things and remained bedridden for a year. It was a year out of her life, and now she is confined in an institution. Wouldn't you think that in itself is enough? Maggie knew full well what she was doing and is a vicious woman. Mother didn't die because of it, but has suffered and continues to be hospitalized as a result."

"Why do you suppose your housekeeper would do such a thing?" I remember meeting your Mother on several occasions. She was bright and full of life. It's hard to imagine anyone cruel enough to bring harm to such a nice woman."

"Well, I hate to admit this, but my father was having an affair with Maggie. I found this out recently. This, I believe, was her motive for wanting my Mother bedridden, or maybe even out of the way! It ended up as a slow poisoning." I was embarrassed to tell him about Dad running around, but I had no choice.

"Jan, I'm sorry, but I don't believe I can be of help. I seriously doubt you will get anywhere with the police. It sounds to me like it's your word against this woman, Maggie. Your Mother could testify, but I'm sure they would rule it out stating her testimony would not be credible since she's been committed. I hate to disappoint you, but your only witness to this is your Mother, right?" He took a few small puffs on his pipe.

"I see what you're saying, George. I guess I'm nowhere. I had this notion I could have this woman arrested and have her pay for what she has done to my Mother and our family. Maybe there is another way—I'll share our conversation with my brother and see what he thinks about my going to the police. To think this woman gets away with this and nothing can be done.... Where's the justice in it all?" I could feel my eyes tearing up, and I didn't want to start bawling.

"Jan, don't despair. In the end, she will get what is coming to her. You and I may not be able to see the justice in it all, but she will get her due." George laid his pipe in the ashtray, got up from his chair, and came around and laid his hand on my shoulder. I looked up at him, "What do I owe you, George?"

"Nothing, I'm just sorry I can't be of more help. I hope things go better for you, no matter what your decision is." He opened the door, had the receptionist show me out. "You take care now, stop in and see the wife and me sometime soon, you hear?"

"I will. Thanks, George." I felt defeated and I let the tears flow. I reached my car and sat behind the wheel and bawled out loud. To think Maggie was going to win. Only the day before I thought I had the upper hand, and she would pay for what she had done. I guess not.

CHAPTER 22

When I got home Les was out and this was Dad's last day at work. In the meantime, I was desperate. If only I could find something to prove I was right. I began searching frantically around the dining room not really knowing what I hoped to find. Did Maggie leave anything in the corner cupboard or in her night stand? It was so long ago. If only I had known about Dad and Maggie before this. I never thought about it till now. How did she get her personal things after Mother chased her out? It had to be through Dad. He would've gathered up her things or else left her in the house when Mother and I were not there. I went through her night stand. It was cleaned out. I remembered looking there when I did house cleaning, but I looked again—it was empty.

I opened the corner cabinet and shuffled through loose papers on the bottom shelf. There were old bill statements and paper napkins. The upper shelves contained glassware and some collectibles. As a last resort, I yanked the fold out couch she used as her bed from the wall. I folded back the bedspread and crawled part way underneath. I saw a small white envelope stuck in the metal part that releases the couch into a bed. I couldn't reach it, and knocked it loose with a yard stick. Oh, my God! It was one of Maggie's small prescription envelopes with her name on it. I pulled open the flap. I couldn't believe my eyes. Inside were a few pills identical to the ones I found in Mother's dresser. I sat down on the floor, tears of joy running down my cheeks. This is it! The proof I needed. I closed my eyes and said, "Thank you, God!" Margaret Horner was hand written in blue ink on the label.

That evening I tackled the switchboard with a vengeance. I agitated the girls sitting on both sides of me. I reached for every light appearing on the switchboard, plugged in a cord and said, "Operator,"

No one really cared, since I was doing their work. Each hour I tried to beat the hour before with the number of long distance signals I picked up. What a night! I couldn't wait to tell Les what I had found. I rushed home and ran upstairs to Mother's bedroom.

"Les, are you awake?" I asked.

"Yes, now that you woke me." He replied jokingly.

"I've got it! Wait till you see what I found."

"I can tell you've been up to something. What is it now?"

I removed the envelope from my pocket and threw it on his lap, "This is what we need—I found the proof."

"What proof? What's this?" Les sat up and propped his back against the head board. I emptied the pills onto the bedspread. Les stared at the writing on the label, Margaret Horner twice a day as needed, "Where did this come from?"

"You'll never believe it! I was so mad I began to rummage around the dining room, looked through her night stand, at everything in Mother's corner cupboard. As a last resort, I pulled the couch Maggie used as her bed from the wall, and crawled half way under. I found this envelope stuck in the spring that releases the couch into a bed."

"Oh boy, this is some find. It was meant to be—they look like the same pills all right. Jan, I've never hated anyone before this, but if that bitch stood in front of my car, I believe I could run her down with no remorse." Les, confessed.

"Les, will they believe me now?"

"Yes, Jan. There's no doubt."

"Les, did you run into Dad today? This is his last day. I wonder if he has seen Maggie?"

"I don't know. I didn't see him," Les said. I was out most of the day and visited with Aunt Beb till about 10 o'clock. He's probably hanging out at the Derby, drinking with his buddies, I hope he doesn't get too drunk."

"If he went to Maggie's we're in for it tomorrow. You're supposed to go out and have a drink with him, remember? If he sees Maggie, your night out together will be off, just when he's starting to warm up to you after all these years."

"Well, I'm waiting. What did your attorney friend say?"

"He wasn't very encouraging about having a case against Maggie. He said it would be difficult to prove with Mother being the only witness against her, especially since she's a patient in the state hospital.

He thinks they wouldn't find her testimony credible. However, that was before I found the envelope."

"I didn't want to discourage you earlier, Jan, but this find does change things. We stuck our necks out going over there and accusing her. If only we would've had this envelope then. We need to think this through. He ran his fingers through his crew cut. I'm not sure how this find changes things. Let's get some rest and discuss where to go with it tomorrow." Les made a lot of sense.

"The fact that Maggie may get away with this crime makes me sick. She's the cause of Mother being where she is. I'm sure of it. She's destroyed our family and I hate her for it! There must be some way to make her pay for the damage she's done. At least, she knows we're wise to her now." I became teary eyed and looked over at Les, "I'm glad you were here to see what's going on. You've been a big help. It will be hard to see you go Les, you've always been there for me."

Les got up and put his arm around me, "Yeah, Yeah, I know. Don't go getting sentimental on me. We better get to bed. Try to get some sleep now. You've been going at it non-stop. By the way, Aunt Beb did say she thinks Judge Cummings was the one Maggie was in thick with."

I pounded my fist against the bedroom door, "I knew it! The more we know the better. See yah in the morning." I went to my bedroom thinking of all the things George said. I'll never give up trying to make Maggie pay for what she has done.

The next morning I was prepared to defend my actions to Dad. If Dad were in touch with Maggie the showdown would be today. But it would spoil Dad and Les getting together. There was no telling how long it will be before Les comes home again. Dad came into the kitchen as Les and I finished breakfast. I was all geared up, ready to let him have it.

"Son, you haven't forgotten about us getting together this evening, have you? I want to take you out to a nice supper and have a few drinks together afterwards. I thought perhaps you would enjoy meeting the guys who have stuck by me all these years. Jan, you're welcome to come along." I took a deep breath. What a relief. There was no mention about our meeting with Maggie.

"No, Dad, I haven't forgotten. What time do you want to go?" Les asked.

"How about 6:00 p.m.? We can go to the Italian restaurant over cross town, or out to the Fish Bowl Inn. Do you have a preference, son?"

"No, either place is fine with me."

"What are you hungry for Jan?"

"Count me out. It's time the two of you get together and talk man to man without me tagging along." I sounded off. Les glanced over at me and I knew exactly what he was thinking. He was hoping Dad didn't take him to the Brown Derby afterwards. If the same bartender was on duty he might recognize Les and ask if he was able to locate Maggie—that would be a real problem.

"Jan, can I borrow your car? I want to drop over to say good bye to Jerry and Bob this afternoon."

"Sure, go ahead. I'm not planning on going anywhere. What time do you need to leave from here tomorrow to catch your train?"

"The train leaves at 12:05 p.m. so let's leave an hour earlier."

"Okay, sounds good. I'm going to wash clothes. Is there anything you want washed before you leave?"

"There are a few dirty clothes up in Mother's clothes closet in the green laundry bag. I appreciate you throwing my clothes in the wash for me."

"It's no problem."

CHAPTER 23

The next day I was anxious to hear how Les and Dad spent the evening together. I ran to wake Les and see how they got along, "Well, how did it go brother?"

"You are not going to believe it, Jan. He was apologetic about admitting Mother but said there was no other place that would take her under the circumstances. Her trip that time to the hospital claiming to be pregnant put him on edge. That's when he met with her doctor and asked for help. He said he hoped I would understand he made mistakes and had no excuses for his behavior with Maggie. But he added, 'You don't know what it's like to have a sick wife?'"

"After two big mugs of beer and stopping at the Brown Derby for a night cap I was ready to let him know how I felt growing up. Before I began to complain about his always criticizing me and never really accepting me, Dad said, 'Hey guys I want you to meet my son. He is a writer for the Air Force and worked his way through college without any help from me.' When I heard those words acknowledging me as a writer I was stunned."

"I'm glad he finally realized your accomplishments, Les. I guess the bartender didn't recognize you after all."

"Lucky for me it was a different guy last night. I saw one of the same men sitting at the bar but he was half smashed and wasn't paying much attention to Dad. Dad was in his element bragging to his buddies and I let him have his moment. I remember vividly those arguments and rejections from him while I was growing up. What hell he put me through. I wanted to at least be able to stand up for myself tonight. Let him know exactly where I stood all those years and I didn't get the satisfaction. There's no use now, what purpose would it serve?"

"I think it better you had no confrontation because you're leaving and with Mother coming home I need his cooperation. I can't find it in my heart to forgive him for being with that whore. I kept picturing in my mind Maggie sashaying down the steps at the cottage after lying in Mother's bed with Dad moments before. And to think she's the reason Mother isn't here right now."

"Jan, I smiled to myself as I watched Dad bragging. For the first time in my life, my father accepted me for who I was and what I do for a living. I watched him as he talked about his last day and how he would be enjoying retirement. He kept looking my way and his voice resonated in my direction. I knew he talked and laughed louder for my benefit."

"He said, 'Son, I'm glad you came and could finally meet the guys I worked with. I'm sorry we don't have more time to spend together before you leave. Maybe on your next furlough we can go up the river bass fishing like old times. I really enjoyed our time together.' He had a straight shot at the bar and I offered to drive but he declined. With all those beers and a couple shots it was amazing he didn't appear drunk and drove okay."

"Did he say anything about what he plans to do now that he's retired?"

"No, but I think he has done some serious thinking about our relationship, obviously. Jan, somehow the two of you will have to come to some sort of a truce, especially with Mother coming home for Thanksgiving. You'll probably need his help when it's time to take her back to the hospital."

"You're right, as usual. I'll do my best to see everything goes smoothly during her visit. It'll take time for me to see how he behaves in retirement. By the way, I ironed the two shirts hanging there on the door knob, and folded your clothes and laid them on the dresser."

"Gee, thanks, Sis. I'm so used to rolling things in a ball for a duffle bag, I forget about folding my T-shirts anymore. The dress shirts you ironed I'll fold carefully and put them in my B-4 bag. The rest of my clothes don't matter."

"Les, I'm happy for you. I just wish Dad would have come to his senses years ago. I'll go down and start breakfast."

CHAPTER 24

"Les, did you hear Dad stirring around upstairs before you came down?"

"Yes, I heard his bedroom door open on my way down."

"I just wanted to make sure he got up in time to go with us to the train station. I know he wanted to see you off. It's going to be difficult to see you leave, Les." My lips began to quiver as I faced the fact he was going.

"Jan perk up! Let's enjoy our breakfast together and not think about it for now. I'm glad you made the oatmeal. I watched Les pour on brown sugar and raisins. I only wished he were home to stay. I heard Dad coming down the stairs as we began to eat.

"Dad, can I fix you something for breakfast?" I asked reluctantly.

"Nothing, right now, I'll have coffee and toast later. Are you all packed, Son?" He inquired, as he opened the refrigerator and had his usual of milk with a raw egg floating on top.

"Dad, I'm in your seat." Les said as he went to get up.

"Stay put, Son. Eat your breakfast. I want to glance at yesterday's paper in the parlor." He took his glass and headed for his favorite chair. I looked over at Les, stuck out my tongue and shrugged my shoulders in disgust at what Dad was drinking. Les cracked up. He had to hold himself back from laughing out loud. It was ten thirty and time to get ready to go, "Les, you better get your bag while I rinse the dishes." I looked into the parlor and Dad was still going through the paper. I walked part way out of the kitchen, "Dad, it's time to go. Do you want me to drive or are you driving?"

"You can drive. I'll sit in the back." Les came down the stairs with his uniform on. He looked so handsome and professional. He was carrying his overcoat, bag and dress hat.

"Let me get your bag, Son." Dad put on his jacket, picked up the bag, and went out to my car. I grabbed my coat and Les and I walked out together. Dad was sitting in the back seat.

"Do you have everything?" I asked, as I slid under the steering wheel and straightened my coat underneath me.

"Yep, as far as I know."

"Well, we've plenty of time, but you never know how many people are taking the same train."

"Son, you sure look sharp in your uniform. They take good care of you, don't they?"

"Sure, Dad they provide us with everything we need. I'm glad I brought my overcoat, but I didn't need it. I wasn't sure how cold it would be. Remember there were years we had a couple feet of snow by now and times we went rabbit hunting in November and had to take our hunting jackets off because we were sweating. It was like an Indian Summer."

"That's right. Remember when your Uncle Bill shot a bunny that ran right in front of him. He was too close and we laughed when he retrieved it. There was nothing left except its' hind legs and the tail, remember?"

"Yes, he was embarrassed about blasting a little rabbit to pieces. He saved the tail to take home to his kids. We had a lot of fun hunting by the river. We will have to do it again, one of these days, Dad," as he looked over his shoulder at Dad in the back seat.

"We will, Son." I drove up Sixth Street, down Eighteenth Avenue, and passed by Aunt Beb's house by the cemetery. Everything looked bare since the fall leaves were down from the trees. I continued toward downtown. A few people were walking around downtown window shopping. The department stores were closed. As I pulled around the corner to the train station I began to realize this was it. Oh, how I hated for Les to leave. I could feel my eyes starting to well up and my heart began to beat faster as I stopped the car. "Dad, get Les's bag out of the trunk and both of you go in and find out if the train is on time. I'll park the car in the lot across the street."

"Okay, we'll look for you inside." Dad removed the bag from the trunk and Les smiled at me as he got out of the car. I watched the two of them walk together across the street. I found a parking place and ran over to the station. Les and Dad were sitting on a wooden bench in front of the ticket counter. "Is your train on time?" I asked.

"Yes, she's on time." Les said, with a funny grin. I watched as the different service men gathered with their families. The men were dressed in Navy and Army uniforms. I saw a couple with uniforms like Les's. "What's his rank, Les?" An older man passed with a lot of medals on his chest.

"He's a sergeant first class. See all those diagonal stripes on his sleeve. That tells you how many years he has in the service, one for every three years," Les explained.

"Gee, he's been in a long time." I was fascinated with all the different men in uniform, their medals, and families as they walked out of the building to the train tracks.

"I need to use the rest room. I'll be back in a few minutes," Dad said.

"Les, before Dad comes back I just wanted to say how much I'll miss you. You've helped me a lot while you were here. I hope they don't send you to Korea or some God forsaken place. Please call and let me know you arrived safely and keep your letters coming—I worry when I don't hear from you. I don't know how things will turn out once you're gone. Here are some crumpets in case you get hungry." I began to choke up, but I held back the tears for I knew he felt bad enough already.

"Jan, you're a strong one and you'll be fine. You may have to stand up to Dad and tell him exactly what you expect from him. It looks as though Maggie is too scared to say anything to Dad. I don't think you'll have to worry about her bothering you. As to what to do about the pills and the effect it has had on Mother, I don't have the answer. It will be up to you. I'll support you in whatever you decide to do. The first thing is to get Mother home and see how she does. I'll try to telephone you Thanksgiving Day. That is, if I can get to a phone. Sometimes it's hours to reach a public telephone. All the guys line up at the phones on holidays and weekends. I'll do my best." He reached over, lifted my chin up and said. "Now, don't be sad. I'll be back before you know it"

"I wish I were going with you. About as far as I get is to the cottage and back. And now going to the cottage is out of the question. One of these days I'm going to travel like you, Les, you'll see."

"I don't doubt it for a moment. You can do whatever you make up your mind to do. And, don't forget it!" The train was pulling into the station and everyone was walking down the stairs and out to the platform. Dad appeared and picked up Les's bag and we began to make our way slowly behind the crowd. Les, had his overcoat over his left arm and wrapped his other arm around mine. We walked together and Dad followed behind with his bag.

Everyone was getting on board and Les patiently stood back with us. The conductor said, "All aboard." Les pulled me toward him and hugged me tight. He shook Dad's hand and took his bag. I watched him walk up the steps and go aboard. He looked back at us standing there, "Bye, Les. Be sure and write. Take care of yourself." I yelled out.

"Be good, Son." Dad and I waved and watched Les walk through the passenger car. He waved from the window as the train began to move. We walked along side until it picked up speed. Dad and I stood there and watched until the train became a tiny speck on the tracks in the distance. As we walked back through the station a few people remained working their way back to the street.

"He's a good boy and he'll be fine." Dad remarked, as we approached my car.

"Yes, I know he'll be all right. I wish he could have stayed longer and be here for Thanksgiving." I had nothing more to say to Dad. He could tell by my actions I still was disgusted with him. Dad and I didn't say another word as I drove back through town and pulled up in front of the house. I parked the car and we walked up the porch steps and into a quiet house. Dad immediately turned on the T.V., and I went upstairs to hang up my coat. Inside my bedroom, I sat on the edge of the bed and the tears began to flow down my cheeks. I didn't want Dad to hear me, so I lay down and buried my head into my pillow and sobbed. I missed Les already.

CHAPTER 25

It was Wednesday the day before Thanksgiving and I was to pick Mother up at the hospital after 1:00 p.m. Dad didn't want to ride along. I arrived a little early and asked the receptionist, "Please tell the nurse I'm here to pick up my Mother." In minutes the elevator door opened. There was Mother with a brown short sleeved house dress hanging on her like a sack. They had her in black oxford shoes and white bobby socks. At least her hair was combed. They tried to make her look good with a little bow fastened on the left side of her head with a hair pin. What a sight she was, but I had big plans for Mother once we got home. Mother's dark brown eyes were sparkling and she was all smiles. The nurse walked over to meet me holding onto Mother's arm.

"Mother, are you ready to go home?" I asked, as I took hold of her other arm and helped her get both arms into a heavy sweater I had brought from home.

"Yes, Where's Les?" She asked looking all around.

"Les had to go back to Louisiana. His leave was up, Mother. I was interrupted by the nurse, "Remember you're to have her back here on Friday before 5 p.m. her supper time. Have a nice visit, Naomi," she said.

Mother answered, "I will," without glancing back.

I took Mother out to my car, opened the passenger door, and gathered up the bottom of her baggy dress so it wouldn't get caught or ripped. Once I got behind the wheel I looked over, "How do you feel, Mother?" I reached over and locked the door.

"Fine, now that I'm out of that place."

"I bought a turkey, the celery, onion and everything I could think of to cook a dinner like you used to. You can help me make the pumpkin pie tonight," I said.

"Where's the old man? Why didn't he come along to pick me up?"

"He's afraid of what you might say or do to him. I agreed it was better for him to wait at home. Besides, I want to help you change your clothes before he sees you. After all, you two haven't seen each other in months."

"I've been waiting for this moment. It seems like an eternity." She gazed out the window and seemed preoccupied the whole way home. The road was familiar, but there were a few changes in the businesses along Sixth Avenue. It was a typical fall day. The woods look barren, and I only wished Les were here.

My plan was to get her upstairs, slip on one of her pretty dresses and fix her hair before Dad saw her. I hoped there wouldn't be a big scene between them first thing. I parked in front of the house and walked around to unlock the car door with my key for Mother. I took hold of her arm and lead her up the porch steps, through the living room and to her bedroom. She managed the stairs better than I thought she would. Dad was nowhere in sight. So far, so good. I was overwhelmed with excitement to have her home. I could see her eyes get brighter and she smiled as she entered her bedroom. I had washed the windows, curtains, and the bed spread. I wanted everything to smell fresh for her visit.

"Mother, here are a couple of your favorite dresses to wear. Do you want to wear a red, green, or a brown one today?" I said, jokingly.

"I'd like the green one. I want to wear a brassiere, a slip, and a pair of my silk stockings. I'm sick of these ugly socks."

"Sure, whatever you want." I opened her dresser drawer and got out her lingerie. I helped Mother slip off the house dress and get into a satin bra, slip, and stockings which I rolled with a garter below her knees. It would be like old times, except for Les. "Les said to tell you he would call tomorrow if he could get near a telephone."

"Where's your father? I want to see him." Mother looked up at me when I accidentally pulled her hair while trying to comb it another way. I removed the silly bow and did my best to fix her hair right.

"He's around somewhere. Let me see how you look, Mother. Stand up." She turned and looked into her dresser mirror and smiled. "I think you need some rouge. What do you think?" I asked.

"Yes, and I want some lip stick, too." She answered.

"Okay, now you're talking. Let's do up your face a little, for a change." When I was finished putting on her makeup, I heard the door open and close downstairs. "Guess, that's Dad, let's go down and surprise him." I took her right arm and she held onto the banister with her left hand as we walked together down the stairs. It was like Loretta Young used to do when she graciously walked into a room in the latest fashions on her afternoon T.V. show.

Dad got up from his chair, "You're looking good woman. How have they been treating you?" He asked.

"What do you mean old man? Don't ask how I've been treated. You know very well what's going on in that place. After all, you put me there, remember? That's where you belong, not me," Mother scolded.

It was time for me to change the subject and separate the two of them. "Mother, I need your help in the kitchen with the pie dough. Dad, I think your news is on the television." I pulled Mother's arm and steered her toward the kitchen. She kept staring at him over her shoulder. I could see Dad's Adam's Apple go up and down. He was nervous. I tied an apron around Mother's waist and lined up the spices, eggs, canned milk, sugars, and canned pumpkin to mix. I went over the recipe and gave her instructions with the right measuring spoons to mix the ingredients. She spilled some, but I corrected the mistakes. I always had trouble trying to keep the pie dough from sticking on the rolling pin.

"Sprinkle more flour over the rolling pin," She instructed. I could hear the television blaring. Dad had a hearing problem in one ear and he drove me crazy with the T.V. so loud. After we got the pie in the oven, I started to prepare supper. I had ground beef for hamburgers and frozen French fries to bake. I placed the fries on a tin pie pan and put them in the oven with the pie. "Mother, can you get the relish, mustard, ketchup and anything else you want from the refrigerator?"

I yelled at Dad, "Do you want me to slice up some onion for your hamburger?"

"Yep," He answered.

Mother went to get up and rinse the measuring cups. "Don't bother, Mother. I'll take care of them later. You might get water on your dress." I started setting the table, and Mother finished placing the dishes and utensils at each place.

"Dad, supper will be ready in a couple of minutes," I shouted into the parlor.

"Okay, I'll be but a minute." Dad, replied. I heard him go upstairs.

"Mother, are you hungry?"

"Yes, I'm sick of the food they give us."

"Good I'll help you fix your hamburger. Once I got her burger fixed Dad appeared in the doorway.

"Dad, will you sit over here?"

Mother glared at him as he went to the other end of the table. It wasn't his usual chair, but I wanted to sit between them. Mother looked up, but took a bite of her burger. It was falling apart so I cut it in halves for her. I dished out the fries on our plates and from then on there was total silence. "Dad, Les said he would try to call tomorrow. He wants to speak to Mother and us. Will you be around all day tomorrow?"

"I don't know. What time will he call and when do you need me to carve the turkey?"

"I thought we would eat around 1:00 p.m. and have leftovers for supper. I'm not sure when Les will telephone. What do you think?"

"Okay, by me."

"Mother, what's your opinion? That's about what we used to do, right?"

"Not always. When your grandparents came we didn't eat till around three. Are they coming this year?"

"No, Mother, remember Grandma has a broken hip and it hasn't been set and Grandpap is not doing well. His left side was affected after his stroke. Aunt Betty is driving up from Lancaster to cook for them."

"That's too bad." Mother added. Supper was tense with Mother and Dad glaring at each other between bites. But at least there were no more harsh words. For once, I was at a loss to keep a conversation going. I kept my eye on both of them and could feel the tension building between them. Dad got up after he finished, got a bottle of beer from the refrigerator, and walked into the parlor. I was glad he left. Mother started gathering up the dishes and knocked her glass over as she reached for my dirty plate. Her hands didn't shake, but it seemed she over or under estimated when she reached for things. She managed, but I could tell it was hard for her to coordinate carrying the plates to the sink, but I left her do what she wanted.

Mother, sat down and I handed her the dishes to dry. I placed my hands on her shoulders and rubbed my cheek against hers. "It's so good to have you home, Mother." As I finished putting the dishes away, I heard the front door open and shut. I glanced into the parlor. The T.V. was off and Dad was gone. Trying not to be too obvious to

Mother I looked out the back door window. I saw Dad going into the garage through the side door. I was relieved because they both needed time to adjust. I wasn't sure how short fused Mother would be if he got her agitated. "Mother, do you want to watch T.V.?"

"Yes, where's the old man?"

"I just saw him go into the garage. He's probably going down to the Derby for a night cap."

"He's got a guilty conscious, and did you see how he tried to avoid looking straight at me. Does he have any idea of what I've been through because of him? How would he like to be placed in a tub of ice until he shivers and shakes until he wonders if he'll make it another day?"

"What are you saying, Mother? Is that what they've done to you?"

"Yes, several times. They insist it's good for the brain. The first time I didn't know what to expect. I screamed to be let out, but they harness you in and make you stay for what seems to be an eternity. The other times I did not get in the tub without a fight. They had to get those attendants to hold me down and fasten me. I kicked and tried to prevent them from pinning me down. They have left me alone lately because they know how hard it is to make me get into that tub. I hear other women screaming different days of the week."

"Oh, My God! That's terrible. Why are they putting you through that torture? I've talked to the doctor before about these so called treatments. You need to tell Dad about what goes on. He doesn't have a clue. But don't get into an argument with him. It won't do any good. I know how hard it must be, but I want us to have a good old fashioned Thanksgiving without the two of you fighting. After all, he did consent to let you come home."

"He did, did he? Who is he to give me permission to come home? Russ took me there and lied about me meeting my doctor who had ordered tests for me. Dr. Hill never did show up. These treatments and humiliation are Russ's fault, and you know it!"

"Mother, I can't begin to imagine the hell you've been through, but you've got to keep your emotions intact. I convinced him you're better, and if you lose your temper you'll ruin everything. C'mon you can sit in his chair, closer to the T.V." I turned on the main channel and showed her how to change the station, but she didn't seem to be paying attention. "If you need me, I'll be in the kitchen getting organized for tomorrow."

I looked in at Mother several times. She seemed fine. I cleaned up the kitchen after cutting celery, onions and breaking up bread crumbs for the dressing. I joined Mother in the parlor. Her eyes were closed with her head hanging down hugging her chest. "C'mon Mother, let's get you upstairs and ready for bed. You'll get a stiff neck sitting like this. Tomorrow's the big day. We've a lot to do in the morning with finishing the dressing and stuffing the bird." I took hold of her arm and we walked together upstairs to the bathroom. I put her toothbrush, towel, and washcloth at the sink and left the bathroom door slightly ajar. I waited outside in case she needed help. When she entered the hallway we walked together to her bedroom. I laid out one of her newer nightgowns. "Mother, I'm putting your house coat across the bottom of your bed. Your slippers are right here if you have to get up in the night. Better still, call me. Do you want me to leave the hall light on and your bedroom door slightly open?" She sat on the edge of the bed and thought for a moment. "Leave the door open." She kicked off her shoes. I rolled down her stockings, helped her undress and got her nightgown stuck pulling it over her head. We both started laughing trying to get it on.

She lay back against her pillow and I pulled the blanket and bedspread up under her chin. It was wonderful to see her there in her own bed. I felt a warm tingle go through my body, and my eyes were watery with happiness to have her home. I felt like crawling in bed and snuggling up beside her for a while, but I didn't. "Good night, Mother, I'm so glad your home. Pleasant dreams."

"Good night, honey. Thanks for supper and everything."

I went downstairs turned off the lights and barely had the strength once ready for bed to brush my teeth. I wound my clock and set it for 6:30 a.m. Once plopped into bed I rolled back and forth mulling the previous events in my mind. Mother barely mentioned Dr. Hill. I was relieved. I thought if Maggie tells Dad or the judge about Les and I barging in on her I might have to seek George's help. My mind shifted to what I had to do for the Thanksgiving meal. I fell off to sleep, but was awakened by the squeaky stair outside my bedroom door. I turned and glanced at the clock. It was 2:20 a.m., I knew it had to be Dad headed to his bedroom or the bathroom. I fell back to sleep.

CHAPTER 26

My alarm rang and I pushed the button. I rolled over, raised the bottom of my window blind and looked out. It was day break, I jumped up and pulled on a pair of black slacks and slipped over my head a black and white stripped T-shirt. I hurried into the bathroom, threw cold water on my face, brushed my teeth, and went over to see if Mother was awake. Her bed was empty! I was frantic. I ran downstairs, looked in the parlor, the kitchen, dining room, looked out the bay window to the front porch. Mother was gone! I opened the back door to see if for some reason she had walked out onto the back porch. My heart was pounding and I felt empty inside. She was nowhere to be found. I panicked! She wouldn't go to the cellar, but I ran down to check. There was no sign of her. I thought maybe she was in her walk-in closet and I had missed her when I was in her bedroom. That's it. She probably walked into the clothes closet for something, and I didn't see her. I ran back upstairs to her bedroom, checked the closet—Mother was not there. The last thing I wanted to do was involve Dad. He would be furious. Surely she wouldn't go out of the house, and head for Dr. Hill's. I didn't know what to think, or do. Dad's bedroom door was closed, but I had no choice. I banged on the door and barged right in. "Dad, I can't...I mean, Mother, what are you doing in here? I was looking all over for you!"

"Did you need me to help?" Innocently she looked up from the other side of Dad's bed. I was shocked! If I had had false teeth they would have been on the bed bedside them. There was my Mother in bed with the man she couldn't wait to get her hands on. Dad's back was toward me. I wanted to slap him and scream, but I held my tongue.

"Russ, I've got to get up and help with the turkey," Mother said. I turned around and slammed the door behind me. I leaned against the wall in the hallway and took a deep breath. I could not believe the nerve of him coaxing her to crawl into bed with him. Had he lost his mind? What could he possibly be thinking of? She's been sick in the hospital and home less than 24 hours. And as mad as she has been at him, it's a wonder she didn't slug him or strangle him in his sleep. This was Dad's fault. To think he was sleeping with that whore across town and now Mother. What's his problem? I was so mad at Dad I didn't know how I would control my anger. I ran downstairs, dumped milk into a pan for my hot chocolate. Mother is the innocent one here. He has his nerve. Mother came down to the kitchen with her house coat and slippers on. "Mother, what's going on?"

"Nothing, your Dad and I decided to call a truce. He still loves me, you know. He says he's sorry for everything."

"What? Sorry. Oh, Boy, that's a good one? Mother he's off base. This is not right. He should not be asking you for favors when you've just got out of the hospital." I shouted.

"It's okay, Jan. He's going to make amends. He promised me."

"Promised you what? Was he drunk, or is he out of his mind?"

"Well, he's lonely. It's been a long time, you know, since...."

"Never mind Mother," I interrupted her, I did not want to hear the details. "Do you want to get dressed or have breakfast first?"

"Jan, it's all right. You'll see. I'll go up and get dressed before breakfast." She left the room and headed for the stairs. I ran after her to be sure she was steady enough to take the stairs alone. She seemed okay holding onto the banister. Was she acting coy and up to something, or was this an honest to God make up? For months she went on about getting her hands on him and getting even. This was weird. I'd been worried about them getting into a real fight and her pitching things at him and now this. I couldn't wait to hear his explanation. Dad startled me when he appeared in the kitchen doorway. "Dad, what are you thinking getting her in bed with you? Have you lost your mind? This is not a good situation." My heart was pounding and at the same time I wanted to cry. I turned away and walked toward the backdoor.

"This is none of your business. This is between your Mother and me. She's my wife and I have every right."

I turned toward him, "No. No, you don't, not anymore. You're totally out of line! She's barely out of the hospital and you drag her into bed with you." I shouted, "This has got to stop! I don't want it to happen again. Do you understand?"

"Don't get smart with me, young lady. You have no right to talk to me like this. After all, I've been through." He added.

"All you've been through? Give me a break. Your behavior is disgusting. Mother has no idea about your affair with Maggie." I looked right into his face. He had a mean look in his eyes. "Dad, Mother may be capable and seem well, but she's still a sick woman and should not be in bed with you. I don't understand how it happened, but it just can't happen again. I can't allow it! She's under my supervision and if I have to, I will sleep with her myself." Dad opened the refrigerator and left the door bang back against the cupboard. I stood watching as he made his morning cocktail of milk, dropped in a raw egg, picked up his glass and left the kitchen. He knows he's in the wrong, I thought. No wonder he's walking away from me. He hasn't given a thought to the consequences. Why, she could even get pregnant. Had he even considered that? He must have been drunk and out of his cotton picking mind.

Minutes later, Mother joined me in the kitchen still in her house coat. I thought she was going to get dressed, but it didn't matter. I slipped a full apron over her head and tied it in back. She helped as much as she could. Her dexterity was not what it used to be. I gave her the easy things to do, mix everything for the stuffing and set the table. I melted butter on the stove and she mixed it in. Few words went on between us while Dad stayed in the living room in front of the blaring T.V. He came in for a bottle of beer a couple of times while Mother and I prepared the turkey and all the trimmings. I was glad he kept his distance. I got the bird in the oven which was crucial to eating on time.

"Mother, let's go up and get our clothes changed for dinner." Mother wanted a bath, so I helped her in and out of the tub. She went to her bedroom and started laying things out she wanted to wear. I bathed and got dressed. When I looked in on her, she was sitting on the bed trying to decide what to wear. She chose her red dress and I helped her fix her hair.

Dad was half asleep in his chair in front of the T.V. when Mother and I went back downstairs. I turned the volume down and let him sleep. The entire downstairs smelled good from the turkey baking. Mother sat down on the davenport while I went to check on the bird. I had the sweet potatoes to peel, the dried corn to bake, and fruit salad to make.

I felt like downing a bottle or two of Dad's beer but I pressed onward.

I knew I would have to call Dad to carve the turkey when I would've just as soon carved it myself. When the bird was done I let it sit for five minutes. I yelled, "Dad the turkey is done and you can carve it now." I laid the knife and fork on the stove beside the cooling roaster and went into the dining room to place hot pads on the tablecloth. On my trips carrying the fruit salad, potatoes, baked corn and dressing into the dining room I glanced over at him doing the carving, our eyes did not meet. I mixed the flour and water for the gravy, stirred it in with the turkey drippings and brought it to a slow boil.

"It's turkey time," Dad remarked, as he carried the plate of sliced turkey into the dining room. He actually had a half smile on his face.

"Wait, Dad, I need to cover the plate with tinfoil to keep it warm while I pour the gravy. Mother, dinner is ready. I hope you're hungry." Mother walked into the dining room and sat down in her usual place. I plopped down with a sigh of relief. It was sort of a typical Pennsylvania Dutch Thanksgiving, but not the kind I had planned in my mind ahead of time.

Dad and Mother didn't exchange words at the table except to pass the potatoes, how the breast of the turkey was moist and a remark here and there about the food. Mother choked on her turkey. I got up and cut it into smaller pieces. I don't know why she chokes on her food. At the hospital she chokes on the sundaes I take her frequently. She continued to shuffle her feet under the table during the meal.

I tried to talk about Les and all the exciting places he had told me about. The two of them listened, and Dad didn't look my way. I could tell he was still mad at what I had said earlier. But he had only himself to blame for my harsh words. We had pumpkin pie for dessert. Dad took a cup of coffee and a cigarette into the parlor. As Mother finished her pie, she said, "That was a good meal, Jan." She helped clear the table. We carried everything to the kitchen table and I started rinsing the dishes in the sink. Dad got a beer from the refrigerator. I ignored his trip in and out of the kitchen. Thank heavens he went back to his chair in the parlor. I heard the telephone ring, "How are you son?" Dad said.

"Mother, it's Les, go into the parlor, so Dad and you can take turns talking. I'll go up and use my bedroom phone." As I lifted my bedroom phone I heard Dad say, "We sure had a great meal. Wish you could have been here. How's everything going?"

"Fine, Dad, How's Mother doing?" Les asked.

"She's right here. Let me put her on, so you two can talk."

"Mother, Happy Thanksgiving. How are you feeling?" Les inquired.

"Fine, Where are you?"

"I'm in Lake Charles, Louisiana for now, Mother. Remember I told you about it when I was home. They had a real big feast for us at the chow hall at noon. Of course, it's still not the same as being home." Les, went on.

"Les, I'm here on the upstairs phone," I replied.

"Jan, it's good to hear your voice. I got your Thanksgiving card and it sounds as if everything is going okay, since I left."

"Yes, so far, so good. We miss you. What's this I hear about you going to Korea?" I asked.

"There's talk about our squadron being transferred. So far it's only talk."

"Les, isn't your time about up?" Mother asked.

"No, Mother, I've got a long way to go yet. It will go fast though. Don't worry about me. Have a good time over the holiday, Mother. Jan, I need to wind this up. There's a long line behind me to use the phone. Wanted to wish you all a Happy Thanksgiving and let you know I'm thinking of you. Bye, Mother, take good care of yourself. Put Dad back on, so I can say good bye." Les said.

"Dad is that you?"

"Yes, Son, I'm here."

"I wanted to say good bye, got to go."

"Okay, Son. Take care and keep in touch. It's good hearing from you."

"Bye, Les. I'll keep writing and let you know how everything turns out." I blurted in.

"Bye, for now, Jan." I heard the phone click and I was sorry I didn't have a chance to tell him what was really going on. He wouldn't believe what had happened. Everything went smooth through the evening because Dad went out, as usual. I was glad because Mother and I could watch the programs we wanted without the T.V. blaring. Aunt Beb came by to visit and Mother was glad to see her.

"Noan, you're looking good." Aunt Beb hugged her and sat down beside her on the davenport.

"Where is that no good husband of yours?"

"Oh, he's gone out for a drink, I guess." Mother replied.

"He should stay here where he belongs on Thanksgiving. What kind of a man is he anyway?"

"Aunt Beb, let's not discuss his problems. So far everything is going pretty good." I winked at her to stop, "Have you had your turkey yet?" I inquired.

"No, I've everything almost ready. The bird is in the oven and we're having ours at supper time."

"Jan made a good meal," Mother offered.

"Yes, it turned out well, considering," I added.

"Well, Noan, I'm sorry I don't get out to the hospital much. You know how it is with keeping up with our son and all."

"Sure, it's okay, I understand," Mother replied.

"Well, I'd better get up the street and keep an eye on the meal. Take care of yourself, Noan." Aunt Beb headed for the front door. Mother tried to get up, but fell backwards since the davenport sits rather low. "It's okay, Mother I'll see her to the door." As I stepped out onto the front porch, Aunt Beb whispered, "Is everything okay?"

"Yes, but Dad is out of line as usual. I'll call you later, when I can. Have a good Thanksgiving." She waved back at Mother while I held the door open. Wait till I tell her about Dad's actions. She'll have a fit. Mother walked into the dining room and sat down at the piano. She started playing The "Old Rugged Cross" without a hymnal in front of her. Her fingers went from hymn to hymn by memory. I joined her at the piano bench and my eyes welled with tears. How wonderful it was. I sang along with what words I could remember. It was just like old times. To see her play after all she had been through. I was amazed at her ability to remember those hymns. Thanksgiving turned out to be one of my happiest. If only Les, were here. "Mother, it's so good to hear you play. How do you remember those hymns?" I asked.

"I don't know. It's strange, but I've not forgotten."

We sat there for over an hour. I got out some sheet music and she played some of her favorites, *As Time Goes By* and *September Song*. "Mother, you must be getting hungry, I know I am."

"Yes, I guess. Where's the old man. Isn't he coming home for supper?"

"I have no idea. Keep playing Mother. I'll heat up the gravy, some turkey, and potatoes. When it's ready I'll call you." We had a nice quiet supper. She helped me put the leftovers away, and I had her sit down to dry the dishes. I went into the parlor and changed the channel on the television. We watched Sid Caesar, and I saw Mother's head begin to droop down to her chest again.

"Are you ready to call it a day, Mother?"

"Yes, I think so."

"C'mon let's go up and get ready for bed. It's been quite a day. Hasn't it, Mother?" She nodded. I walked upstairs with her. As she was using the bathroom I went back downstairs and turned off the lights. When I got to the top of the stairs she was already headed down toward her bedroom. She didn't need much help except to get that nightgown over her head again.

"Mother, please do not let Dad talk you into sleeping with him tonight. You need your rest. If he bothers you call me. Do you understand? I mean it!"

"Uh-huh." She replied.

What a day this was. I couldn't wait to get to bed. I was pleased the turkey turned out as good as it did, and I fell asleep. I woke in the middle of the night, went quietly down the hallway to look into Mother's room. She was in her bed fast asleep. Dad's door was partly closed and I wasn't sure if he was there or not. I tip toed back to my bed so glad Mother was in her own room. Morning came and I peered into Mother's room again and she was still there. What a relief. I got dressed and went downstairs to check to see if Dad's car was in the garage. It wasn't. To think I worried through the night about him coming home and coaxing Mother into his bedroom. I can guess where he spent the night. If he went across town, I may be in for it real soon. Maggie might spill her guts to him. Mother was awake when I checked again. "Mother, how about I fix you a nice tub of hot water this morning?"

"Where's the old man?"

"I guess he got up early and went out already," I answered.

"That's strange. I didn't hear him come in."

"Well, Mother, I'm not surprised with the big day we had yesterday. You probably were in a deep sleep." I couldn't share my suspicions about where he spent the night. It undoubtedly was across town with Maggie the whore. Lord knows what Mother would do to him if she knew the truth, especially after the other night.

"Can you help me wash my hair, Jan?"

"Sure, why not. Then we can style it better." Mother, I planned on taking you down to see your mother, "Mom" and Aunt Shirley this afternoon. Mom's been looking forward to seeing you. The reason she hasn't been out at the hospital to visit lately is her health hasn't been good."

"What's wrong?" Mother looked worried.

"It's her blood pressure and her heart isn't that strong. She's on heart and blood pressure medicine."

"I didn't know about her heart. Did you tell me?"

"Sure, I did, but that was before you were getting those special treatments at the hospital." I helped her get in and out of the tub and washed her hair. I laid out a nice dress, her underwear, brassiere and stockings. Her hair looked great. So good, it was hard to believe she had been in the hospital. I telephoned Mom and told her we would be down in early afternoon. Mother and I had a late breakfast with time to sit and relax at the kitchen table.

After clearing the dishes I turned on the T.V., and Mother sat in Dad's over-stuffed chair. I went upstairs, took a bath, and got dressed to visit Mom. When I came down stairs Mother's head was hanging down to her chest again; she had drifted off to sleep. I decided to let her nap. She needed the rest. I removed the tablecloth and placed it in the upstairs dirty clothes basket and carried the basket to the cellar to wash later. It was about 1:00 p.m. when I awakened Mother for left-overs before going to see Mom. "Mother, are you hungry?"

"Yes, I'm hungry for a hot turkey sandwich with gravy on it." She replied.

"Sounds good to me." She ate well, but once again started choking on the turkey. I cut it in smaller bites and gave her a glass of water. I rinsed the dishes and set them in the sink to wash later. I could tell Mother was anxious to see Mom for it had been a couple of months since she had visited. Mother looked out the car window the whole way to Mom's. I held onto Mother's arm when we climbed up the steep front porch steps. Mom opened the door in her apron and baking cap. The house smelled so good.

"Noan, it's so good to see you." She put her arms around Mother and the two of them hugged. Shirley came out from the kitchen and hugged Mother too. Mom had tears in her eyes, and my eyes were tearing too. They were tears of happiness for Mother and Mom.

"Noan, you look good. How are you feeling?" Mom, asked.

"Fine, I'm doing much better now," Mother answered.

"How was your Thanksgiving?" Shirley, spoke up.

"Great. Jan and I stuffed the turkey and we had the works."

"It's too bad Les couldn't have been home. Was Russ there?" Mom inquired.

"Yes, he ate, but shortly thereafter he left for the beer garden."

"He couldn't even stay home for a Thanksgiving. What's that man's problem, anyway?" Mom, asked.

"He's the same old Russ, but lonely. He hasn't changed. But he's still my husband."

"He may be your husband, but what good is he? Is he really retired now?" Mom continued.

"Yes, he retired a couple of weeks ago. A couple of days before Les left," I said.

Shirley interrupted, "What's he going to do with himself now that he's retired?"

"Lord knows. He's still drinking a lot." I replied.

"It's high time he straightens himself out. He hasn't been worth a darn lately," Mom added. It was a nice visit and Mom gave us a piece of date and nut cake right out of the oven with whipped cream. Mother loves Mom's cake. I had intended to bake one before Mother got home but didn't get a chance. Mother choked a little, but thanked Mom for remembering her favorite. We said our good byes. I helped Mother back down the rickety steps to the sidewalk. As I looked back, I could see the sadness and concern in Mom's eyes as she waved goodbye.

"Mother, how do you think Mom looks?"

"She looks awfully tired. She does entirely too much work around there, with Shirley and Glen working and the two kids."

"Mom wouldn't have to do as much as she does, but it's not her nature to take it easy. She asks about you all the time, Mother. I keep her informed." When we arrived home, Dad was there glued to the T.V. He barely glanced up at us as we walked in the front door and went straight to the kitchen. If he saw Maggie I'm in for it, I thought. He didn't say a word when I walked back through the parlor to go upstairs and gather up Mother's clothes. I dreaded the thought of having to take Mother back to the hospital. Mother sat on the davenport quietly looking out the bay window than at the television. Dad and she did not exchange words.

"Mother, you can wear the dress you have on to show the women and nurses at the hospital how nice you look."

"I'm not going back! Not ever again. Isn't that so, Russ?" Dad turned in his chair and was silent. Did they both know something I didn't?

"Mother, I promised the nurse I'd have you back before supper."

"Well, I'm not going back, and it's final!"

"Woman, you're under a doctor's care and you need to go back for now. The nurses are trained to help you get well."

"But you promised, Russ. They're not doing anything except making me miserable. I can't go back. I won't survive if I do."

"Give it a little more time, woman. I meant when you're well."

"You're a liar! I am well. You've seen for yourself." I expected Mother to get out of control and start pitching things and was ready to intervene.

"There's no one here 24 hours a day to look after you."

Dad got up from his chair and walked briskly into the kitchen. My eyes followed him through the door way. He turned, waved his arm for me to join him. I walked into the kitchen and he whispered, "She can't stay here and you know it! We've got to get her back to the hospital. It's your responsibility. This was your idea to bring her home."

I kept my voice low, "I can't force her to go back. Besides you're the one who coaxed her into bed with you. What in heaven's name did you tell her? Can you blame her for not wanting to leave? What do you suggest?"

"Convince her to get in the car and I'll help you get her there."

"I'm not going to lie to her. I say we call an ambulance."

"No, our insurance won't pay for it. You'd better figure out a way to get her to calm down and cooperate," Dad scolded.

"That's great, now it's up to me. I've got to think this over. I need to get back into the parlor before she wonders what's going on between us." My mind was spinning, and at the same time my heart ached for Mother. I closed my eyes for a moment and prayed, *Oh, God, help me find a way to get Mother back to the hospital.* I hurried to the parlor and sat beside her, "Mother do you think you are well enough to stay by yourself when Dad and I aren't around?"

"You saw for yourself. I'm perfectly fine and only need a little help now and then."

"But Mother, you need help with your bath and the cooking. I don't think you should be here all day by yourself. What would you do all day?" I asked.

"I'll be fine, you'll see. When I need help I'll wait till one of you are home."

"Mother, I'd be afraid of you falling like you used to, and not be able to get up, or choke, or something." She looked away and began shifting her legs back and forth. I knew she was nervous and there was no changing her mind. What a mess.

"Mother, I've got to go to the bathroom, I'll be right back." I went upstairs and sat on the edge of my bed trying to think of a plan. Perhaps, if I told her we were going to view the Christmas decorations on Eleventh Avenue and take a look at the big tree all lit up down town. That might be enough to get her into the car. She always loved Christmas. We used to drive around and look at how beautiful the houses were decorated. The Santa Claus parade was today, and tonight the store windows would be bright with Christmas lights.

I'd need to stall at least until dusk. Thank God it gets dark early. I'd be late getting her back, but it was worth a try. I hated to deceive Mother. Would she ever forgive me? But I believed it was the only way. I had to play a part now, one I knew I would hate for a long time to come. I took my time walking downstairs and over to the davenport. "Mother, I have a headache, and I'm going to take a couple of aspirin and lie down. Would you like to take a little nap upstairs, or stay here and watch television?"

"I'm okay. You go and get rid of your headache, honey."

I walked to the kitchen to ask for Dad's help. I was so angry with him, but I was in trouble and knew I had to get his help to get Mother to the hospital. I whispered to him my plan.

"Okay, but this had better work. If we don't get her there tonight, I don't know what the consequences will be," he added. I thought to myself, *Dad's got a lot of nerve blaming this whole situation on me.* I went back upstairs, and lay on top of my bedspread. I raised the window blind so I would know the moment it got dark outside. It had to be dark enough to persuade Mother to get into the car. We would go see the Christmas lights all right, but on the trip to the hospital. My forehead was beginning to pound. This was one of the longest afternoons of my life.

Finally, it was dark outside. I ran downstairs and tried to show some excitement. "Mother, I've a great idea. Why don't we take a drive to see the Christmas lights before supper? I brought down your heavy sweater." I yelled to Dad, "Do you want to go along to see the Christmas lights with Mother and me?" I really didn't give Mother a chance to answer. Her dark brown eyes lit up, and I helped her put on her wool sweater. I knew she wanted to go.

"Mother, tonight will be the first night of the tree lighting in the center square and the biggest shopping day of the year. All the store windows will be beautifully decorated," I rambled on. Dad came into the parlor with his jacket on. He looked straight into my eyes. I could have cried, but I looked away.

"I'll run outside and start the car to get the heater going. Dad, will you help Mother to the car?" I didn't wait for an answer and ran out ahead of them. I took a deep breath of fresh air, jumped behind the wheel, started the engine and turned on the heater full blast. It wasn't freezing cold—unusual for the day after Thanksgiving. As Dad approached the car, I motioned for him to take her around front. "Mother, sit up front with me, you'll be able to see better." I opened the car door from inside and Mother slid onto the seat beside me. As soon as Dad closed the door, I reached over and pushed the door lock button down. Dad got in the back seat behind Mother. I drove by the cemetery, down Eleventh Street to Eleventh Avenue to the main shopping district. A lot of shoppers were bustling from store to store. When I reached the center square where the tree stood I slowed down. "Look, Mother, how big the tree is this year. They put only white lights on it for a change." Mother's eyes sparkled with excitement. I steered the car close to the curb, so she could get a closer look. I drove up the street to the largest department store.

"Woman, check those windows in Gable's Store. Those reindeer and Santa are in motion." Dad wound down the rear window for her to look over her shoulder.

"The lights along the eleventh avenue are pretty, aren't they, Mother?"

"Yes, they're beautiful." Mother looked over at me and smiled. I drove through town slowly, dreading what I had to do. Luckily there were a lot of houses trimmed with Christmas lights and yards with reindeer and nativity displays. Mother was occupied looking back and forth to see both sides of the road as Dad and I pointed out different displays. I hoped by the time she recognized the road that winds up the hill to the hospital there wouldn't be a problem. Dad kept making comments and pointing out different houses. When I reached the turn off leading up the hill to the hospital, she stiffened her legs and her face went pale.

"No, Jan, No!" She started screaming at the top of her voice. "How could you, I can't go back to that place." She started kicking her feet against the floor boards and swinging her arms combatively. Dad had to grab both her arms from behind and pin them down along her sides.

"Calm down, woman. You are making matters worse." She kept kicking with her feet and slid almost down to the floor boards. Dad leaned over the back of Mother's seat, to keep her arms pinned down. She continued to kick and struggle to get free. She tried to bite his arm, her head thrashing back and forth. I could see the tears running down both her flushed red cheeks. She was hysterical, her eyes looked terrified, "You son of a bitch. This is your doing. God damn you, Russ!"

It was all I could do with her struggling and Dad hovering over her to steer the car up the hill. She screamed every cuss word she probably ever heard working at the railroad. I pulled up to the back entrance, jumped out of the car, ran to the doorway, and rang the emergency bell. The door opened and a nurse I didn't recognize appeared.

"Hurry, I need help to get my Mother, Naomi Bryar, out of my car. She's terribly upset, and I'm late bringing her back." The nurse yelled over her shoulder, "Jim, we need your help over here." A large muscular looking male attendant appeared with a wheelchair. They followed me to the passenger side of the car. Mother's face was crimson and wet with tears. Her sweater was half off and her dress up above her knees from struggling to get free from Dad's grasp.

I opened her door with my key from the outside. Thank heavens I locked it after she got in, or she may have tried to jump out when she recognized the road. Once she saw the attendant and the nurse matters got worse. She kicked harder and struggled with all her might. "Mother, stop it! Let them help you," I cried out.

"Get away from me, you bastards!"

"Now, now, Naomi calm down. You're only hurting yourself carrying on like this," the female nurse pleaded. The male attendant grabbed her under the arm pits as Dad let go, and dragged her backwards from my car and plopped her into the wheelchair. The nurse tried to put the foot rests down but Mother was kicking too hard. She fastened the safety strap tight across her arms while the attendant held her arms firm against the wheelchair. She continued to struggle and screamed. "You fuckin, son of a bitch, let me go"

"Mother, please calm down, I'm sorry, but I promised your doctor." I don't believe she heard a word I said.

"Damn you, let go of me. You're hurting me!" I followed beside the wheelchair helpless, while Dad stayed back by the car.

"We can handle her from here," the male attendant said over his shoulder as he wheeled Mother through the doorway. I stood there with tears in my eyes as the heavy metal door banged shut in front of me. I could hear her screams as I turned and headed for the car. I knew she would be upset, but never expected her to be so out of control. My dear Mother was now someone else—someone different than had just spent Thanksgiving with me. Dad was standing by the car smoking a cigarette. Tears rolled down my cheeks dropping to the ground as I opened the car door. My forehead pounded with each beat of my heart. I felt a sick emptiness inside. She will never forgive me for what I've done.

The expression on Dad's face said it all. He opened the car door and slid onto the seat beside me. I wiped my eyes with the back of my hand and glanced over at him. He was beyond upset. Thank heavens he came along. There was no way I could have driven and controlled Mother at the same time. She fought with every bit of her strength. It's such a shame she has to endure this hell. I slid behind the steering wheel and gripped my hands around it in despair.

"Well, that's it. There will be no more visits home. Not after this type of behavior. Now do you believe me? She's not as well as you thought. Is she?" He prodded.

"Dad, please, not now. We tricked her and you know it. Who wouldn't react like this? You've no idea what it's like to be penned up in this place. This is the first time you have had a taste of what goes on out here. I'm ashamed of myself for what I've just done."

"This was no picnic for me either. She scratched my face. It was difficult trying to keep her arms still so she wouldn't hurt you or bang them against the windows. There won't be any more of it, I can assure you," Dad added.

"I pray they won't hurt her, and she calms down now that we're out of sight. She probably will never want to see me again after this." I closed my eyes for a moment as Dad took another long drag on his cigarette. My thoughts were with my poor Mother back there being wheeled down the hallway in this institution. I said a silent prayer to God, *Please forgive me and watch over my dear Mother.* Dad interrupted my thoughts. "Don't be ridiculous. Why would they bring harm to her? If anything she's more apt to hurt herself with her kicking and thrashing about." He smashed his cigarette into the ashtray, and I started the car. I knew there was no convincing him this place was torture for Mother. My chest felt tight as my head continued to pound. All I wanted was to get home. There was nothing but silence between Dad and me from then on.

I drove by the same Christmas lights we had admired on our way out, now just a blur through my tears. It was a constant chore to keep my car on the road.

Once home, Dad headed for the refrigerator, and it wouldn't be for only a beer but something stronger to go with it. I ran upstairs and threw myself across the bed. My head pounded, my eyes were burning, and my nose running. I grabbed a tissue and blew my nose. How would I be able to make my case about Mother being poisoned after this? The nurses would make notes in her chart about her combative behavior and being late coming back to the hospital.

Dad didn't say a word or give any indication that he knew about Les and me going to Maggie's. I guess Maggie realized she'd better keep quiet especially knowing she was guilty as hell. After Dad's behavior over Thanksgiving I'm sure he knew nothing about what Maggie had done to keep Mother bedfast.

Sunday, I decided to visit Mother at the hospital. I was scared after leaving her the way I did on Friday. After asking the receptionist to call the nurse to bring Mother down to visit, I became more nervous by the minute. Would she even want to see me after all that happened? The elevator door opened. Mother stood there beside the nurse with her head hanging down. She was in one of those baggy dresses and her hair uncombed. Tears filled my eyes as I walked to greet her, "Mother, how are you today?" There was no answer. She raised her head slightly and didn't speak.

"I brought you your favorite peanut butter sundae." I took hold of her arm and led her to the visiting cubicle. She didn't pull away from me, but I was devastated. Mother sat down, I pulled up a chair to the table, and took the sundae out of the bag.

"Here's your spoon and a napkin, Mother." Her eyes were glassy with not a trace of excitement. She paid no attention to her sundae.

"Mother, please forgive me. I had to bring you back, we promised your doctor." Her eyes were watery, and vacant. She remained silent. Then it dawned on me. She must have had another shock treatment. That had to be it—they punished her for acting out! Since Mother was combative when I brought her back it gave them an excuse to zap her again, or maybe she was heavily sedated. I put my arm around her and placed my face against her cheek.

"Mother, let me help you with your ice cream." Her arms remained at her sides, her hands in her lap. I fed her one spoonful at a time. She choked a little, it went slow, but I got her to eat about half of it. I knew there was no need to worry about her forgiveness for now. She was far removed from Friday night's memory. It was a one way conversation. I rambled on about being tired of leftover turkey, what the pastor said at church, and that I saw Mom and Shirley at Sunday School. She seemed to hear me, but there was no reaction or response to any of it.

I was relieved she showed no anger toward me, but as the moments went by I could feel my own anger building about what they were doing to her. She was very still, even her legs weren't shifting around like usual. I walked over to the receptionist to ask her to call the nurse. I looked over my shoulder to ensure she was okay sitting there. I went back to the visiting area, threw the rest of the melted sundae in the trash and sat down beside Mother.

Mrs. Claney came out of the elevator and headed toward us. I walked to meet her and in a low voice said, "Mother is withdrawn and sad, what's going on?"

"She's fine. It will take a few days for this to wear off. It's just the treatment, you know." She showed little concern.

"Well, I don't like all these treatments Mother is getting. I don't think it's necessary to torture her like this. Look at her! It's pitiful!"

"My, Oh My! How you continue to fuss about her. You have no idea what you're talking about. This is helping your Mother calm down and get things straight in her head. I assure you, we are doing what is best for your Mother." She took hold of Mother's arm and helped her up from the chair. I took Mother's other arm and walked with them toward the elevator.

"Mother, you'll be feeling better in a few days and I'll be back soon," I said, trying to be reassuring. I waited for the elevator door to open. "Mother, take care." The nurse walked her into the elevator, and turned her around facing the door while she pushed the button.

The elevator door was closing and Mother stood there with her head hanging down. She never looked up, or attempted to wave. It broke my heart. As I drove down the hill I kept wondering how I could stop these shock treatments. Dad was no help, and showed even less understanding now. I didn't want to worry Mom, but I needed to talk to someone. They are ripping the life and spirit out of Mother. If only Les were still here, we could go together and plead once again to her doctor.

CHAPTER 27

Months passed, Mother was getting weaker and more restless. She couldn't keep her feet, arms or fingers still. There was no brightness or excitement in her eyes anymore. Her words were difficult to understand and there were fewer of them. It got to the point I would ask questions. She would nod at times, but there was no spontaneity to speak of. Mother needed more help getting up from a chair and walked very slow and awkwardly. I mentioned to Dad about her going downhill and not being able to keep her legs from shuffling back and forth.

"Quit worrying about her. She's getting good care. There's no more that can be done. Why do you fret over things out of your control?"

"I had high hopes for her getting well one day and returning home."

"I tell you, it ain't gonna happen and you might as well get used to it." Dad had a smirk on his face, a beer in one hand and a cigarette in the other. I didn't like what I saw. So this was how he was handling retirement—with more alcohol and chain smoking. He was more upset with me about trading my car in for a Volkswagen convertible than Mother. I was tired of trying to get around in the snow.

"You'll never get me inside a rag top," he said.

It was noon the next day, when I got a call from the hospital. The nurse said, "Naomi has taken a turn for the worse and has developed pneumonia. You'd better come right away." I rushed to the hospital, and for the first time I was escorted upstairs.

Mother's bed was in a cubicle very much like the ones dividing the visiting area downstairs. The side rails of Mother's bed were padded with sheets and taped down. Mother was restless and kept banging her arms and legs against the padded side rails. Black and blue bruises were on her thin arms and legs. Her eyes were closed and her face was pale and moist. She looked frail against white sheets. "Mother, I'm here. It's me, Jan." Her eyelids fluttered opened, but there was no response. I lifted up her little hand and held it against my cheek. I stood there for some time watching her head rotate back and forth. Her legs thrashed about, and I could feel her fingers twitching against my cheek.

I stood there thinking about what had happened in the last months. After Thanksgiving she never was the same. Did she give up all hope? Or was it those damn treatments—Lord knows what effect they had on her? I placed her hand back down on the bed and walked over to the glass-enclosed room where a few nurses were gathered. A big buxom nurse with a heavily starched hat walked out the door to greet me. She had a large ring of keys in her hand. "Is Mother any better?" I inquired.

"No, not really. We did get her high fever down. These next twenty-four hours will be crucial. We have her on oral medicine, but may have to start an intravenous line." Her expression was stern and sober. I went back to Mother's bedside and tried to rouse her. Her eyes opened but closed again when I repeated, "Mother it's me, Jan. I kissed her cheek. It was moist and clammy. "Mother, I'll be back. I love you. Please don't give up." Prickly needles went through my whole body as her legs continued to thrash against the padded rails. It was the same feeling I experienced each time she hurt herself, whether it was burning her fingers on the stove or falling and bruising her knees. I always cringed inside. I stopped where the tall buxom nurse was sitting, "Will you call me if there's any change?"

"Yes, I work till eleven and will pass it on to the night shift at evening report. We're doing all we can."

"Thank you. I'll say goodbye to Mother and please call me." When I arrived home, Dad was in his usual spot and more tipsy than usual.

"The hospital called. Mother has pneumonia. They urged me to come right away. She really looks bad, Dad. I'm worried."

"Is that so?" How did she get pneumonia?"

"I don't know. She hasn't been well for months. I'm having a harder time trying to understand what she's saying. It gets more difficult week by week."

"That's too bad. I really am sorry to hear it," he said not looking straight at me. This was more like what I had expected all along from him, I thought. This must have been one of his more compassionate moments. I was glad this was my day off; I could stay near the phone in case the nurse called. I decided to telephone Mom, Aunt Beb, and Aunt Oak to let them know Mother wasn't doing well. I could tell by Mom's voice she wished there was a way she could help. Aunt Beb offered to go along to see Mother the next day.

Aunt Beb and I made the trip and Mother was a little better. She seemed to recognize us, but only nodded her head to our questions. She was short of breath and had a needle in her lower left arm which was strapped with gauze to a board to keep it straight. Even with the board attached she banged her arm back and forth against the side rail. She was restless and constantly moving her legs back and forth. Mother was trying to make words with her lips.

"Mother, don't try to talk." Aunt Beb stepped closer and took Mother's other hand. I could tell by Mother's eyes she was happy to see her.

"Noan, we're praying for you. Mom, Shirley, and Oak will try to get out and visit soon." We stayed for a long time watching, hoping for an improvement as we glanced back at each other in despair. I could tell Aunt Beb was having difficulty seeing her older sister this way. I placed my hand on Mother's forehead, her eye lids blinked, "Take care Mother, I'll be out again tomorrow."

"Bye, Noan," Aunt Beb returned Mother's hand at her side.

We walked to the Nurse's station and Nurse Claney said, "It has been touch and go till now. But she's improving as you can see." It didn't look like much of an improvement to me. Aunt Beb and I walked slowly out the door, took a deep breath of fresh air and walked slowly to my car.

"Jan, it's such a shame your mother ended up in a place like this. Your father is to blame with his running around and bringing that whore into the house. It probably played on your Mother's mind. It's no wonder her mind is mixed up."

"I believe Maggie was the cause all right. If only I could prove it." I didn't want to discuss what I knew with Aunt Beb. When it came to gossip she was right up there with the rest of my nosey neighbors spreading the news.

For the next few weeks my visits remained much the same. Mother recovered from pneumonia but remained frail and weak. Maggie's name was never brought up and I realized there was nothing more I could do to prove her guilt. Mother's condition was such that it would do no good to share my opinions with her. Nor, would she be able to testify. Only Les and I would ever know what happened to our family and Mother. It would haunt us forever.

If I were to reveal my findings with Dad—he would refuse to believe it. I was certain Dad was still sneaking around and sleeping with Maggie. There were nights he didn't come home. The close relationship we had prior to my finding them together at the cottage never returned. I tolerated him, but he was no longer my confidant. I went about my life doing what I had to do without sharing my thoughts or dreams with him.

Mother never got all her strength back. She needed help and most of the time was brought down to the visiting area in a wheel chair. She had difficulty talking, swallowing and continued to be restless. Mother lost a lot of weight and those hospital dresses hung on her like gunny sacks.

One day in particular stood out from the rest. She mumbled something about Christmas. As near as I could tell she was expecting me to bring Christmas presents along with her frozen custard. I wheeled her over to the glass vestibule window, "Mother look outside. The tulips are in bloom. Do you see them there along the path? It's spring." Her eyes wandered back and forth as I slid my finger against the window glass. Tears came to her eyes. She was upset. There was no way I was able to convince her it wasn't December. Following each visit with Mother, I stepped outside, took a deep breath, looked across the rolling fields and thanked God silently or spoke out loud, "Thank you God." I was so grateful to be free to leave.

I didn't mind going straight into work after leaving the hospital. When it wasn't busy I visited with girls sitting next to me at the switchboard. At work I laughed and joked with everyone. Nobody at work knew my life was filled with sadness and despair. Dad told me he stopped drinking the hard stuff. I believed him until I found empty vodka bottles in our coal bin. Each time I brought up his drinking habit he promised to do better. When I started upstairs to bed at night, I said, "Good night, Dad."

His response was always the same, 'I hope I go tonight.' I encouraged him to get a part-time job, or at least find something that interested him to occupy his time.

"I'll try. I'd like to start an antique shop." He sounded positive, but he didn't make the slightest attempt. One evening having heard his same old phrase night after night, I snapped back. "Dad, I'm sick of seeing you sit here week after week drinking. And, hearing you say, you hope you go tonight. It's no wonder I'm getting depressed."

"So, you're depressed, are you? Well you don't have to suffer with arthritis pain, nor have you been through all that I have. I might as well tell you what's been on my mind lately. I want to sell this house, get out from under this responsibility and move into an apartment."

"What? Are you serious?" I was shocked when he nodded to the affirmative.

"If you move into an apartment you'll drink and smoke yourself to death. You mean to tell me, after paying a lot of the bills and working hard to keep this house clean and orderly this isn't what you want? Tell me the truth! If you think I intend to move into an apartment across town you are badly mistaken—I won't! I'll move, but not anywhere in this town."

"I'm sick with worry about taking care of the problems around this house. We need a new roof and there is painting to be done."

"Since when have you been doing any painting around here? I have painted all the wood work, the walls, and do all the scrubbing and cleaning, not you."

"Well, there's more that needs to be done and it's too much to think about. It's final! I'm putting the house up for sale." I watched his expression as he took a big drag from his cigarette.

"Okay, I hope you know what you're doing." I walked away from him. My heart ached to think he didn't care about our home anymore. I had made a profound statement that I would leave here, but what about Mother? Where would I go? All evening at work, I thought about losing the house.

CHAPTER 28

I remembered the fun traveling by train with Mother and Les one summer when I was twelve. We visited my Aunt Anna in California and other relatives in New Mexico. I also, remembered the year I lived and worked in Philadelphia after high school. Those were happy times. Les seemed content in the Air Force. No wonder, he was away from here. Every time Uncle Bob visited he was telling us to get out of town. The question remained could I leave home for good? I explained to Mom, Aunt Beb, and Shirley about Dad wanting to sell the house. They saw no reason for me to stay any longer. They promised to visit Mother for me.

"Go and move somewhere where you'll be happy," Aunt Beb, said. I telephoned Mother's doctor at the hospital. "Naomi has lost all sense of time," he said. She doesn't realize when you visited last or what day of the week it is. If her sisters and mother agree to visit Naomi, you are free to live your life wherever you chose." For the first time, Dr. Martin seemed sympathetic toward me. I couldn't sleep worrying about making a decision to leave.

The next day, I telephoned Les from our employee lounge, "Les, Dad threatens to sell the house, and I told him I will not move into an apartment. Mom and everyone agree I should leave him and get out of this town. I'm thinking about moving to California where it's warm. Dad's drinking more and staggering by nightfall. He has no interest in anything. I fear his smoking while drunk will burn the house down with both of us in it. I've no confidence in him any longer. My big problem would be leaving Mother behind, not him."

"Jan, I can't believe he wants to sell the house. Is he in his right mind? How is Mother? I couldn't believe what you wrote about his behavior while Mother was home at Thanksgiving. He has his nerve.

Your letters sound bleak."

"I talked with Dr. Martin about leaving town." He said, 'she's unaware of the change of seasons or even what day it is.' I began to choke up and tears were rolling down my cheeks. My voice started getting hoarse and could barely continue. He said, 'if her mother and sisters agree to visit Naomi, I should be free to move wherever I choose.'

"It's okay, Jan. Pull yourself together, I know what you're going through. Remember the day I telephoned you in Philadelphia to come home. I couldn't take Dad's ridicule any longer. At the time, I was working forty plus hours a week, finishing my finals at Penn State and helping Mother. Mother was still home, but unable to do much. It was impossible for me to go on. You were provoked and upset with me when I telephoned you to come home."

"How could I forget? I was so mad I hung up the phone and cursed out loud. I knew I had no choice with you leaving home. I had to think of Mother instead of myself, leaving my friends, a good job, and losing my freedom. It didn't take long after I got here to realize why you joined the Air Force."

"Jan, I am surprised at Dr. Martin's remarks. I've got an idea. Can you hang on awhile longer? There's talk in our squadron about over strength, too many 1st Sergeants. If it's true, I might be in line for an early out. I'll go see the captain when I hang up. There's a slight chance this is not a rumor. Don't do anything yet. Give me a couple of days to get back to you."

"Les, could we be that lucky? My thoughts and prayers will be with you. I'll keep my distance from Dad till I hear from you." I was elated with the thought of Les coming home. I closed my eyes and asked the Lord to intervene. The next two days I stayed home close to the phone before going to visit Mother. On the 3rd day I was awakened by a ring and the light on my princess phone.

"Jan, it's me. I got it! I was right about an early out."

"Oh, I can hardly believe it! This is the best news I've heard in a long time. Wait till I tell Dad."

"Wait, do you think you should tell him? I would like it to be our surprise. I need to put him in his place, Jan. He's out of control."

"Perhaps it would be better for you to see him in this state. If I tell him you're coming he will try to sober up and act different. When can you get here?"

"I'm given a week to process out. It may not take that long—I've got to clear base. If I'm lucky I can get a hop up to Andrews Air Force Base outside of D.C., and catch a bus from there. At the latest, I should be home ten days from now. This is happening fast, and I'll be home before you know it."

"I can hardly wait to see the expression on Dad's face when you walk through our front door. Good luck! Keep me posted. I can pick you up at The Greyhound or the train station."

"I'm looking forward to it, Sis. Take care and I'll be in touch. Bye for now."

"Bye, Les, See you soon."

I avoided Dad and went about my regular routine of visiting Mother and going into work. I told Mother Les was coming home. She smiled and I knew she understood. My mood was light and I told everyone at work Les was coming home for good. I wanted to share the news with the relatives, but thought it might somehow get back to Dad. I sneaked by Dad in his chair on my way to the kitchen after work. I got a dish of ice-cream and took it upstairs. Luckily he was groggy. I didn't say good-night for fear he would bring up selling the house again. I sighed with relief.

A week later, Les telephoned from D.C., "I'm catching a Greyhound tomorrow morning and will arrive in Altoona at 2 p.m. Is every-thing okay?"

"Yes, I'm avoiding Dad. I'll change shifts or trade days off. I'll be there to pick you up. Mother's the same. Dad has no idea about you're coming home. I can't wait to see his face."

"I hope it isn't too much of a shock, but he deserves a talking to for sure. I'm staying at the guest house at Andrews for the night. If there's any change I'll call you in the morning."

"I can hardly wait, Les. Have a safe trip and I'll be at the Greyhound." I traded days off and was standing where the Greyhound parks at the curb of Eleventh Street. My heart began to pound when I saw the bus pull up. I watched as each passenger exited. There was Les in his Class-A's, as he called them. He grabbed me and lifted me up from the sidewalk, "You look good, Sis. How are you holding up?"

"Les, how does it feel to be a civilian again?"

"It's too early to tell. I can't believe it. It's happened so fast. Hold my B-4 bag while I get my blue duffle bag." On the drive home I brought Les up to date about Mother's condition, Maggie's silence and how I kept avoiding Dad. I was on edge for fear of any arguing about selling the house. Les standing beside me would make it easier.

Dad's car was parked out front by the curb, I pulled up behind him and turned off the engine. I opened the trunk and helped Les with his bags. I set the bag I was carrying down on the front porch and threw open the door. Dad was sitting in his chair in front of the T.V. as usual. The look on Dad's face was priceless.

"Son, how did you get here?" He rose from the chair and almost fell backwards. Les dropped his bag, extending his hand, "Dad how are you?" Dad placed his right hand in his and patted him on the shoulder with the other.

"How long are you home for, Son?"

"I'm home for good. I've been discharged on an early out."

"Jan why didn't you tell me Les was coming?"

"I just found out myself and besides I wanted it to be a surprise." This was one of those half-truths. Dad didn't need to know my real reason.

"Dad, I'll take my bags upstairs. Should I use Mother's bedroom, again?"

"By all means, sure, that's fine."

I carried the B-4 bag behind Les to Mother's room. Once inside, Les gave me his devilish look, like when we were kids. We both started laughing and we put our hands over our mouths to keep Dad from hearing us. We gathered our composure before going back downstairs, "Les, should we get straight to the point about his insisting on selling the house or wait a day or two?"

"Let's wait. I would like him to be sober when I talk with him man to man."

"Okay, are you hungry for anything special? It would be nice to sit down to supper together."

"Can you make sauerkraut and pork? The mess hall has it about once a year. Dad likes the way you make it too."

"Sure, why not? I have a pork roast in the freezer. I'll need to run to the market to get fresh kraut. This will give you a chance to visit with Dad alone." Les and I ran down the steps, "Dad, Les is hungry for sauerkraut. I'll put a roast in the oven before I go. Is there anything else we need while I'm at the store?"

"Get a gallon of milk, we're getting low."

"Can you think of anything else, Dad?"

"No. What about you, Son?"

"I could go for Tasty Cakes, the peanut butter ones?"

I started laughing, "Wait, I've something to show you, Les." I ran to the kitchen and brought out a box I bought when I knew he was coming. "Do you want one now?"

Les chuckled, "I might have known you would have some." He took a pack of three and couldn't wait to bite into one. I set the box on the coffee table, "Don't eat too many and ruin your supper." I left wondering what they would talk about. I hadn't seen Dad look that bright in months. I hoped Dad didn't bring up selling the house. If he did Les, would let him have it.

The pork and sauerkraut hit the spot. Dad ate more than usual, "How about another beer, Son?"

"No thanks, Dad. I've had a long day. I'll help Jan with the dishes and hit the sack."

"Whatever you say, don't mind if I do." He said, jokingly looking up at Les, as he opened another bottle and walked to his favorite chair in the living room. Dad loved seeing Les in uniform and had a change of attitude toward him since he joined the Air Force. Les and I cleared the table, put the left overs in the refrigerator and did the dishes. He shared with me his experience writing for the squadron newspaper and The Stars and Stripes Magazine.

"Jan, I want to get a job in television as a writer, work for a magazine or newspaper."

"With your experience and talent I don't see why you can't." It was an exciting day, and when I checked on Dad he was asleep with the T.V. blasting. I turned off the television and walked behind Les upstairs. "Les, do you need anything? You know where everything is, right? Good Night, Les."

"It will be strange when I wake up tomorrow and don't see the barracks wall. Good night, Sis. Thanks for everything."

"Don't mention it. I'm glad you're home. Hope you sleep well."

I was awakened by loud voices coming from downstairs. I grabbed my housecoat and ran to the stairwell in my bare feet. I could hear Dad raising his voice at Les, "You don't understand what I've been going through. Face it, Son, your Mother will never be back home to stay and this house is too much worry."

"Dad, I can't believe you'll be happier in an apartment. What about Jan? She's worked hard around here. Have you given her any consideration in this decision?"

"She nags me about my drinking and won't let me alone. There's no peace around here. You've been home only a day; what do you know about what goes on."

I wanted to barge in on the conversation, but it would have made matters worse. It was hurtful to hear Dad accuse me of nagging him.

"Dad, my opinion is you're making a mistake and drinking may be clouding your thinking. You had a vodka double header in your glass of milk and are chasing it with beer and it's only 9 a.m."

"Son, don't you start on me. This is the way I deal with my pain. It's better than being on pills all day. You've no right to tell me what to do! My mind is made up and there's no changing it. I don't want to discuss it any further."

"Dad, let's be clear, you brought up this discussion. Jan has tried her best to keep this house running smooth. You will lose your daughter if you sell. I'm certain she won't move into an apartment. She will be gone. Is that what you want?"

"I told you I don't want to talk anymore about it. I've got to do what's best for me. I can't help what she does. Jan's a grown woman and has to make up her own mind."

I tiptoed back to my bedroom. I heard enough. So, he doesn't care what I do. It was hard to think my concerns about his drinking and taking care of this house were in vain. At least it was out in the open. Dad was selling the house and Les coming home wasn't changing a thing. I delayed going downstairs for breakfast. I didn't want Dad to know I overheard his comments, or get into another argument with him. What I had done for him and this house meant nothing. Les rapped on my bedroom door, "Jan, are you okay?"

"Yes, come in. I'm trying to decide what to do."

"You overheard our conversation. I had a feeling you could hear us. I wanted to tell him off, but he was already tipsy. He's a depressed alcoholic and wants to be left alone."

"I've paid a lot of his bills, cleaned house, cooked meals and tried to get him to eat. I ate alone because the alcohol ruins his appetite. I was pleased he ate at supper last evening. He grabs a piece of cold meat, and glass of milk with a raw egg in the morning. After I leave to visit Mother, I see little evidence when I get home that he ate much of anything. His face is sunken in and his arms are thin. He probably is mal-nourished. I'm glad you're here to see how frail he looks. Dad isn't here a lot of evenings, he probably stays with Maggie. Or he could be sleeping drunk in his car after the bar closes. Only the Lord knows where he hangs out. I know now he doesn't care about me and sees me as a nag. I'm finished trying to hold things together!"

"Jan, don't take this personally. He isn't the same Dad we knew growing up. He's selfish, depressed and an alcoholic. He swears the drinking kills his pain. He's probably suffering from guilt about his affair with Maggie and sending Mother to such a place."

"Where will we go, Les? There is no sense in staying in this town any longer. But how can we leave Mother?"

"Jan, we have each other and we can make it. Speaking of Mother, what time are we going out to see her?"

"As soon as we finish breakfast, better yet, let's stop for breakfast on the way. I don't want to face Dad this morning after what I overheard."

The nurse brought Mother in a wheelchair, and as the elevator opened Les hurried to greet her. Her eyes lit up and she tried to speak, but no words came. Les kissed her on the forehead, "I'll take over, nurse." He wheeled her to the visiting area.

"Mother, How are you?" Mother looked up and gave a partial smile.

"I've been discharged from the Air Force and glad to see you." Mother tried to respond but her tongue was thick. No words were clear. I could tell by her eyes she was excited. This was the day she had waited for. If only this had been months earlier, when she was still talking. Les looked at me, tears welling in his eyes. It was sad. For what seemed like an eternity she had talked about Les coming to rescue her. It wasn't going to happen. Les fed Mother her frozen custard, and he told her about Louisiana and his plans to get a job writing for a magazine or newspaper. I'm not sure Mother understood, but she did eat most of her custard. Her feet shuffled about, the foot rests had been removed, and her arms were in constant motion. I went to the receptionist and requested the nurse be called to take Mother back upstairs. Les wheeled Mother to the elevator. "I'll be back soon, Mother." The nurse turned Mother's chair around facing the door, and Les and I waved goodbye. She made an attempt to raise her arm as the door closed.

"Good heavens, what have they done to her? She must be heavily sedated. She can't talk or feed herself. How long has this been going on, Jan?"

"For weeks, since she had pneumonia. At times she nods her head to my questions—today wasn't one of those days. She tries to talk, but her words are hard to understand. You're lucky she didn't choke on her custard."

"When you told me over the phone what Dr. Martin said, I was shocked. I'm not sure what Mother understands. Do you still think you want to move to L.A.? That's a long way from here."

"Les, let's face reality. We no longer have a home. Are you willing to move into an apartment? I've had enough of this town and I cannot picture myself cooped up in a second story flat."

"I don't know. It's too soon to even think about it. I need to check things out. Can I find the type of job I want, and what about Mother? I need to meet my buddies again to see how they are doing." We looked at each other as I started the engine. We both sighed at the same time as we looked back at the hospital and I slowly drove away.

That evening I loaned Les my car to meet his friends. He picked me up at work at eleven p.m., "What did Jerry and Bob have to say about job opportunities?"

"They aren't sure I can find the kind of job I want. There's only one television station and our one and only newspaper, The Altoona Mirror. They don't know anyone personally at either one to make a recommendation. I'd have to apply and see what happens."

"I think you would have a better opportunity in Los Angeles. I could apply for a transfer to ensure one of us is employed while you look for the type of job you want. We could go together. And we have Aunt Anna out there to help us."

"Oh Boy, that's a big decision. I'm not sure I could leave at this time. Jan, you should go. I'll stay here and look after Mother. You've done more than your share and deserve a chance at a better life."

"Les, please reconsider and come with me. I've made up my mind. If I'm moving it will be where there's no snow. It won't be easy. I'll call Aunt Anna tomorrow from work and get her opinion."

The next day I telephone my great aunt. "Aunt Anna I'm thinking of moving to Los Angeles. Dad is putting our house up for sale and I refuse to live in an apartment in this town. Could you put me up till I can find a place to stay?"

"Oh my, that's the best news I've heard in a long time. Come ahead. You can stay here as long as you like." Her voice was positive and uplifting.

"I'm going to request a job transfer and will let you know when I find out if it's possible." Aunt Anna wished me good luck and I hung up the telephone with a big sigh of relief. I went to my supervisor and requested a transfer to Los Angeles. It was on a whim and I couldn't believe I had really asked for a transfer.

My supervisor advised, "You will have to accept whatever opening, and it may not be the same type of switchboard you're accustomed to." At this point, I didn't care what job it was. My mind was made up and there was no turning back.

I was excited with the thought of leaving, I temporarily lost sight of the fact that I'd have to leave Mother. As far as Dad was concerned, he wouldn't care where I went. Not knowing how much money I would need once I got to L.A., I decided to sell the furniture I'd bought over the years. I prepared a list and sold end tables, lamps and the big T.V. Once sold, I replaced them with old ones stored in the attic. The parlor looked dim with the old lamps and end tables. When a friend bought the television I felt bad replacing it with Dad's old table T.V. and placing it on a stand in front of his favorite chair. When I got home from work, Dad was waiting up for me. Les was out with his friends.

"What's the big idea selling all the furniture out from under me?" Dad asked with a vengeance.

"It was your idea to sell the house, not mine. I told you I wasn't going to move across town. I'm moving to California and these were things I bought over the years. I don't know how much money I'll need, and I'm selling what I can."

"So that's it! You're robbing me blind." He raised his fist getting up from the chair. Swinging wildly he lost his balance and fell back staggering drunk.

"No, Dad, I'm not selling your things. You haven't bought any furniture around here in years, and you know it!"

"Don't get smart with me. I don't want anything else sold. That's final. Or I'll call the police." He was loud with a mean expression that scared me.

"I'm going to bed. Don't worry you won't have to put up with me much longer." I turned away and ran up the stairs. My heart ached, but I began to worry about his behavior. I hadn't seen him like this in weeks. I had another sleepless night. I wished Les was here to hear him. I felt bad about selling my own things. I didn't hear Les come home that evening.

The following afternoon I told Les about Dad's yelling at me for selling furniture I had bought.

"Jan, from now on I'll be here when you get home from work." Les dropped me off at the office and went out to see Mother. Mary, my supervisor, motioned for me to come into her office, "Your transfer request was approved. You are to report to Pacific Telephone at 4th and Olive Street in Los Angeles three weeks from today." She handed me a piece of paper with the address and information.

"Wow, Mary, It seems like a dream come true. They must need switchboard operators out there."

"I'm sure they do. L.A. is a big city, and you will make out fine. I wish you the best, Jan."

"Thanks, Mary I really appreciate your help in getting me transferred." I shook her hand, turned and walked back to the switchboard. I felt like celebrating. What a relief, I would have another chance to pursue my dreams.

Reality set in really quick! How was I going to get everything together and report to a new job in three weeks? I figured it would take seven days to drive to L.A.

Les was parked outside the Telephone Company. "I got the transfer and have only three weeks to get to L.A."

"Gee, Jan, I'm happy for you, but three weeks doesn't give you much time."

"Les, come with me. The chances of you landing the type of job you want here are next to impossible. Please reconsider. It would be fun driving across the country together."

When we got home Dad was asleep in his chair. Les and I went straight to the kitchen, got a dish of peanut butter ice cream and took it up to my bedroom. It was like old times eating ice cream. Les looked discouraged after another day of filling out applications and making calls to set up interviews.

"Jan, my prospects don't look good. I applied for office work at an insurance company. They are considering me."

"Les, reconsider. I know you can find a job in L.A."

"I want to be near Mother. I've been away from home too long. I'll see you in the morning. Good night, Sis."

"See you at breakfast." I had another sleepless night worrying about leaving my dear Mother.

CHAPTER 29

In the morning, I looked at Dad's bedroom door. It was shut. In my pajamas, I ran down to the cellar to use the phone by the washing machine to telephone Aunt Anna. I didn't want Dad to hear my conversation. "Aunt Anna, I got my transfer, and I'm to start work at Pacific Telephone at Olive Street. How far is that from where you live?"

"Honey, I've been waiting to hear from you. What good news. It isn't far away, and you can get there without having to get on any freeway. Don't worry, dear, when you get here I'll take you on a dry run. When will you arrive?"

"I want to give myself a week to drive across country. I leave next Saturday and will call you along the way. I would like to stop in Galveston and see my uncle who's in medical school. I'm not certain the exact day, but I'll telephone the moment I cross the California State Line."

"We will be waiting for your call. Your room will be ready, don't you worry about a thing. It will work out, and be careful driving. It's a shame you don't have someone to drive out with you."

"It's okay. I'll be seeing parts of the country I've not seen before. I'm trying to get Les to come with me. He is reluctant to leave here. He just got discharged from the service and worries about leaving Mother. It's hard for me, too. But I can't live with Dad any longer. I can't wait to see you again, Aunt Anna. I'll be talking to you soon, bye, Aunt Anna." Her voice was up-beat and sounded happy about my coming. I ran upstairs. Dad's bedroom door was still shut.

The worst part would be saying goodbye to Mother without knowing when I would return and see her again. Les wasn't up yet. I had breakfast and sorted some dishes, a few pots and a skillet I packed to take with me. I would need things to start an apartment. I went through the linen closet and pulled out a couple of newer sheets and 4 towels and washcloths to pack. Les met me in the kitchen. His friend Bob was picking him up for another job interview. I stopped at the grocery store on my way to see Mother and picked up cardboard boxes from the grocer. I told him I was moving to California and he remarked, "Boy that's a long ways away. Good luck to you." I threw the boxes in the back seat of my Volkswagen and felt better about my decision.

Mother was sitting in a wheelchair with her head hanging down. Her chin was resting on her upper chest. I held it, while I spoon fed her frozen custard. Mother was weak and listless and kept shuffling her feet back and forth. There were bruises on her arms and legs from bumping against the chair and Lord knows what else. I rubbed her frail skinny arms while bringing her up to date about Mom and everyone. In the back of my mind, I knew moving away was one of the hardest things I would ever have to do. I decided to visit her as often as possible before moving. She wouldn't know I wasn't coming back as usual. The week flew by with the small get-togethers. My last day at work was Wednesday to give me time to pack.

I made a special trip to see Mom and Aunt Shirley to ensure they would take my place and see Mother. Also, Aunt Beb and Aunt Viola agreed over the telephone to visit. After all, they were her sisters. All my relatives gave me their blessings and wished me well. Friday came and I made my last trip to the hospital. Mother was the same. I got choked up. I wanted to tell her I was going to California, but was afraid of her reaction. She always recognized me, but for months there had been only nods of the head and no spontaneous conversation. She may not be sure about the day of the week, or time of year, but Mother understood I would show up. If not today, or tomorrow, it would be the next day.

I spent extra time holding her head against the back of the wheelchair and kept smoothing her forehead. When the nurse came to take her upstairs, I kissed her on the cheek and said, "Mother, take care. I'll see you." I waved goodbye as the elevator door closed in front of her. She didn't see me wave, her head was hanging down. I swallowed hard, tears swelled into my eyes as I walked over to the receptionist, "I'm moving to California and my brother, aunts, and grandmother will be coming to visit Mother."

"I wish you luck. I'm sure your Mother will miss you." She looked up from her desk as she spoke.

"I talked with her doctor and he's aware I'm leaving." I walked away and was about to open the door but turned back and added, "I hope she will be all right. It's difficult to leave her."

"It will be all right, she's in good care."

I thought to myself, *oh yeah, this last year had been hell for Mother.* I pushed the heavy glass door open and walked outside like hundreds of times before-this was the saddest. I wouldn't be coming back in a day or two. I looked out over the fields starting to green over. The gray gloom of winter was gone and spring was here, but Mother wouldn't know it.

By the time I reached my car tears were dropping from my chin. I sat with both hands on the steering wheel and looked back toward the second story where Mother would be sitting. She was somewhere all alone in her world and lined up with all the rest. I brushed my tears away with the back of my hand and started the engine. I drove down the long driveway glancing back at the hospital on the hill. I realized it would be a long time before I would return.

When I walked into the parlor, Dad was sitting in his chair. He must have seen the boxes in my bedroom and knew the time was near. "Dad, I'll be leaving tomorrow for California. I got a transfer to Los Angeles and Aunt Anna is putting me up until I get established."

"Well, I hope you're happy with the mess you've made around here. What kind of person did I raise? You've taken advantage of me. Go ahead, leave me alone."

"Dad, have you forgotten whose idea this was? I want you to know I'm leaving for good in the morning."

"Well, go ahead. I don't care anymore. Get out of my sight!" He raised his fist at me once again, but didn't try to get up from his chair. Startled, I knew saying anything more was hopeless. I turned, ran upstairs and slammed my bedroom door. My heart ached after leaving Mother, and I didn't need him yelling at me. I was invited to supper to celebrate leaving Altoona, but when I should have been happy, I wasn't. I telephoned my good friend, Beverly, and agreed to meet my closest colleagues at Olivio's restaurant. I had a glass of wine which helped me to relax. Kathy said, "If you're afraid to go home, stay with me tonight." Dad's tone of voice, and being drunk every evening was scary. I was excited about going to California, but my life had fallen apart at home. I hugged my friend's goodbye, one by one.

Dad was asleep in his chair when I arrived home late. I checked and Les's bedroom door was closed. I didn't want to disturb him and went to bed. It was another totally restless night.

After breakfast, I finished loading the car with my bedspread, books and suitcase. Dad was nowhere in sight. I thought it best not to say goodbye anyway, after the way he had been acting. I ran upstairs for the last time, picked up my purse, sweater, and took one more look around my room. It looked bare without my pictures and bedspread. This is where I'd spent much of my time growing up. I checked in on Les to say goodbye. I was shocked when I opened the bedroom door and peeked in. His bags were packed.

"Sis, hold on. I'm going with you. Jan, I've put in applications everywhere. I even applied for a sales position but I have no desire to be an insurance salesman. Having a job here isn't meant to be. You were right about leaving Altoona. I'm sad and hate to leave Mother after being away so long. I need to see Mother one more time to say goodbye. Can we stop on our way?"

"Yes," I threw my arms around him and we held each other tight. I didn't know when I'd been so relieved.

"You've made the right decision, and I believe in my heart you won't be sorry. I admit leaving town is frightening, but with you along I know it will turn out okay."

When we got half way down the stairs my heart was racing and I could feel the warmth flushing my face. Dad got up from his chair and walked slowly toward us. I watched not knowing what to expect. When I reached the last stair, my arms stiffened, I was prepared to protect myself. I felt more secure knowing Les was behind me.

Dad's eyes met mine straight on. His look was not the mean stare I saw the night before. I stood firm on the last step. I wanted to grab Dad by the shoulders and shake him. My chest wall tightened and my heart continued to race. I felt sad and angry at the same time. I wanted to shout, *"Why are you killing yourself with alcohol. Don't you see what's happening? I wanted to scold him and plead for him to stop drinking. I had lost him as a father long before."* His eyes were glassy and watery, and I took in a large gulp of air and released it. He placed his hands on both my shoulders, kissed me on the cheek, "Good luck and both of you drive careful." This was the first time in a long time I saw my real father, the way I used to see him. Les and he shook hands, and he patted Les on the shoulder. He didn't seem upset or surprised Les was going with me.

"Dad, I'll look after her. Take care of yourself. Bye." We walked out the front door, got in my car, and glanced at each with a sign of relief as I started the engine. I drove away and neither of us looked back. Aunt Beb was standing in the middle of the street in front of her house. I pulled on the emergency brake. Les and I got out of the car with the engine running and hugged her goodbye. I looked into her eyes and we hugged again real tight. I choked up when I said, "Be sure and see Mother for me." I turned, got back into my car and Les followed.

"Les, I'm glad you are going along to help drive. Take care of your sister and the best of luck to both of you. Tell Aunt Anna I said she's to watch over you." Aunt Beb walked over to speak to Les through the open window, "Les thanks for calling last evening to let me know your decision. You've made the right choice. Your Dad brought this on himself with his goings on. I'll come and see you in L.A. one of these days."

"I hope you do, and soon," Les remarked. She kept waving and Les waved out his open window as I pushed down harder on the accelerator to the top of the hill and rounded the corner by the cemetery. I could see her still waving as I drove out of sight. This was what I had looked forward to and yet the tears kept coming and my nose began to run. I looked over at Les, he smiled and I knew things would be all right.

We stopped to see Aunt Viola and Uncle Ralph. They insisted we come inside. I told Aunt Viola and Uncle Ralph about Dad kissing me on the cheek, "If I remember correctly it was the second time in my life he ever kissed me."

"It's about time he acknowledges you. It was through you he even had a home. I still don't trust him. Les, I'm happy you're going with her. I was worried about Jan driving alone," Aunt Viola remarked. It was sad, and Les and I took turns hugging her. Uncle Ralph kissed me on the cheek and patted Les on the back. They followed us down the porch steps to the side of the car.

"Have a safe trip." Uncle Ralph said. Aunt Viola ducked her head partway into the car window on the passenger's side, "Bye, Jan. Let us know when you and Les get there."

"I will, and please visit Mother for me, Bye." As I drove up the street I could see them waving in the rear view mirror. I beeped the horn as I turned the corner toward the main highway. Well, this was it! My final good byes as I drove beyond the city limits. I half smiled to myself and looked over at my brother who smiled right back.

I hated to stop at the hospital and see Mother after what I had gone through the day before. But Les needed to see her one more time. Perhaps it would be easier this time with my brother beside me. Les carried a one way conversation about applying for jobs and his feelings about leaving the Air Force. Les and I had tears in our eyes as we took turns kissing Mother good bye. She didn't know it would be a long time until we would see her again, if ever. The fear of not knowing when was hard to accept. Les and I said "Good Bye, Mother," in unison as the nurse wheeled Mother into the elevator. Mother never looked up. The drive down the hill from the hospital was difficult. We both couldn't hold back the tears and were bawling out loud. My heart ached and I wanted to believe we were making the right move under the circumstances.

Les, wiping the tears from his face in a raspy voice said, "Jan, before you got home from your party last night I told Dad my decision to accompany you. He respected it and seemed to understand there just wasn't a job in this town for me. In fact, I think he was relieved to know you wouldn't be driving alone. He was civil and of course tipsy, offered me a beer and I drank it."

"I figured you probably had words last evening since he made no fuss when we left." We took turns driving across country and Les had me stop at Vicksburg, Mississippi Cemetery, and Lake Charles, Louisiana. He was proud and excited to show me his old barracks where he was stationed in Lake Charles. The University of Texas at Galveston was our next stop. It wasn't far from Louisiana and we were anxious to visit Uncle Bob while in medical school.

Uncle Bob took us into the medical laboratory where his classmates were using cadavers to trace arteries, nerves and locate body organs. There was a pungent odor about the room. We went to a large delicatessen for lunch after watching them working on corpses, it took away my appetite. It was a wonderful visit and Uncle Bob's friends took us out to supper. I stayed in one of the women's dorms for the night and Les, slept on Uncle Bob's couch in his room. Uncle Bob was ecstatic to hear about Les and me finally breaking away from Dad and Altoona. He knew how difficult it had been with Dad's drinking and Mother's illness.

When Les and I crossed the California State Line, I started singing 'California Here I Come'. We stopped and called Aunt Anna from a pay phone. I had forgotten in all the excitement to telephone her that Les was coming too. She was standing in front of her house when we drove by. I didn't recognize the house after all these years. The huge palm trees on Riverside Drive were gone and when I turned onto Newell Street I drove past her house. If it weren't for her stepping out from her driveway and waving her arms I would've kept on going. I made a U-turn and pulled into her driveway.

I was only 12 and Les was 14 when we had visited Aunt Anna. We got out of the car and she hugged us both. She seemed so happy to see us. She pointed to the freeway embankment. "The state purchased one half of my property as part of the Golden State Freeway project. My house next door was bought and demolished. They provided a sidewalk and a six foot high chain link fence to keep anyone from going up the bank—the freeway is up there." I could hear the car traffic going like crazy.

Aunt Anna had a large bedroom made up for Les and me. She placed a divider between two twin beds—it was like two rooms made out of one. It was an exciting trip and I found it hard to believe I was in California at last.

After supper I telephoned Aunt Beb to tell her we had arrived safely. She said, "Have I got news for you! The day after you left, on my way to church I walked passed your house and guess who I saw with your Dad, that whore, Maggie! She was moving in."

"Oh, no! I can't believe it. No wonder Dad was congenial the day we left. So that's what putting the house up for sale was all about. Maggie must have been behind the idea to get us out of the way."

"Don't worry. We will have nothing to do with her whether here in town or at the cottage." Aunt Beb, went on.

"How is Mother and Mom?" I asked.

"Your Mother barely recognized me. Mom is doing okay."

"I miss Mother and everyone already. Les and I had a good trip, visited Uncle Bob and the base where he was stationed. I'll get back with you soon, Aunt Beb. Tell everyone I miss them. I'll pass the phone to Aunt Anna. She wants to talk with you. Aunt Anna and Aunt Beb had a lot of catching up to do about all the relatives. While they were talking I told Les, "Maggie's moved in with Dad."

"I'm not surprised. Dad is a lonely man who is easily swayed by that whore. She's got what she almost killed for—our Dad. I still don't believe our father was part of the poisoning scheme. But his lie about selling the house leaves room for more doubt. We will never know. One sure thing is we have lost our real father and our home as we knew it."

The next day Aunt Anna took me to Pacific Telephone at Fourth and Olive, in Los Angeles, as she promised. For six months I continued to make the trip downtown from where she lived. Les landed a job as assistant editor of a magazine two weeks after we arrived at Aunt Anna's. She kept prolonging our leaving her. She had delicious food each evening along with cocktails. I envied her talents for cooking and entertaining. She had big family gatherings to introduce us to all the relatives and bragged, "These are Andy's grandchildren and they have to be great coming from the dearest kindest person I ever knew, my brother." Every apartment we drove her to see didn't meet her expectations. I think Aunt Anna felt responsible for our safety, and I'm sure enjoyed having us. But we worried about her doing all this fussing and cooking for us. Aunt Beb kept in touch frequently.

I applied for a transfer with Pacific Telephone to the Gower Street Business Office in Hollywood not too far from there. About the same time, I got a call from Aunt Beb, "Your Mother's doctor stopped to talk with me during a visit. He had news about her condition. I was prepared for the worst. They have determined she has a disease called Huntington's."

"What? You mean to tell me after years they finally think they know what's wrong with her?" Aunt Beb continued, "Yes, they're sure it's Huntington's Disease."

I interrupted, "Is there a cure? Will she get better?"

"I can't answer all your questions, but he's sure it's Huntington's," Aunt Beb stated. I thought, *to think they gave her treatments for God knows what, and now they think they have it right. Mother went through hell and torment while they couldn't figure it out. Would this change anything and could she recover? I had never heard of the disease.* "Aunt Beb, see what you can find out and give us a call as soon as you can." Aunt Anna, Les and I went through old medical books and couldn't find any information on Huntington's. Aunt Beb told us later there was no cure and very little could be done for Mother at this time. The cause was unknown, but they were certain it was inherited.

"Jan, the way you describe the involuntary movements of your Mother's feet and arms and her difficulty swallowing and talking....

Well years before your grandfather, Andy, died he was having similar problems. It was difficult for him to get around especially with that wooden leg. I heard he had problems swallowing and choked on his food. Your grandmother, Mom, said he insisted on eating alone because of spilling things on the table. They said he had a nervous disorder, or St. Vitus Dance. My hunch is your Mother's father had this same condition. Your Mother must have inherited the disease from him."

"That's got to be it, Aunt Anna. If only the doctors would have known earlier, Mother may not be where she is today. She wouldn't have received cruel and unusual treatments and medications for a crazy person. Only God knows how they effected her." I telephoned Aunt Beb and requested she ask Dr. Martin to telephone me about any new medicines or treatments which would help her. It was as I expected. The next time Aunt Beb called she reported, "Dr. Martin said 'Naomi's disease has progressed to the point where nothing more can be done. She receives custodial care, and her blood pressure has to be controlled with meds."

"Thanks, for letting me know. It's a pity Mother inherited a disease the doctors knew nothing about. Why were they treating her like a crazy person. Keep me posted, Aunt Beb. I appreciate you going to see Mother. Tell her Les and I miss her." Finally, I understood why Mother's feet were rarely ever still and the symptoms began to fall into place. Les said, "It's a damn shame they treated her for mental problems without knowing what she suffered from."

This information didn't make our living in California any easier. I had difficulty handling the grief of leaving Mother behind. I was homesick for her, my relatives and friends.

I could not afford a plane flight back to Pennsylvania. Besides, I started the new job in Hollywood. I had no vacation time accrued.

Maggie won, at least on the surface. She lied, betrayed, poisoned and coerced. I wish we could have proven her guilt and sent her to prison for destroying our Mother's life and ruining our family. Maggie ended up with our house, summer cottage and Dad. She got Dad 100 per cent, but he was a beaten down, desperate and depressed alcoholic. Dad had lost his self-respect. He was now a man with no dignity who let a cunning whore dominate his life.

Mother endured and suffered most from the betrayal of her husband and housekeeper. Maggie poisoned her causing weakness and confusion. A cheating husband with no patience arranged for her to be locked behind closed doors. In the beginning, he was unaware of the bedlam. When he was told how Mother suffered with these special treatments, he did nothing. Mother was tortured and used for experimentation. Her faith sustained her through the worse days from frigid ice-baths, shock treatments, strait jackets, strange medicines and the humiliation of being locked up. Then the doctors realized Mother was overcome by an unknown inherited disease, which took over her mind. Huntington's Disease must have begun to influence Mother's thinking and reasoning years earlier.

However in the 1950's a man or woman could be locked away in a state institution with as little as hearsay from a spouse. Only the husband or wife's signature was required. It could be as simple as a disagreement in marriage. In my Mother's case she was accused by Russ of having an uncontrollable temper, being crazy, assaulting and chasing Maggie out of the house.

There were no real winners in these previous chapters. As it turned out, Les and Jan made an extremely difficult decision to leave their Mother behind but it was the right one! They've begun to experience a new beginning and look toward a future happiness in California.

ABOUT THE AUTHOR

Joan Foor, MN, RN graduated from UCLA's Nurse Practitioner Program. She worked for Kaiser Permanente for over 35 years beginning in Pediatrics at Kaiser, Sunset Boulevard Hospital, Hollywood, CA. She held positions in Nursing and Patient Education and served as Clinic Administrator at The Antelope Valley, Kaiser, Medical Offices. In retirement she taught at California State University, Bakersfield, and Antelope Valley College in Lancaster, CA. She enlisted in the U.S. Army during Viet Nam.

She continued her career in the U.S. Army Reserve Nurse Corps 26 more years retiring as Lt. Colonel. After completing graduate writing courses in fiction and non-fiction she published her first book, *Homeward Journey*, (I Universe), 2003 and co-authored two children's books *It's Tough Growing Up*, 1st edition (Tate Publishing), 2009 and 2nd edition (Creative House Kids Press), 2011. She's a member of The Palm Springs Writer's Guild, Military Officer's Association, and Benevolent & Protective Order of Elks, USA. She loves writing, tap dancing, golf, gardening, traveling, manicures over an acre of fir trees and desert terrain at her high desert country property. At her winter home she maintains a rose garden surrounding her pool near Palm Springs. She travels back and forth with her two rescue cats and terrier dog by her side.

www.ingramcontent.com/pod-product-compliance
Ingram Content Group UK Ltd.
Pitfield, Milton Keynes, MK11 3LW, UK
UKHW041856190726
13854UKWH00002B/930

9 781634 521062